The
UNDER-GROUND SISTERS

ALSO BY SORAYA M. LANE

The Secret Librarian

The Pianist's Wife

The Berlin Sisters

The Secret Midwife

The London Girls

Under a Sky of Memories

The Secrets We Left Behind

The Last Correspondent

The Girls of Pearl Harbor

The Spitfire Girls

Hearts of Resistance

Wives of War

Voyage of the Heart

The UNDERGROUND SISTERS

SORAYA M. LANE

Published by Lake Union Publishing, Seattle

www.apub.com

EU Product Safety Contact:
Amazon Media EU S.à r.l.
38, avenue John F. Kennedy, L-1855 Luxembourg
amazonpublishing-gpsr@amazon.com

ISBN-13: 9781662523212
eISBN: 9781662523229

Cover design by The Brewster Project
Cover image: © Laura Ranftler / ArcAngel; © Kletr © sergio34 © aziseptian
© Krivosheev Vitaly / Shutterstock

Printed in the United States of America

For my readers – thank you for choosing my books to read!

Prologue

30 April 2015

Aletta sat at her dressing table and stared at her reflection. She barely recognised the white-haired, wrinkle-skinned woman looking back at her; her slow blinks, the hollowness of her cheeks, and certainly not the frail hand that trembled as it lifted to touch her face. The woman she remembered had been bright-eyed, quick to smile and with thick chestnut hair that brushed her shoulders.

She closed her eyes, holding back her tears and wishing she could go back in time, to have even one last day as she remembered herself.

When Aletta opened them, she saw her daughter standing behind her. Aletta smiled as warm, soft hands came to rest on her shoulders, her daughter meeting her gaze in the mirror. She could see that she, too, had tears in her eyes, and she watched as one slipped from the corner of her daughter's eye, sliding down her cheek.

'We don't have to go.'

Aletta nodded, understanding that her daughter wanted to protect her. But today of all days, she needed to be brave. There was no other choice. What would it say about her if she stayed home instead of facing the past? She smiled as a warm cheek brushed hers, her daughter's lips whispering a gentle kiss to her skin. She inhaled her perfume, reached up and placed her hand over her daughter's as she took a deep breath. Aletta cleared her throat, the words hard to find, knowing she needed to say them.

'If we don't go, they will have won,' Aletta said, her voice catching. 'We fought too hard to let that happen.'

She closed her eyes again, wanting to remember but at the same time wishing that her memories couldn't still haunt her. Remembering the past was a blessing, but sometimes, on days like today, it could also be a curse.

'All these years later and she's still the bravest woman in the room,' her daughter said, her smile kind as she dropped a kiss to her mother's head. 'Shall I give you a little bit longer, or are you ready?'

'I just need a moment,' Aletta said, looking at her reflection again. 'I promise I won't be long.'

'You take all the time you need, there's no hurry.' Her daughter turned to go, but Aletta reached for her hand again.

'Thank you, for taking me today. I wouldn't be able to do it without you.'

Her daughter's eyes glistened with fresh tears. 'It's my pleasure, Mum. I would never, ever let you do this alone.'

And she wouldn't, Aletta knew that. Her daughter had always stood bravely by her side, always there for her when she needed her. She also knew that attending today was a privilege of the living, and one she couldn't allow herself to miss, and certainly not because she was too scared.

For those we lost, and those we loved, she told herself. *Today, we honour you. Lest we ever forget the sacrifices we made, all those years ago.*

Chapter One

Amsterdam, April 1940

Aletta

Aletta tipped her head to Cecilia's shoulder while they walked, sighing contentedly as the sun brushed her skin. When her friend passed her the still-warm cinnamon roll again, she eagerly took another bite before passing it back to her, stifling a groan as the sugar touched her tongue.

'I've never tasted anything so delicious in all my life,' Aletta said with another sigh, licking the sugar and cinnamon from her fingers. 'I could eat these every day for the rest of my life and never get sick of them.'

'There's a reason my father can barely fit through a door these days,' Cecilia teased. 'He can't stop eating what he makes!'

They both laughed, heads bent close together as they slowly strolled, taking turns to have little bites of the sweet roll. They'd called in to see Cecilia's father at his bakery on their way home, and he'd been delighted to see them, insisting they take one of his famous Zeeuwse *bolussen* with them for the short walk home. He'd started making it for his Jewish customers, but she didn't know anyone who didn't love it, Jewish or not.

'Do you ever just wish you could get married?' Cecilia asked. 'Imagine how nice it would be strolling like this, but with a baby in a pram in the sunshine.'

Aletta felt her eyebrows shoot up. 'Get married? What about teaching?' She couldn't imagine that having a baby was all sunshine walks and smiles either. From what she'd seen, being a mother looked like the hardest job of all, and it certainly wasn't one she was rushing to have.

Cecilia sighed. 'I didn't much like school, and now I'm studying to become a teacher. It doesn't seem right.'

'You'll make a great teacher,' Aletta insisted, gently bumping her shoulder. 'The children will love you, and you've been doing so well with your studies. I've loved this first year of having my own class, and it'll be you next year. Besides, there might be no young men around to get married to for a while.'

That made them both sigh, their walk slowing the closer they got to home. It was always Aletta's favourite part of the day, strolling back with her best friend, arms linked, chatting about the day. They were so different – Aletta wanted nothing more than to work and earn her own money, enjoying her independence for the first time in her life, but then again, she'd loved school and enjoyed learning. Cecilia had always insisted that she'd only gone to school to see her friends – if college wasn't so social, Aletta might have found it impossible to get Cecilia to join her on the same career path. As it was, it had taken Cecilia a year of working odd jobs for her father before following Aletta to teachers' college, which meant her friend would graduate a year after Aletta.

'Do you think we'll join the war?' Cecilia asked. 'I keep thinking about all the young men who might end up fighting if we do.'

'It's seeming less and less likely that we won't become part of it, don't you think?' Most of the time Aletta tried hard not to think about the war, or the young men they'd gone to school with who'd left to serve, but lately it seemed to be all anyone was talking about.

'I keep thinking of what it must be like for them, how much they must miss home, and they haven't even left the country yet.'

Aletta linked her arm tightly with Cecilia's. 'You're worried about Peter.'

Her friend nodded. 'I wish I'd told him how I felt before he went. I just—' Aletta knew her friend was trying hard not to cry. 'I just hope I get the chance to. I hope they all come home, all our boys. I hope they don't get sent away.'

Aletta knew what Cecilia meant. She didn't have a sweetheart herself, but she couldn't stop thinking about all the families she knew who were missing someone, or more than one someone, at their dinner table each night. And all those men were still relatively safe; the Netherlands hadn't joined the war yet, but their troops were mobilised. They were ready and waiting, and she knew that it would only be so long before they were thrust into the war like some of their European neighbours. Even the young children she taught were whispering about the brewing conflict, repeating what they had likely heard at home around the dinner table.

'My parents want me to take my brothers and move to my aunt's place, in the country,' Cecilia said. 'They don't think it's safe here for them.'

'When will they want you to go?' Aletta asked, thinking how boring it would be if she didn't have Cecilia. They barely ever went a day without seeing each other, except for the summer holidays if one of them went away with their family.

'I don't know, but I think it might be soon. I found my father with his head in his hands last night,' Cecilia said. 'I've never seen him like that before.'

They always tried hard not to talk about the war on their walks, but often it was impossible not to. Every part of their lives was being touched by it; that feeling that every day they were edging closer and closer to being part of the conflict. But Aletta had never truly imagined they might be parted, not after so many years of friendship. They'd met as six-year-olds, linking arms then just as they still did, their long pigtails and ribbons tossed over their shoulders as they marched around the playground and refused to let the boys tell them they couldn't climb trees. Nothing much had changed, except for the fact that their walks were now strolls home, the talk was more about the boys they liked than the ones they didn't, and they were more interested in sunbathing and listening to music than risking their necks by climbing trees.

'Do you think they'll make you, or is it just them worrying?' Aletta asked. 'Surely they wouldn't actually send you away?'

Cecilia shrugged when Aletta glanced at her. 'Honestly? I don't know. My mother is beside herself; she's wringing her hands so often I think she's going to give herself an injury, and I've tried to tell them that I'd be best to take my brothers there and then return myself. I don't want to be stuck in the country.'

Aletta didn't want her friend to be stuck in the countryside either, but she didn't say anything – the last thing she wanted was to make her feel worse than she already did.

'My father is worse than my mother,' Aletta said. 'My mother is quiet and resolute, as if she thinks her one job in life is to make our house one of calm, but my father is looking older by the day. He has dark lines beneath his eyes now and I keep hearing him in the night, restless and walking around the kitchen like he just can't sleep anymore.'

They kept walking, lost in their thoughts, until they rounded a corner and found a young boy flapping his arms selling newspapers, with people beginning to cluster around him.

'What do you think that's all about?' Aletta asked, reaching into her pocket to see if she had a coin. Whatever paper he was selling must be hot off the press to draw such a crowd.

They edged closer, and when the crowd dispersed, with people darting away as if their house were on fire, Aletta gave her coin to the young boy as he thrust a paper at her. She froze, understanding now why so many people had stood and stared at the newsprint in their hands.

Cecilia's little gasp and her fingers digging tightly into Aletta's arm told her that her eyes weren't deceiving her, that what she was reading was real.

A heaviness settled over Aletta's heart as she let her eyes trace the five words emblazoned across the front in bold black type. The five words that had the people before her running for home.

MARTIAL LAW DECLARED IN THE NETHERLANDS

'What does this even mean?' Cecilia whispered as they were jostled out of the way by people rushing over to the boy on the corner.

They exchanged worried glances as passers-by began to shout around them, as more and more men and women read the news.

'It means that it's happened,' Aletta said. 'The war has finally reached us.' She gave Cecilia a quick hug, holding her tight. 'We need to go home, but shall we meet tonight? After dinner? If it's safe to do so?'

She didn't have to say where; they always met at the little park near their apartments.

Cecilia nodded, and they hurried off in opposite directions. Aletta's heart began to pound and by the time she saw her apartment block ahead of her, it was thundering so loudly she feared it might beat straight out of her chest.

*If martial law has been declare*d . . . Aletta swallowed a hard lump in her throat. It meant that the boots of Nazi soldiers would soon be heard on the pavements of Amsterdam.

◆ ◆ ◆

It had only taken Aletta minutes to reach home, and she fumbled with the door handle as she hurried inside, her heart still racing, finding her mother standing in the kitchen.

'Have you heard the news?' she asked, breathless as she held out the paper to her mother, thrusting it into her hands. 'Look at this!'

Her mother's mouth fell open, as if she'd been about to say something but the words had frozen in her mouth. And then the newspaper fluttered to the ground between them, slipping from her mother's hand as a news presenter began speaking, the wireless crackling as Aletta reached over to adjust it, meeting her mother's shocked stare. She was usually pink-cheeked and busy as she prepared dinner at this time of day, but today she stood so still it scared Aletta, her skin so pale it appeared ashen white, as if all the colour had been leached from her.

'The news has been confirmed,' came a steady, loud voice through the radio. 'Martial law has been declared by the Dutch government.'

Aletta didn't even try to reassure her mother, because neither of them were fools – there were no words that could sugarcoat what they'd just heard broadcast for all to hear.

They'd all known this moment might come, had prayed and hoped that it wouldn't, but Europe was at war, and it had only been a matter of time before their country was impacted. Aletta had felt as if some of their neighbours' homes were on fire, and theirs was one of the last standing, miraculously spared as the fire continued to rage around them.

'What do we do?' Aletta asked, knowing as she said the words that her mother would have no great solution for her. 'What are any of us expected to do now?'

'We wait until your father comes home,' her mother said, her wide eyes meeting Aletta's. 'He'll know more. He'll be able to tell us what's happening. He'll know what to do.'

Aletta nodded, bending to pick up the newspaper from the floor and setting it on the kitchen table. But her mother immediately leaned forward and turned the paper over, clearly not wanting to see the headlines blaring at them from their own table, her hand lingering as if she wanted to ball it up. Aletta would have preferred if she'd screamed and thrown it across the room compared to this still, silent version of her mother that she didn't recognise.

Because the news could only mean one thing: war was about to reach them, whether they were ready for it or not.

Chapter Two

Aletta

When Aletta's father walked through the door, it was obvious that he wasn't bringing any good news. The shadows beneath his eyes seemed to have become even darker, his shoulders slightly stooped. Only a year earlier, he'd still seemed youthful, with a bounce in his step, but the threat of war had taken its toll. Now, with the conflict at their doorstep, she couldn't imagine the worries resting upon his shoulders.

'You've heard the news?' he asked, dropping his leather brief-case to the floor and coming towards them.

Aletta nodded, rising to pour her father a glass of wine. Her mother was still fussing over the cutlery drawer – something she'd been doing for the past hour as they'd waited for him to arrive home – even though Aletta had pressed a glass into her hands to try to get her to relax. They usually only opened a bottle of wine for special occasions, but she'd felt they might all need it tonight. And she'd rather that than it be left for Nazis to loot when they arrived in Amsterdam.

'Thank you,' he said.

Aletta turned her head slightly rather than acknowledge the tremor in her father's hands. That was new; she'd never seen her father shake before. He was usually unflappable.

'What are we to do?' her mother asked, as if she'd suddenly realised her husband was home and had woken from her trance.

Aletta watched as he set his glass down on the table and rubbed at his eyes before sitting heavily in his usual chair. It struck her that perhaps he didn't actually know what they should do.

'All we can do is eat dinner and carry on as normal tonight. We can worry about tomorrow when it comes.'

Her mother nodded and reached out to her husband. She squeezed his hand and pressed a kiss to the top of his head before turning and putting her apron back on. It was as if she'd been waiting for someone to tell her what to do, as if she was now ready to resume her usual duties.

'Father, what will happen though?' Aletta asked as her mother busied herself with dinner preparations. She leaned closer to him across the table. 'What will happen to your clients?' She didn't need to specify – they both knew that she was referring to his Jewish clients.

His frown furrowed deep lines between his eyebrows and around his mouth, and he sighed and took a sip of wine before answering her.

'I've been fielding appointments and walk-ins from clients all afternoon,' he said. 'They're worried, some more than others, but they're right to be. The threat they face, it's like nothing I've ever imagined in my lifetime before, the news more horrific by the day, what's being said about them, what's being done, all over Europe.'

Aletta nodded. Her father was a lawyer and many of his clients were Jewish businessmen and families – it was what kept him awake at night, she was certain, worrying about their fate if Hitler's army ever crept close to them. And now that worry was more than a threat; it was reality. It also meant she had her own personal worries to contend with, as she thought of the handful of Jewish children in her class. It made her sick to the stomach to think of those beautiful children and the challenges their families were certain to face now.

'What will they do?' she asked, softly. 'Is there anywhere they can go?'

He rubbed his hand over his jaw as he spoke. 'Yes and no. The ones I helped leave when all of this was just a threat, they went to America or England, with much of their wealth intact, but now . . .' Her father sighed. 'There is so little any of us can do, other than sympathise and offer help in any little way we can, but I fear they might lose everything. If they haven't left yet . . .'

Aletta nodded, understanding why her father couldn't finish his sentence as her mother placed potatoes in the middle of the table. If someone was watching them and hadn't heard their conversation, they would have mistaken it for a regular family dinner.

'Cecilia's father has talked of sending their younger children away to the country,' Aletta said, watching as her father took another long, slow sip of wine. She was pleased to see that the shake in his hand had disappeared. 'He thinks it will be safer for them there.'

'Perhaps. At least they will be away from the worst of it, and bombings will likely target the city areas.'

It was Aletta who began to shake then. *Bombings?* She hadn't even thought about the possibility of that, about how their safety could be compromised not just from enemy troops on the ground but from air strikes too. And it wasn't just herself she was worried about. She immediately thought of the children in her class; all the families that would be affected. If the city was bombed, what would happen to the school?

'What's happening to them elsewhere throughout Europe,' her mother said, placing one final dish on the table, 'do you think it will happen here?'

Her father's expression was sombre, and Aletta suspected that if he could hide the truth from his family, he would. 'I fear that there is no Jew in Europe safe from Hitler,' he said. 'The persecution they face . . .' He took a breath and looked between them. 'It's like nothing the world has ever witnessed before.'

Aletta reached out to touch her father's arm, holding her hand there as she sensed the weight of his pain.

'We just have to keep doing whatever we can to help,' he said. 'Even when it feels as if all hope is lost, we have to keep trying.'

Aletta's mother joined them, sitting down beside her husband. And she did something that they hadn't done for many years at their family table, not since Aletta's grandmother had passed away and was no longer there to demand it of them.

'Emma?' Aletta's father said, his eyebrows raised as her mother reached out to each of them.

'If there has ever been a time to pray, Jan, it is now,' she said. 'Please, take my hand.'

Aletta took her mother's hand on one side and her father's on the other, but she didn't close her eyes, and she noticed that her father didn't, either. Instead, their eyes met, and he gave her a small smile as her mother spoke.

'We thank you Lord for the food on our table, and pray for the safety of all those around us. Protect us from those who want to harm us and others, and give us strength as we face the evil of our enemy.'

When her mother opened her eyes and finally let go of the hold she had on Aletta's fingers, she could see that something had changed within her. It was almost as if she'd wallowed in her worries all afternoon, and had re-awoken with a steely determination in her gaze.

'We will survive this,' her mother said. 'I refuse to believe that anything could divide our family, and we will do anything we can for your Jewish clients and for our neighbours and friends, too.'

Aletta found herself nodding, and she knew that her father agreed, despite his stillness – it was what he'd been fighting for since the whispers of war had begun the year prior, to do anything he could to help those who needed him.

'I walked home with Cecilia today and we ate the best cinnamon bun I've ever tasted,' Aletta said, as she hovered her fork over a carrot. 'I think her father's tinkered with his recipe.'

Her father laughed then, and her mother's lips turned up at the corners, and Aletta grinned straight back. Soon they were all laughing, and her father reached over and placed his hand on hers.

'Cinnamon buns,' her mother said, her cheeks still creased with her smile. 'I've never heard of a more perfect topic to distract us from war.'

'Our Aletta, huh?' her father said. 'Always finds a way to make us smile. I bet those children in your class thank their lucky stars they have you as their teacher.'

'Well, they'd think they were a *lot* luckier if I arrived at class with cinnamon buns.'

They all grinned, eating their dinner and sipping their wine, and Aletta couldn't help but think that they might not have many more nights like this: just the three of them, with the street quiet outside and the low hum of the wireless in the kitchen. She wouldn't trade quiet nights with her parents for anything in the world, and there was nothing she wouldn't do or say to make them smile.

An hour later, Aletta was in the kitchen doing the dishes, trying to be as still as possible so she could listen to her parents speak. They were talking in low voices and she didn't want to miss a word, even though they weren't saying anything she didn't already know. They were worried, as she was – it was the worry of the unknown that was churning her stomach – and she only wished that they wouldn't try to shield her from anything. Whatever concerns they had, she wanted to understand them.

'Should we be sending Aletta away?' she heard her mother ask.

'She's twenty years old, Emma,' her father said. 'She's a teacher with her own duties and obligations now.'

Aletta bit down on her lip, grateful that her father saw her as the young woman she was, instead of a child, although she knew that her mother was only wanting to protect her.

'If things become worse for your Jewish clients, for their families, we must act, Jan,' her mother said. 'If we can find safe places to send them, if *they* can be sent to safer homes in the countryside—'

'We will, we'll do everything we can, but there will come a time when people in the Netherlands must choose whether to keep their own family safe, or take in a Jew,' he said. 'The Nazis don't tolerate those who stand against them.'

'What are you saying?'

'I'm saying that we have to decide as a family how far we're prepared to go to help others, if it means putting our own lives at risk.'

Aletta blinked away tears, imagining how frightened so many families must be right now, how terrifying it was to think that someone might turn a Jewish person away for fear of retribution. She knew it would break her father's heart to ever be put in that situation, but she also understood he would do anything to protect his own family – most likely above all else. It was a choice no one should ever have to face, but as she thought of the handful of Jewish children in her class, she wondered what might change. Would they even be allowed to stay at school? Would they be spared because they were children?

She glanced at the clock on the wall then as she dried the final dish, knowing she'd have to go soon to meet Cecilia. Being within the four walls of her apartment was beginning to suffocate her – no offence to her parents – and she needed to breathe in some fresh air and sit with her friend.

Aletta cleared her throat so her parents knew she was coming and that she could hear their conversation. They both fell silent and looked up when she entered the room.

'Unless there's anything else I can do, I'm going to meet Cecilia at the park.'

Her father smiled up at her, and she walked over to press a kiss to his cheek. She turned to her mother, touching her hand as she leaned in to kiss her too.

'Don't stay out past dark,' her mother said. 'We have to be careful now, even in our own neighbourhood.'

'I won't, I promise,' she said.

Aletta went to her room, dabbed a touch of perfume to her wrist, put on some lipstick, and collected her bag. It felt strange to just go about her normal routine on the cusp of so much change, but if ever there was a time she wanted to be with her best friend, it was now.

When Aletta arrived at the park, she saw Cecilia sitting on the ground, her back resting against their favourite oak tree, a cigarette dangling from her fingers. Aletta lifted her hand in a wave when Cecilia looked over, crossing the park and dropping down beside her, close enough that their shoulders were touching.

Cecilia offered her the cigarette and she took it. Aletta didn't smoke often, but if there was ever a time to partake, it was now.

'How did your parents react?' Cecilia asked. 'Is your mother all right?'

Aletta passed her back the cigarette and rested her head on her friend's shoulder. 'She's better now that she's had time to process it, but I can tell how scared they both are. I wish I could be a fly on the wall, listening to what they're talking about now that I'm not home. How about yours?'

'My mother was near hysterical,' Cecilia said. 'The moment she heard it on the wireless she ran to the boys' bedroom and started to pack their clothes into suitcases.'

Aletta took another puff. She knew what Cecilia was telling her.

'So, the decision is made? About the boys being sent away?' Aletta asked. 'How long do you think you'll be gone?'

Cecilia was silent for a moment. 'They, well, they want me to stay in the countryside now, too. They think I'll be safer, and they want me to look after the boys so they're not too much trouble for my aunt.'

Now it was Aletta who was silent. She'd never imagined being without Cecilia – never thought that anything would truly part them.

'You could come too,' Cecilia said softly. 'We could look after the boys together?'

Aletta kept her head on her friend's shoulder. 'I can't, not now that I have my own class. I can't just leave.' She sighed. 'It's just so hard to imagine that everything's changing, that the life we know . . .' She stopped talking, not even wanting to finish that sentence. She also didn't want to give up her job, but that decision might be taken out of her hands now. She had no idea whether they would even be allowed to continue teaching.

'My father told us that there are Dutch citizens doing everything they can to stop the Germans from advancing. They've even placed explosives on railway lines,' Cecilia said. 'They're trying to stop the Nazis, but . . .'

Aletta lifted her head to look at her. 'But what?'

'Aletta, there's, well, there's something else I've been wanting to talk to you about,' Cecilia said. 'Something I've been sitting on for a while, since Thomas left.'

Aletta sat up properly and turned to face her, wondering what she could possibly have to say when they usually told each other everything. But she supposed if it was to do with Cecilia's older brother, then it might have been a family secret.

'The night Thomas left, he told me about an underground movement. He said there's a group of people getting together to prepare for some sort of resistance against the Nazis.'

Aletta felt her eyes widen. 'A resistance?'

'He told me that they need more people to join, that they have meetings every week, but my parents forbade either of us from so much as speaking about it again.'

It had only been a few hours earlier that Aletta's heart had raced as she'd hurried for home, but it was beginning to pound all over again.

'What sort of things do you think they'd be doing?' she asked. 'Who are they hoping will join them?'

Cecilia lit up another cigarette and took a long drag before passing it to her. 'I don't know. All he told me was they were looking for as many young people as possible to be part of their underground network, to work against the Nazis, and he said there's a similar movement taking hold in France. But it would be a very dangerous affiliation now.'

Aletta let her head fall back against the tree trunk as she digested Cecilia's words. She'd never heard anything about an underground movement, but if Thomas had mentioned it, then she didn't doubt it was true. She couldn't deny that she was curious about the types of things they might do, and the people who might join such a group.

'Would you ever consider joining?' Cecilia asked. 'Do you think your parents would let you? I mean, your father is already taking a stand by keeping his Jewish clients, right?'

'Me? Joining a resistance movement?' Aletta thought about it. It wasn't that she objected to the idea, but she didn't even know what she'd have to offer them. 'I don't know. I mean, I'd like to think I was brave enough to be part of something like that, but . . .' *Would I be brave enough though? To fight against the Nazis?*

'I know what you mean. I don't know if I could do it.' Cecilia sighed. 'Thomas told me they meet on Thursdays, but I'd have to write to him in code if I ever wanted to find out more. Just promise me that you won't tell your parents what I've told you. I don't want them thinking I'm a bad influence or anything.'

'I won't, I promise,' Aletta said. She doubted she'd ever be brave enough to go along to something like that, anyway.

They sat for a while in silence before she finally spoke again. 'Do you really think they'll make you stay in the countryside? That you won't come home until the war is over?'

It was Cecilia dropping her head to Aletta's shoulder now. 'I hope not. Just promise me that you'll write, because I don't know what I'll do without you.'

Aletta didn't admit that she couldn't imagine a week without her, let alone an entire war, and it only made her want to enjoy sitting in the park as darkness slowly fell around them all the more.

Without Cecilia, she would feel like she had no one.

When Aletta arrived home, she let herself in, locked the door and then took off her shoes. She didn't want them clicking on the floor if her parents were asleep, but when she tiptoed down the hall, she saw the light was still on in her father's office.

She was about to walk in when she heard her mother's voice, so she leaned back against the wall instead. It wasn't that she wanted to eavesdrop, but she found it impossible to walk past without listening.

'I just feel like there should be more that I can do,' her father said, and she could imagine the way he would be massaging his temples with his thumbs as he spoke. 'They trust me, and they keep turning to me for help, for guidance, and it doesn't matter which way I turn. We're running out of options to keep them safe.'

'You're doing more than most,' her mother said. 'Truly Jan, you are, and I'm so proud of you for it.'

There was silence for a moment.

'Those that are still here . . .'

'Shhh,' she heard her mother whisper, and she heard a shuffle and imagined that she now had her arms around him, comforting him. 'One of the reasons I fell in love with you was your compassion, but there's only so much one man can do. Can you help to arrange any more marriages?'

He shook his head. 'I think the window for that has closed, and if Hitler continues on his current path of success, then it's anyone's guess what their fate will be.'

Aletta knew her father had been helping some of his Jewish clients to find non-Jewish husbands for their daughters. He was the one who arranged payment, and she'd heard him say that some of the couples barely even met, they certainly didn't live together, it was simply a business deal that involved the groom being compensated with a large sum of money. But if it kept those girls safe, then she supposed it was worth every guilder.

'Just promise me that if I'm caught helping them—'

'Don't say it,' her mother said. 'We will get through this together, as a family, like we always have. You just have to be careful, promise me that? Promise me that you'll be careful.'

'I promise,' he murmured.

'I love you, Jan, and I couldn't survive you being taken from me, do you hear me? I couldn't survive it.'

Aletta slid down the wall, quietly, until her bottom hit the carpet, and she pulled her knees up, hugging them tight. The way her parents loved each other was something she'd never had to question, but hearing the worry in their voices, knowing how scared her mother already was at the risks he was taking, told her that she didn't need to tell them about the resistance movement. She'd never be brave enough to be part of it anyway, and the last thing her mother needed was something else to fret over.

But it wasn't just her parents she was worried about. Many of the children in her class were going to be frightened, and not just her Jewish ones. They would all be scared about bombings and the uncertainty of what came next, and she resolved to do everything she could to keep things as normal as possible for them during school. No matter what happened, she would keep teaching; she would show up for them every day, so at least while they were in her class, they could feel safe.

Chapter Three

10 MAY 1940

Aletta

Aletta stood and surveyed her class, a pit forming in her stomach. The announcement about the Germans arriving had been devastating, but nothing quite compared to the realisation that three of her Jewish children weren't in class. Everyone else was accounted for, which made it even stranger.

'Else,' she said, beckoning one of the girls over, once she'd settled her class with their books.

The little girl rose from her chair and came to stand in front of her. She'd been her favourite from her very first day, although Aletta would never admit it to anyone and tried hard not to show her favouritism.

'Do you know if Luuk, Maria and Julia are unwell?' She felt bad singling her out, but as one of the Jewish children, she thought Else might know.

Else shook her head, her eyes wide like saucers. 'They're not coming to school anymore.'

Aletta felt her eyebrows shoot up in surprise. 'They're not? Do you know why?'

The little girl's cheeks stained bright pink, and Aletta quickly got up from her seat and came to crouch in front of her, taking her hands.

'It's all right, I'm so sorry for asking. I should have known better,' Aletta said, giving her a hug. 'I'm only worried about them, that's all. Thank you for telling me.'

After reassuring Else and ushering her back to her seat, telling the rest of her class to get on with their writing, she went back to her desk, turning to stare out of the window. She'd naively hoped that the war wouldn't touch her classroom. *How wrong I was.*

When Else's seat was vacant a day later, Aletta didn't ask any of the children questions. But as soon as class was dismissed for the day, she tidied up the classroom and packed her bag, hurrying down the street and heading in the opposite direction to her apartment.

If Else and the other Jewish children no longer felt safe coming to school, she wanted to find out what she could do for them, whether it would be helpful for her to drop off schoolwork, or even call around some afternoons to give private lessons. But after knocking once, then twice at Else's family's door, she started to think that something was very wrong.

'Mrs Zilversmit?' she called out, knocking again. 'It's Else's teacher here. It's Aletta.'

There was still no reply, and just as she was about to turn away, another door opened and an old, grey-haired lady looked out.

'You won't find them here,' she said.

'This isn't the house of the Zilversmits?' Aletta asked. 'I—'

'They left in the middle of the night.'

Aletta swallowed. 'Did they say when they'd be coming back?'

The lady just shook her head, her expression sad, and Aletta stood for a long moment after she'd shut the door. There was only one Jewish student left in her class. *One*. A week ago, there had been five.

She clenched her fists, tightly balling them as she left the apartment block, anger rising inside her while she tried to make sense of what was happening.

And after she walked into her apartment on autopilot, she found herself standing in the middle of her living room.

Write to Cecilia. Ask her where the resistance group meets and whether they're still looking for new members.

A terrified shudder made its way through Aletta, but she knew that feeling heartbroken wasn't going to help anyone.

But writing that letter will.

Chapter Four

Aletta

It had been almost dark when Aletta tiptoed through her apartment and slipped out of the door, putting her shoes on outside so she didn't make any noise. Cecilia had left a note for her that morning before she left, telling Aletta where the Resistance met, and she'd known from the moment she read it that she had to go. Every time she doubted herself, she thought of little Else, wondering where her family had fled to, and she couldn't just stand by and do nothing.

She was looking for an industrial building about a twenty-minute walk from her house, and although she'd initially imagined there might be a guard outside or a codeword needed to enter, she was simply greeted at the door by a young man of a similar age to her with nothing more than a smile and a nod.

'You're here for the meeting?' he asked.

Aletta nodded, her pulse racing as she wondered for the hundredth time that night whether she should have come in the first place. But instead of letting on how nervous she was, she just replied: 'I am.'

She was taking a huge risk in coming – they all were – but she imagined that every single person inside had a good reason for being there, just as she did.

Aletta walked nervously past him and into a space full of people, many of them as young as she was, some a little older, and all she could think was that the energy in the room was contagious. But then someone let out a loud whistle, which made everyone fall quiet. The noise in the room went from loud to a low hum.

'We'll get started soon,' a man of about thirty said at the front, and she imagined that he was standing on an apple box to be able to see out over the crowd so well. 'Talk to the people next to you, make friends. We're all in this together.'

Aletta's stomach fluttered as she glanced around her. Standing in the crowd listening was one thing, but striking up conversations with strangers was something else. For some reason, she'd imagined none of them talking to each other, trying to keep their identities hidden, perhaps. She folded her arms around her middle, nervous all over again, but she'd barely crossed them when a girl of a similar age stuck out her hand.

'I'm Sara,' she said with a grin. 'Is this your first meeting?'

'Is it that obvious?' Aletta asked, shaking her hand, her cheeks flushing hot. 'I'm Aletta.'

'Your eyes are like saucers, so I'm going to say that it was kind of obvious, but I'm almost certain I looked the same last week. This is only my second time.'

'It's . . .' Aletta looked around. 'I don't know how to describe it. There're so many people here, more than I could have imagined.'

'Just wait until you hear what they have to say,' Sara said. 'Because if you're anything like me, you won't be able to stop thinking about it. It's like it sets something on fire inside you, and you can't wait to find out how you can be part of it all.'

The person on the other side of her tapped her shoulder then, and Aletta turned, meeting another young woman and the man with her. When she finally spun back around, Sara was gone, but it didn't matter. Aletta was certain she'd see her again, and by the sounds of it, it was time to listen anyway.

She glanced over her shoulder, nervously expecting that they could be found at any moment, that someone might come and arrest them all for attending such a gathering. But despite the risk, she had the most overwhelming feeling that it was worth the risk.

Aletta slipped in the door, expecting her parents to be asleep. It was dark, but there was a light on in the kitchen and her father was sitting in his armchair, facing the door. She saw him immediately because of the burning tip of his cigarette in the almost-black of the living room. She knew then that something was wrong; her father was often up this late in his office, but he was never waiting for her when she got home. Worry curled in her stomach.

'You frightened me,' she said. 'What are you still doing up?'

'I've been sitting here waiting for my daughter to arrive home. My daughter who has seemingly forgotten the curfew we set for her.'

His voice sounded different, and she could tell that he was cross with her in a way she wasn't used to. *Because you never usually break his rules, that's why.*

'I know it's late, but—'

'Aletta, where have you been?' he asked.

She dug her nails into her palms as she stood before him. Her father never usually asked her where she'd been or was upset with her for staying out a little late, certainly not now that she was twenty. But things were changing, she understood that, and perhaps it wasn't so unexpected. Besides, this time she was more than just a little late.

Aletta took a deep breath, understanding she was going to have to answer his questions very carefully. It wasn't that she intended on keeping her whereabouts a secret, it was simply that she'd expected to have more time to figure out how to break the news to them. She also wasn't certain how she felt – her thoughts were a jumble and her heart had raced since she had listened to the beginnings of this resistance movement.

'Aletta, I want you to tell me where you've been,' her father asked, his voice rising. 'Because in case you missed the news, our country has been invaded by the enemy, and you're choosing now to disappear at night and not return until well after dark! Anything could have happened to you!'

Aletta lifted her chin. She wasn't going to lie to her father, but she was also a grown woman who'd made a decision to attend a gathering, not a child in need of berating. It was he who'd said as much to her mother only a week or so earlier.

'You're speaking to me as if I'm a little girl again,' she began.

'This is my house, which means you *will* obey my rules!'

Aletta took a slow, shaky breath. This was not a version of her father she was used to, but she could tell he was worried, so she wasn't going to hold his outburst against him. She spoke as calmly as she could. 'I've been at a meeting.'

'What kind of meeting?' he asked, extinguishing his cigarette in a glass dish and standing up to face her.

Aletta cleared her throat. 'I've been at a meeting of like-minded people who want to help our country,' she said, repeating something she'd heard a woman at the meeting say. 'I don't want to just sit idly and not do anything, so I've taken it upon myself to investigate what other young people are doing. How they plan to stand up to what might, what *will*, happen here.'

'You attended a meeting for the underground movement?' he whispered, his voice barely audible. She wasn't sure what was worse – his raised tone of earlier or the quiet, disbelieving way he was speaking now.

'Yes.'

His face fell. 'Aletta, are you mad? You can't go to those meetings! You can't risk your life by being caught working with the Resistance! Do you know what could happen to you?'

Anger simmered deep inside her as she faced him. It was one thing to be worried about her, but another entirely to act as if he wasn't taking risks, too. Risks that he would most definitely be punished for if he were caught. 'So, it's all right for you to risk your life by helping your Jewish clients, but I can't even—'

'This is different, you're my daughter, Aletta! I need to know you're safe!' he demanded.

'Safe isn't going to save lives! Safe isn't going to bring back the Jewish children who've disappeared from my class,' she cried, turning slightly when she realised that her mother was standing in the dark near them, stepping out of the shadows with one hand pressed to her mouth in disbelief as she listened to them argue. 'I won't stand by and do nothing, Papa. I can't.'

They had never been a family who quarrelled, never usually raised their voices to one another, and she could see the shock on her mother's face to find her husband and daughter at odds in the living room so late at night. Aletta stood, silent now, the only sound the rasp of her breath as her mother looked between them.

'What's going on here?' her mother asked. 'Aletta, where have you been? Have you only just arrived home?'

'Tell her,' her father said. 'Tell her where you've been!'

She faced her mother, finding it even harder to say the words.

'Where have you been, Aletta?' she asked. 'Why are you both yelling loud enough for our neighbours to hear?'

Before she could answer, her father spoke.

'She's been at a meeting of the underground movement,' he said, turning to face her mother, who was as ashen-faced as she'd been when they'd listened to the news on the radio. 'The *Resistance*, Emma. She thinks she's going to join the Resistance!'

Aletta closed her eyes after seeing the look of disbelief pass over her mother's face.

'You've joined the Resistance?' her mother asked. 'That's where you were tonight?'

'I was,' Aletta said. 'I know it's a lot to take in, and I should have said something at dinner, but I didn't want you to talk me out of it. I wanted to see for myself what it was about, to understand how we could work together, to know whether I even wanted to be a part of it.'

'And you were impressed by these people? By this movement?' her mother asked. 'They made you want to join them?'

'I was, and they did,' Aletta said, feeling a warmth spread through her as she remembered the energy in the room, that feeling that there was nothing they couldn't achieve if they all worked together. She met her mother's stare. 'It was like nothing I could have imagined, and I'm sorry but nothing either of you has to say will stop me.'

She didn't think to ask how her mother knew about the movement as she saw the surprise on her face turn to something else. But it wasn't the look that fazed her, it was the way her mother walked forward, the colour slowly returning to her face as she reached for Aletta's hand. Her mother, who'd never been anything other than a sweet, obedient wife, a woman who'd never openly disagreed with her husband as far as Aletta could remember.

'If you're brave enough to join, Aletta, if you truly believe it will make a difference, then I'll support you,' she said.

'Emma, you can't be serious!' Aletta's father cried. 'You can't—'

'She's right, Jan. Safe isn't going to stop the Nazi soldiers from killing our fellow countrymen or trampling through our front door and taking our home—' Her mother's voice caught, her voice a gasp as she continued. 'Or heaven forbid, helping themselves to our daughter when they do. We have to do *something*. We have to prepare.'

'What do you mean *we*?' he asked, his face draining of colour as he stared at his wife.

'I mean that maybe I will go along to the next meeting too, and hear what they have to say. Maybe there's even a contribution of value that a woman my age can make.'

Aletta hated being at odds with her father, the last thing in the world she'd ever wanted to do was upset him, but she was filled with pride at her mother's words. Her mother who had never done anything other than care for and love her family, so bravely declaring her support.

Her father looked between them then, his shock slowly turning to understanding, almost as if he knew better than to argue with the two women he loved the most in the world, who were standing so resolutely before him. And surely he must have been proud, after all he'd done to help others, that his wife and daughter were wanting to do something, too.

Aletta watched as he sunk back into his armchair, suddenly looking so much older. He buried his head in his hands for a moment as she sat on the sofa, turning on the lamp, her mother on the arm of his chair, her hand falling on his shoulder. They might have argued, but it hadn't stopped her mother wanting to be near him, to comfort him as he struggled with their decision. Aletta had never been the type of girl who yearned for marriage, but if she ever did marry, she knew she wouldn't accept anything less than the kind of partnership that her parents had.

'If you both do this, if there's truly nothing I can do to talk you out of it, then we need to have some rules,' he eventually said when he lifted his head, his eyes pleading. 'We have to promise each other that we'll all abide by them, to do everything we can to keep our family safe. That has to be something we all agree on.'

Aletta nodded. She could live with that. Her father was taking risks every day too, and they all needed to understand what the others were doing, and just how far they could go, how much they were endangering the family. Each of their individual actions had a knock-on effect, and it was unfair not to be honest with one another.

'There is no shame in being the one at home looking after us, Emma,' her father said, his gaze fixed on her mother. 'You don't need to do anything else for me to be proud of you.'

Aletta watched as her mother shut her eyes and took a deep breath before opening them again. 'If we don't join, if *we* don't all do something . . .'

'Then how can we expect others to,' Aletta finished for her. 'We all have a duty to do whatever we can to help our country and all the people in it. We don't have a choice. We simply have to try.'

Her father's nod was solemn, as if something in her words had resonated with him. 'Emma, how about you make us all a cup of something hot. I have a feeling it's going to be a very long night.'

Aletta knew then that her father had accepted their decision, but also, that their conversation wasn't over. He had that look in his eye she'd only ever seen when he was working on an important case, which meant he would be very thorough in his interrogation of them, and even more thorough when it came to establishing exactly what they were and weren't allowed to do.

Aletta wasn't complaining though – despite the confrontation, she was still thrumming with excitement about the evening she'd had. And she couldn't wait until the next meeting so she could take her mother with her and see the look on her face when she realised just how many people were prepared to fight for not just their country, but for the people. Even if her mother chose not to volunteer, she still wanted her to feel the energy she'd sensed herself tonight.

They were going to make a difference. They were going to fight for what was right.

There was power in numbers, and if what she'd heard was correct, there were going to be resistance groups formed throughout Europe.

As far as she was concerned, this was only the beginning.

Chapter Five

Aletta

'I don't think I can do this.'

Aletta reached for her mother's hand. 'You can, and you will,' she said. 'If you're not comfortable once we're in there, we can leave.'

Her mother's eyes were caught in Aletta's gaze. She hadn't truly believed that her mother would come, but the following night, they were going to Aletta's second meeting together. Usually they were held no more than once a week, but with the German forces on their shores, everything had changed.

'Mama, if you need a reason, think about the children I've lost from my class. This is about more than just us, it's about standing up for what's right.' She'd had to be so careful at school, reassuring some of the little ones who were worried about their friends, without saying anything that might get her in trouble. Aletta had read more books to them and come up with more art projects than she ever had, in an attempt to keep them all distracted.

'I just—'

'Come on,' Aletta said, leaning in to whisper to her mother. 'What happened to that brave woman who stood beside me and declared to her husband she would support me?'

She received a sigh in response, but the feet that had been planted to the ground beside Aletta finally moved. A little shiver of anticipation ran through Aletta as she entered the room again, and she glanced around to see if she recognised anyone from last time. The girl she'd spoken to wasn't anywhere she could see, but the faces around them were friendly, and although many were young, there were also plenty of men and women closer in age to her mother. And despite their smiles, there was something about them all, a determination perhaps, that drew Aletta to them all the more. What they were doing put them all at huge risk, but it was obvious that everyone in attendance had decided it was worth it.

'What do we do now?' her mother asked.

'We make friends, I suppose,' Aletta said. 'Until someone stands up at the front and starts talking, anyway.' She realised she was still holding her hand, and she slowly released it, hoping she wasn't feeling quite as nervous now they were inside.

But they didn't have time to mingle, as the same man who'd spoken at the last meeting called out for silence as he stood on an overturned box at the front of the room. His voice easily carried all the way to the back where they were standing, and Aletta felt a familiar shiver run through her as she listened to him.

'The Nazis will be walking through our city's streets within days, as if they belong here, and we've seen what's happened in the countries they occupied earlier. We know the enemy will impose a curfew, that they will come for all our Jewish friends and neighbours, that they will seek out anyone who stands against them. We've seen what's happening in our Jewish communities already, and this is just the beginning.'

Aletta breathed in the almost static feeling in the room, as if an electrical current was charging between all the people gathered there. There were no smiles anymore – they were all focused on the man standing before them.

'But we've seen in Austria, in Poland and Czechoslovakia that what continues to connect their people is their resistance movement. What keeps them fighting and determined to seize back control of their countries are the men and women, just like all of you here tonight, who are prepared to do whatever is needed of them. People who aren't afraid to work against the enemy, people who won't baulk at danger or the challenges we face. Who will keep turning up even when the stakes are higher, the risks greater.'

Cheers erupted from around them and Aletta started clapping. When she looked over at her mother, she saw her hands pressed together as if she'd been about to clap but was so transfixed that she hadn't moved.

'We will be like those great countries who are fighting from the underground, but we will be even stronger. If they come for us, then we will be prepared. We will be ready to fight, and no one, *no one* will be able to stamp out the cells that we create in every pocket of our country. In every city, in every town, we will have people ready and prepared to put their lives on the line for the greater good.'

He paused, and Aletta was taken by how magnetic he was, how impossible it would be to not agree with his powerful speech.

'So, who's with me?' he asked. 'Who in this audience pledges to join our movement? To be ready to act when the time comes? To stand against the Nazis and defend not just our country and our right to freedom, but the rights of all of our people, especially those they seek to persecute?'

'I do,' Aletta said, her voice a rumble in her throat as she held up her hand, as the crowd of people erupted around them. 'I do!' she shouted, louder this time, wanting to be heard.

Her mother's voice surprised her as she shouted her pledge as well, the crowd clapping and cheering.

I do, thought Aletta. *For how could I not vow to defend my country and the people in it?*

'Everyone, every single one of you, can make a difference,' he said. 'We're going to start creating newspapers and flyers to spread among our communities, and we need people to write those articles, to type them, to print them. We need explosives set for ambushes, we need men and women to place them and detonate them. Whatever you can do for us, we will find a way to put you to work.'

'The newspapers and the posters,' Aletta murmured, leaning close to her mother so she could speak into her ear. 'What do you think? That's something we could do, isn't it?'

'We could do some of the writing, or even just all the typing,' her mother said, her eyes widening. 'It'll take me some time to get back into it, but I used to type when I worked for your grandfather. And you'd be excellent at typing and writing, too.'

It didn't take them long to find someone to talk to and offer themselves forward, and when it was finally time to leave, Aletta wished they could stay. There was something about being in a room full of people who were so passionate and engaged, and she wanted to soak up the atmosphere for longer.

But she knew her father would be waiting up for them, and she didn't want him to worry any more than she knew he already was. And sure enough, when they arrived home, he was sitting in the living room, staring at the door in the same way he had when he'd caught her sneaking back in after the first meeting. Only this time he knew where she'd been, and he was holding an almost empty glass of whisky in one hand as his cigarette burned in the other.

She could see the relief on his face the moment he set eyes upon them, as if he'd half expected them not to come home.

'Well come on, tell me what you've signed up for,' he said, as her mother brushed past them both, after kissing her husband's head, to fix something for them to eat.

'We're to help with an underground newspaper they're planning,' Aletta told him, perching on the arm of his chair. 'They said that one of the first things the Nazis will limit is the news we can access, and we need to make certain that the Dutch people know the truth. It will be our job to collate the information and type up the news, and then someone else will print the copies and distribute them.'

He stroked his chin, as if lost deep in thought, but in the end, he only nodded and patted her leg as he rose when her mother called them for supper.

It was the thumping sound that woke Aletta. She pushed herself up on her elbows and listened, wondering what she was hearing. When she still couldn't figure it out, she pushed the covers off and padded down the hallway, realising that the sound was coming from the living room.

What on earth was happening in their apartment so early in the morning?

Her mother came up behind her, her hand skimming Aletta's shoulder as she passed her. 'What on earth is your father doing? He'll wake the entire apartment block.'

Aletta shrugged and they wandered in to the living room to find her father with a hammer in hand and a number of what looked like white boards. They usually called someone to do odd jobs around the place if needed – it certainly wasn't her father, although she did remember that he'd worked for a builder when he was a student in need of work.

'Jan, what are you doing?' Emma asked, sounding exasperated.

A few moments later, looking satisfied with his work, he turned to them both. His expression was sombre, and his eyes were bracketed with a tiredness that she thought might be more from worry than lack of sleep. Or perhaps it was both.

'I'm building somewhere for you to work,' he said, as if he were trying to swallow down thick emotion. 'This is my final condition.'

Aletta looked at her mother, waiting for her to say something. But when she stayed silent, Aletta spoke.

'What is your condition?' she asked, as it slowly dawned on her. She'd been so bleary-eyed from sleep, she hadn't realised straight away.

'If you're going to work with the Resistance, if you truly intend on helping them to create their newspaper from our home, then you must be hidden,' he said. 'I cannot risk you being caught.'

Aletta saw his eyes fill with tears as he looked between them, and it wrenched at her heart.

'I won't be able to live with myself if I don't keep you safe. No one will ever even know this wall is new, we'll make it look as if it's always been here. It backs on to the wardrobe alcove in your sewing room, Emma, so I've been able to create a proper little room for you that is only accessible through the wardrobe door.'

Her mother embraced him, holding him tight and whispering something she couldn't hear.

When she stepped back, Aletta smiled and squeezed her father's hand.

'Thank you,' she said. 'Now how about you show us this hiding place? I'd like to see exactly where we'll be tucked away.'

The relief on his face was palpable, and she dropped her head to his shoulder for a moment, knowing that he'd done this not out of a need to control them, but from fear.

And so all three walked into her mother's sewing room, which doubled as the spare room her grandparents had always stayed in when they'd come to visit, and discovered that the wardrobe door now opened into a large alcove that was almost big enough to call a small room. Aletta had to duck low to get in, but she stood up tall when she was inside, surprised to find a space that was larger than expected.

'I know it's small, but it's safe,' her father said. 'Or at least I hope it will be. It's the best I could think of as I lay in bed awake last night, and we had that alcove in the living room that was easy enough to block off with board.'

Aletta hugged him, holding tight. 'It's perfect. Truly it is. Now come along,' she said, nudging him forward. 'It's time for breakfast and I can already smell coffee brewing.'

He obliged and disappeared through the door, and as he did, she turned and looked back at the space he'd created. It wasn't big, and it wasn't much, but the fact that her father had made it meant it was all the more special.

Aletta didn't know how long schools would stay open, or how things were going to change – no one did. And she needed every distraction she could get, because she couldn't stop thinking about the children, and just what might happen to those who'd already left her class.

'Aletta!'

The sound of her mother's panicked call made her hurry to the kitchen, thinking something dreadful had happened. And from the look on her mother's face, it had.

'What—'

The radio crackled, the strong male voice of the announcer interrupting her. 'Queen Wilhelmina and the Dutch royal family, including the Prince, Princess Juliana and their children, as well as the government, have fled to England. We repeat, the Queen and the Dutch royal family, along with the government, have fled the Netherlands for safety in England.'

'The royal family have left us,' Aletta whispered, clearing her throat as her words caught. 'It means they don't feel safe here any longer. It means . . .'

'They would never leave their people unless . . .' Her mother touched her mouth as tears filled her eyes, which made Aletta's own eyes prickle in response. 'They must truly think the worst is about to happen, it's the only reason they'd go.'

Aletta shuddered. If the royal family have gone, what hope is there for the rest of us?

Chapter Six

Aletta

'Come along, class,' Aletta said, trying her best to sound bright. 'Tidy your desks and pack your bags, and then we'll have time to read another fairy tale.'

She noticed one of the little boys was rubbing at his face, and she went over to him, bending down to check he was all right. When he saw her, fresh tears filled his eyes and began to plop down his cheeks.

'What's wrong?' she asked.

'I'm worried about my brother. He's eighteen.'

The rest of the class had gone quiet, and she turned to see almost every child was watching her. She hadn't thought that they might have worries about their own siblings being sent off to fight, but so far she'd managed to avoid any questions about the newly departed royal family or the war.

'Is anyone else feeling worried about their brothers?' she asked, as it dawned on her just how many of these children could be affected by the war. 'Or your fathers or uncles?'

Every little head began to nod.

'Well, I understand. The thought of war is terrifying, and I'm a little scared too,' she admitted. 'But here in this class, while you're with me, we're all going to do our best to smile and have fun. How does that sound?'

There were more than a few smiles, and she beamed back at them, even though inside she wanted to cry.

'We're going to read and sing,' she said, 'and we're going to think of fun projects that will keep us all busy.'

Aletta gave the boy a hug and stood up, turning away for a second to quickly wipe her own eyes. In that moment, she couldn't look at their innocent, beautiful little faces. They might not all be here by the end of the year, and the thought broke her heart into a million tiny pieces.

As soon as she got home after school, Aletta kept herself busy setting up their little room, not wanting to think of her sad children from earlier in the day. The only consolation was that they'd all been smiling when they left, after she'd read all their favourite fairy tales.

They'd just carried a typewriter through the little door in the wardrobe from her mother's sewing room, which was heavier than it looked, and it was now sitting atop an overturned apple box. There was barely any space, so they'd decided on the box and a cushion each, with another box for a desk. They also had a painting on the wall, to make it appear more homely, and some blankets and other cushions, all ones her mother had stitched herself, that had been gathering dust in a cupboard. It was certainly going to be warm and cosy in there, because there wasn't going to be so much as a breath of fresh air in the small, cramped space.

She passed her mother, pushing her slightly damp hair from her face as she carried in some supplies. Her father had brought home paper from his office, which they would use for the typewriter, and they also had pens and some of her teaching plans just to make it look like a storage area if their new workspace was found. Her mother grinned back at her, looking satisfied as she went back out for another load.

'I think we're almost done,' Aletta said, blowing her hair away when it fell straight back to her forehead.

'I think so, too,' her mother said.

Aletta went back to her room and took some final bits and pieces, knowing they'd be grateful to have everything they needed at their fingertips when their work began. They still didn't know when it would be, but the closer the Nazis got to the city, the more pressing the need for an underground newspaper. And they all knew that it wasn't a matter of *if*, but when.

She paused beside a photograph that had been taken when she was a girl, a portrait of her family, just the three of them. She lifted it, remembering the day. It had been her birthday and they'd gone to sit for a photograph before going out for ice-cream. Her father had taken the day off work, and it had made her feel like a princess, as if no one was more important than her on her special day.

After she replaced the photograph on her bedside table, Aletta took the last of her supplies and made her way back into their little room. She found her mother standing there, and caught her wiping a tear from her cheek.

'What's wrong?' she asked, putting her things down and placing an arm around her mother's shoulder.

'Nothing,' her mother said, smiling as she wiped another errant tear away. 'Nothing's wrong at all. I just needed a moment to look at what we've done.'

Aletta felt her own eyes prickling with tears, but she blinked them away.

They stood, hands on hips, surveying the room. It wasn't anything fancy and it certainly wasn't very large, but it was theirs.

'We did it,' she said, turning to her mother, who replied with a big smile. 'We actually did it, and we did it together.'

Her mother blinked away tears. 'I suppose it's been a long time since I've done anything for myself,' she said. 'I know how that must sound to you, but we didn't have the same opportunities when I was young. It was get married and have a baby straight out of school, and . . .' Her mother smiled. 'I know it probably doesn't seem all that different to you now, but it is. I mean look at you, studying to be a teacher at the college and bravely signing up for this resistance work.'

Aletta smiled back, reaching for her hand and squeezing it.

'Who knows, women might help win this war,' she said, before letting go. 'Now come on, let's have a cup of coffee and make some lunch.' She checked the clock – there was a reason her stomach was rumbling. It was well after noon.

She felt lighter as she walked through the wardrobe door, ducking down low and then emerging into her mother's sewing room, and she smiled to herself as she went through the apartment and into the kitchen, setting the water to boil. But just as she was turning to get the cups down, she heard something – a rumble that left her uneasy. Aletta waited until she heard it again. It was only faint, but it was a rumble, like nothing she'd ever heard before, and she also registered the glasses tinkling together ever so slightly in their kitchen cupboard.

'Did you hear that?' she asked her mother, just as another noise sounded in the distance.

'I heard it,' her mother said, frowning as they both paused to listen again. 'It was . . . I don't know how to explain it.'

Aletta quickly went over to the window to open it, leaning out and listening, seeing that other people in apartments across from theirs were doing the same. Her pulse ignited, and Aletta glanced back at her mother, who was now fiddling with the wireless. Something was very wrong.

'Do you think . . .' but Aletta's voice faded away. She knew that whatever it was they were hearing could only mean one thing, that this was no random noise.

This was an act of war. It couldn't possibly be anything else.

The fighting was getting closer. Close enough that the happiness and bravery she'd felt only moments earlier was fast evaporating.

She forgot about the coffee she'd been making when the wireless crackled to life, and she shut the window as she wrapped her arms tightly around herself and listened. There was a static noise for some time, and they just stood there, waiting, her mother adjusting it as a voice came to life and stuttered through the airwaves. There was another distant shudder as they listened to the broadcast, a shudder that told her that somewhere, something more dreadful than she could possibly imagine was happening.

'The city of Rotterdam is under attack,' came the steady, emotionless voice of the newsreader. 'I repeat, the city of Rotterdam is under attack from aerial bombing.'

Aletta met her mother's gaze. *Rotterdam?* They had friends who'd moved there some years ago, and it was a beautiful city. She couldn't imagine the terror of the people who lived there, what it must be like to hide in fear as bombs were ruthlessly dropped from the air, the fear of realising that the planes overhead were coming for them and their homes. That they were the enemy's target. Was that truly what they'd heard? And if they were bombing Rotterdam, did that mean that Amsterdam was next? She swallowed, trying not to imagine the terror of buildings being ripped apart around her, or heaven forbid, their own apartment block being hit. Or where they might hide.

'Despite a fierce act of resistance to German paratroopers and soldiers who landed on the water and tried to invade the city of Rotterdam not four days ago, today marks a grave day for the people of the Netherlands. Our forces refused to surrender, and now it is feared that hundreds will already be dead.'

Aletta stepped forward, her hand shaking as she turned the radio off. She didn't want to hear any more. She *couldn't stand* to listen to another word, not as fear built inside of her at such a steady rate, threatening to steal her breath away.

'What we're doing . . .' she began, wrapping her arms around herself. 'We're doing the right thing. It makes the work we've agreed to do even more important.'

Her mother nodded, but she couldn't disguise the fear in her gaze. 'I'd hoped that we could fight them off, that we wouldn't surrender, but . . .'

She didn't need to finish her sentence. They were only a tiny force compared to Germany's army; it had only been a matter of time.

'Do you think they'll stop with Rotterdam?' she asked her mother. 'Or do you think the bombing will continue?'

Her mother's wide eyes met hers. 'They want us to surrender.' Her voice was barely a whisper. 'They're not going to stop until they get what they want.'

And what they wanted right now was the Netherlands, and Belgium, and France, and Luxembourg, and then the next country that was in their path. It seemed they weren't going to stop until they'd swallowed all of Europe.

There was another distant shudder and then another, and it took all Aletta's will power to go about making their coffees as her mother took up the place beside her to make them each a sandwich. This might be one of the last normal days they knew, and no amount of worrying was going to help them. But when she glanced over at her mother, she saw the unmistakable shake of her hands as she sliced the bread. Her own hands were trembling, no matter how many times she clenched and unclenched them.

Aletta's mother turned on the wireless again. But this time, they listened to the slightly staticky sound of music instead of the BBC, neither of them saying a word as they sat at the table and chewed, the food like sawdust in Aletta's mouth as she forced it down. Their pledge to join the resistance had suddenly become a whole lot more dangerous, and she imagined her mother would be thinking the very same thing.

But just as quickly her thoughts turned to her friend Cecilia, wondering if she'd be able to hear the faraway sound of bombs falling from the countryside. It had seemed like a knee-jerk reaction when her father had chosen to send her away with her brothers, but now it seemed like the height of good judgement, and it wouldn't surprise her to see families lining the streets by morning, suitcases in hand as they rushed their children as far away from the invading forces as they could.

The next day, Aletta was trying to keep her class settled when another teacher came rushing in, her face pale.

'Miss, would you please come into the hall with me?'

Aletta smiled to her children and excused herself, closing the door behind her as the other teacher thrust a single page of newsprint into her hands.

THE NETHERLANDS HAS SURRENDERED.

Aletta felt as if the world had stopped around her as she read the words over and over again.

'What do we tell them?' she finally whispered. 'The children, what do we say?'

'We stay calm and say nothing,' the teacher said, grabbing hold of Aletta's hand and holding it tight. 'Their mothers will start arriving for them soon, and it will be sheer panic when they do, so we just stay calm.'

Aletta nodded, feeling numb all over, and when the other teacher left, she took a moment to breathe and steady herself. Then she walked into her classroom with a bright smile.

'I think it's story time everyone!'

Later that morning Aletta walked home, the news finally sinking in now that she'd seen all her children safely collected, her class empty. Her mother had come, as worried for her as the other mothers had been for their children, and she was grateful for the company.

Newsprints drifted down the streets, as if people had read the four printed words and then just let them go, like balloon strings slipping from the hands of children. As she looked around, people were either silent, clearly in shock, hurrying for home, or dropping to their knees. One old man she could see had crumpled, his face streaked with tears, his body unable to hold him upright in the face of such devastating news.

It was like the day martial law had been declared, only worse. Then, it had been a stark surprise, but this . . . this was the very worst news.

'Let's go home,' she said to her mother, tucking her arm tightly through hers and pointing them in the direction of their apartment. She glanced around, expecting soldiers, but so far there were none in their neighbourhood. The sounds of fighting only hours earlier had been clearly audible, but for now, there was silence.

Aletta's stomach churned. In truth, she didn't know what they were supposed to do or what to expect, but going to the relative safety of home felt like the only sensible thing to do in the face of such news, especially as schools had closed early.

They hurried home, walking as fast as they could, and Aletta stayed alert, eyes darting around the streets. She felt as if she couldn't properly catch her breath until they reached their apartment block, and her hands were shaking so much that her mother had to take the keys from her to unlock the door.

They immediately locked the front door behind them and her mother made them coffee as Aletta went to the window and stared out, pressing her cheek to the cold glass. She'd known this was coming, they all had, but it didn't make it any easier to accept.

It felt like she'd been standing there forever, but only minutes had passed before her mother pressed a steaming hot cup of coffee into her hands.

'Maybe we'll have something stronger when your father gets home,' her mother murmured.

Aletta nodded, blowing on the drink as she kept looking out of the window.

And then she saw what she'd feared the most. A soldier in an unfamiliar uniform. *He is wearing a Nazi uniform.*

Aletta swallowed, her fingers tightening around the cup as her mother shifted closer to her, their shoulders touching.

'They're here,' she said, her voice barely a whisper. *Where are you, Father? Please come home. Come home.*

She didn't say anything about her fears to her mother though – she'd be worried enough as it was.

When she finally glanced at her mother, she saw a single tear slipping from the corner of her eye and sliding down her cheek. She bit down on her bottom lip as her own tears formed, the emotion feeling as if it were lodged in her chest, fighting to come out.

Nothing is ever going to be the same again.

Soldiers would be patrolling their streets, taking over the city they loved, speaking another language. But worse than that, what would happen to the Jewish families in their neighbourhood? Where would they go to be safe? Where had little Else and the other children and their families gone?

She watched two Nazi soldiers laughing and cheering, with another two following close behind. They had conquered the Netherlands, and she imagined today would be a celebration for them before they began to hunt down those they sought to destroy.

'The underground work,' Aletta began, blinking away a fresh wave of tears. 'This changes everything; this makes it even more important.'

'If we're caught, now that they're here, what we're doing . . .' her mother said with a gasp.

'Don't,' Aletta said, squeezing her hand. 'Don't say it. Don't let fear stop you from doing what we need to do. That's what they want.'

Her mother dropped her head to Aletta's shoulder as they continued to stare out of the window, as more soldiers came, as if there were a never-ending trail of them. 'Heaven help us,' her mother whispered.

Aletta sipped her coffee, swallowing it down and trying to steady her mind. What they were planning to do did come with more risk now. They'd known this was coming. Her only mistake was naively not realising how soon Nazi boots would echo down the cobbled streets of her home city.

Chapter Seven

30 April 2015

Aletta stared out of the window of the train, her face so close to the glass it was almost touching. She closed her eyes and listened to the noise of the wheels rumbling along the tracks, letting her mind wander back. It wasn't often she let herself remember, not like this, but today she didn't stop herself.

For years she'd stamped away the memories. They'd been like tentacles at first, creeping towards her and holding her in their iron-clad grip. Or they'd wake her in the night, leaving her trapped in damp, tangled sheets as she fought to get away from the dark thoughts of the past. But not today.

Today she let the memories find her.

Her thoughts took her back to another train ride, one she'd been forced to take. When she closed her eyes more tightly, she could still smell the inside of the carriage, remembered the fear and terror that had wrapped around them all. Peeking through the gaps and blinking through her tears; the feel of her mother's arm around her, stopping her from falling to the ground.

She opened her eyes, the memories proving too painful.

'Mum?' The voice was familiar, calming. 'Mum, are you okay?'

It took her a moment to realise it was her daughter, and she looked at the warm hand covering hers before glancing around them. They were in a warm train carriage. There were other people sitting nearby; children, families, other women smiling and talking.

She was safe.

It had taken her a moment to pull herself back to the present, but she knew she had nothing to fear, not anymore. She took a deep, shaky breath as her racing heart began to settle.

'If it becomes too much, if you decide you don't want to be there . . .' Her daughter cleared her throat. 'At any stage, Mum, you just let me know.'

Aletta nodded. Her daughter had said the same words to her at the house before they'd left, and again when they were in the car on the way to the train station. She knew it was because she cared, that it was hard for her to see her mother revisit such a harrowing time in her life.

She leaned towards the window again, watching the countryside pass by in a blur and trying to place exactly where they were, how much longer they had to travel before they got there.

If I don't do this now, I might not have a chance to go back again.

Aletta was in her ninety-fourth year, and she knew that time was running out on her. She had her final respects to pay, and this year might be her last.

Chapter Eight

Paris, June 1940

Chloe

Chloe sat close to the wireless. Even though they were permitted to listen to the BBC broadcasts under the occupation, she was always hesitant, preferring to keep it turned down as low as possible to avoid censure. Since the occupation, every part of her life had changed overnight – from what she could listen to, how it felt to walk outside her door, and the worry if her family were even a few minutes late arriving home. And those soldiers in her beautiful Paris – it made her stomach turn seeing them walk down the cobbled streets as if they owned the city, as if they belonged.

But tonight, most of her family were safely home, already in bed, and she was alone in the kitchen, tidying up after supper and listening to as much of the broadcast as she could. The door clicked then and she glanced up, seeing her brother Claude arrive home. It was late; it always was when he slipped back into their apartment these days, but she didn't scold him. Instead, she waved him over, knowing he'd want to hear the broadcast as much as she did.

'It's about to start?' he asked.

Chloe nodded. 'Charles de Gaulle will be on in moments,' she murmured.

When the radio crackled to life, Chloe placed her hand on her brother's shoulder and closed her eyes, listening to de Gaulle's voice.

'The destiny of the world is at stake . . . Whatever happens, the flame of French resistance must not be extinguished, and *will not* be extinguished!'

She opened her eyes to find her brother leaning forward, intently, as if he were listening to the most important speech of his life. And perhaps he was, for he was no different from thousands of other young men in France. Too young to have been sent away to fight, but full of enough bravado and anger to make them determined to do something, *anything*, to save their country.

They listened to the rest of the speech together, and she half expected Claude to leave again, for them to argue as they often did about the hours he was gone, the curfew he flouted time and again. But when she reached for him, he only smiled and gave her a hug, reminding her of the boy he'd been a handful of years earlier. She knew, despite her protests, that he could no more stop what he was doing than he could stop breathing.

'I love you,' she said, pressing a fierce kiss to his forehead and holding him tight. 'You know I couldn't live with myself if anything happened to you, right?'

'I love you, too,' he whispered into her hair.

He squeezed her back, but when he let her go she saw a glint in his eye that scared her. She could see that de Gaulle's speech had only stoked the fire inside him all the more, and it terrified her.

Please keep him safe, she prayed as he turned to go. But Chloe wasn't even sure who she was praying to anymore, because if there was once a higher being who listened to her, they certainly didn't seem to be any longer. No deities seemed to be protecting the lives of men throughout Europe.

◆ ◆ ◆

The next night, Chloe stood in the kitchen preparing dinner, still thinking about the BBC broadcast. She couldn't stop remembering the way de Gaulle had so passionately announced that France was not alone, because in truth, she'd never felt so lonely in her life. Being scared wasn't in her nature, but ever since her mother had passed and the war had begun, she'd never been so frightened. And if she was honest with herself, it was worrying about her seventeen-year-old brother that consumed most of her thoughts. Her younger brother, Adrian, she could manage – he came home from school when he was supposed to and listened to her words of caution – but Claude? Claude was going to be the death of her.

Chloe called out to Adrian to set the table, smiling as she heard him run down the hallway. *As loud as a herd of elephants.* She remembered the words her mother had always muttered, but unlike her mother, she didn't caution him. If all Adrian did was run too loudly down the hall, that was the least of her worries.

He came into the kitchen, his cheeks flushed and his smile kind. She kissed his head, smiling when he squirmed away from her – too big for kisses, but still young enough to be made hot chocolate before bed.

'Go and call Papa for dinner once you've set the table,' she said, turning around to slice the loaf of bread and take the potatoes and vegetables from the oven.

By the time she took the food to the table, her father and brother were already seated. She placed a plate in front of Adrian first, with a small amount of chicken on it, and one in front of her father with an even smaller amount. Hers had none – something her rumbling stomach seemed acutely aware of. Neither of them would want her to go without, but since her mother had died, she'd taken over her role in the family, and she knew without a doubt that she would have gone without too to ensure the boys had enough.

When Chloe finally sat, her father shook his head and took the chicken from his plate, silently transferring it to hers. She in turn gave him half back, which resulted in only a meagre amount for each of them. He barely spoke anymore, but the fact that he'd noticed how little food she had told her he did care.

Adrian didn't even bother offering to share his. He knew by now that it was a fruitless argument because no one at the table would ever let him go without. Just as no one said anything about the fourth, empty place at the table. Chloe had once left Claude's plate there and hoped he'd be in before it was cold, but now she kept it in the still-warm oven, knowing that it could be hours before he returned.

'How is school?' she asked Adrian, as she ate a mouthful of vegetables. She would save the chicken until last and savour every tiny bite.

'It's all right,' he said, his mouth full as he talked.

She glanced at her father. One of them should have reprimanded him for not covering his mouth before answering, but she didn't have the heart.

'And you, Papa?' she asked. 'How was your day?'

He gave her a small smile. 'It was fine.'

Chloe glanced at Claude's empty seat again, wishing she could hear the sound of his keys jangling and see him walk through the door. Her father worried too, she knew he did, but he still seemed able to amble off to bed when Claude didn't return home, whereas she sat up half the night, making a terrible job of her knitting as she waited.

The worst thing was, she knew there was nothing she could do to stop Claude.

'Thank you for a lovely dinner, Chloe,' her father said when they'd all finished.

There wasn't a scrap left on their plates, not with food being so precious now.

'One day I'll find a whole bird to roast,' she replied, smiling as her father reached over to pat her hand, grateful that he'd said more than a couple of words. 'Adrian, you can help me clean up.'

'But I have homework to do!' he cried.

'And I have a house to keep clean,' she muttered. 'You can just clear the table with me, and I'll do the dishes.'

He grumbled but did as he was told, and she playfully flicked him with the tea towel before he skipped away and headed for his room. Which is how Chloe found herself, yet again, standing in the kitchen alone, up to her elbows in soapy water, and still waiting for the click of a door that never came.

Until it did.

She turned at the sound, surprised to see Claude's wide grin as he crossed the living room with his long, loping stride. Usually, he came home brooding or contemplative, but tonight, he looked as if he were on top of the world.

'You look as if the Allies have just taken back France,' she teased, welcoming him with a hug.

He hugged her back, and when she held him at arm's length, she could see that his eyes were shining brightly.

'I've joined the Resistance,' he said, as casually as if he'd gone to the movies.

'You've, you've what?' she asked, her heart skipping a beat.

'I've joined the Free French,' he said.

Chloe swallowed, taking a moment to compose herself as she turned around and took his dinner from the oven. It shouldn't have surprised her. She'd known he was doing something with all the hours he disappeared, and it certainly wasn't because he was studying.

'You heard de Gaulle, we have to fight, Chloe,' Claude said, taking the plate from her and forking the small pile of chicken from it, swallowing it in one mouthful. 'We can't stand by and do nothing.'

'I understand,' she said, nodding slowly. Because she did understand, and if she hadn't had to step into her mother's role, she would have been burning just as brightly to help the cause, sneaking out of the house and joining Claude on his escapades, doing what she could for her beloved country.

'You do?' he asked.

'I do,' she echoed. 'You forget that I'm only three years older than you, Claude.' *That all I want is to behave like a twenty-year-old instead of someone twice my age, she thought.* 'But I still wish you'd talked to me first, that you could have discussed it with me before—'

'Would you have tried to talk me out of it?'

She sighed. 'Maybe.' But then again, maybe she wouldn't have.

'We're going to fight the Nazis, Chloe,' he said, his eyes wide and full of passion. 'We're going to blow up convoys and destroy bridges, we're going to create a network throughout France and fight to get our country back.'

His words scared her, but they also made her proud, and when he set his plate down, she reached out and wrapped him in her arms. 'I'm so proud of you, Claude,' she said. 'Mother would have been so proud of how brave you are, too. I hope you know that.'

'You truly think so?' he asked, and when she looked up she saw tears shining in his eyes.

'I don't just think so, Claude, I know so. She would have been so proud of the man you've become, as am I, even if what you're doing terrifies me.'

He smiled when she ruffled his hair, and Chloe leaned back on the kitchen counter and watched him eat. He didn't even bother taking his plate to the table, just ate standing as if he hadn't been fed in days, and she couldn't help but think how boyish he looked.

'Claude,' she said, as he finished his last mouthful.

He glanced at her. 'I thought you said you weren't going to try to talk me out of this.'

Chloe smiled. 'I'm not, I promise I'm not. But *you* have to promise *me* that you won't bring danger home with you,' she said. 'I wasn't lying when I said how proud of you I am, but Mama would never forgive us if we put Adrian in danger. You have to be careful.'

Claude's expression was solemn. 'I know.'

'So, you make sure you're not being followed, you keep an eye over your shoulder, and you be careful to keep your identity hidden,' Chloe said.

He nodded. 'I promise, Chloe. I don't want to put Adrian in harm's way any more than you do.'

She took the plate from Claude then and rinsed it, waving him away when he attempted to take it from her.

'It's fine,' she said. 'Just tell me all about this Free French movement while I finish cleaning up. I might not be able to join it myself, but it doesn't mean I don't want to hear all about it.'

And she did. There was a yearning deep inside Chloe, wishing that she could go with her brother, but she had responsibilities now, and she'd made a promise to her mother as she took her final breath. Just like she'd given up her dream of becoming a writer and going to university – she had to be content now with reading her favourite books instead of writing one. Her notebooks were in a pile beside her bed, gathering dust, their pages not cracked open for longer than she could remember. Real life had stolen her once-active imagination.

I will always protect Adrian, Mama. There is nothing I won't do to protect that boy and shield him from the worst of the war.

Adrian was still a child, and she wanted him to have a childhood and feel safe and loved, and if that meant sacrificing her own life by looking after him and her family, then so be it.

Chapter Nine

Chloe

Chloe rose from her bed and walked down the hall in her nightgown. She'd intended on staying awake to wait for Claude to get home, but she must have fallen asleep. She'd woken with her novel fallen on her chest, and a quick glance at the clock had told her that it was late. It was a testament to how tired she was that she couldn't keep her eyes open to read. *Rebecca* by Daphne du Maurier was one of her favourite books that she often re-read, and one she'd hoped to emulate in her own writing.

She tiptoed past her younger brother's room, glancing in to make sure he was still covered up, and then paused outside Claude's bedroom. Her heart sank when she saw that he wasn't there. His door was still wide open, his bed still perfectly made as it had been all day; as it had been for two entire days now. Chloe sat on the edge, wishing there was some way to contact him, to make certain that he was all right. She'd hidden Claude's absence from their father, but there was only so long that she could cover for him.

Chloe decided to wait for him there, her eyes closing of their own accord, still so tired from waiting up for him two nights in a row. If he arrived home, he'd find her there and have no choice but to wake her, and as she snuggled down beneath his duvet, she squeezed her eyes shut tight as the faint smell of his cologne wafted up to her from his pillow.

She could have sat up with her notebook full of poems that she'd penned before her mother's death, and tried to write something new, but the words just wouldn't come to her anymore, and she'd mostly given up trying. It all seemed like a dream from the past now, imagining that she might one day be a published writer.

Come home, Claude. Please, just come home.

◆ ◆ ◆

It was in the early hours when Claude finally appeared, and Chloe woke with a start, bleary-eyed and half furious, half relieved to see him. She got out of bed and gave her brother a shove, followed by a hard hug, wondering if she might never let him go.

'I've been so worried about you,' she said, not wanting to wake anyone else up as she pressed a kiss to his temple. 'You couldn't have sent word that you were all right?'

Chloe could tell from the brightness of his eyes, the way they were shining, that she'd regret asking where he'd been. But she was his sister, and she needed to know what kind of trouble he was in.

'Where have you been?' she asked, softly, hoping that if he didn't think she was angry he might answer.

He grinned. 'Do you really want to know?'

She sighed. 'Yes, Claude, I really want to know.' She pulled him down to sit on the bed beside her.

'You remember I told you about the resistance group, about what they had planned?'

As if I'd forget that. But she simply nodded. 'I remember.'

'We have to do everything we can to hinder the Nazis,' he said. 'We have to disrupt their supply chain, their ability to move easily in our country. We have to stop them when they least expect it, or they'll never leave.'

Chloe swallowed. 'What have you done, Claude?' she asked, her voice barely a whisper.

'I was part of a network tasked with blowing up a section of road,' he said, as proudly as if he were a boy announcing an excellent school grade.

'You—' Her voice faded away as he kept talking, her stomach twisting in knots.

'You should have seen us, Chloe!' he said, his eyes wide as he grabbed hold of her hand. 'It was like nothing you've ever seen before. We set the explosives, lay in wait, and then, boom!'

She closed her eyes as a shudder ran through her, imagining how many men might have been killed. 'Claude . . .'

'Before you say anything, if I don't do this, then who does? We all need to step up, Chloe. We need to do what we can, to get our country back. It's our *duty* to fight in any way we can.'

She nodded and reached for his hand again when he pulled it away, holding it tight. 'It's not that I don't understand, it's that I'm fearful of the implications. For our family.'

He shook his head and tried to pull his hand away again, but she held firm.

'I made a promise when our mother died, that I would take care of this family,' she said, meeting his gaze, knowing that he was full of bravado now, but that eventually her words would reach him. 'I held her hand just like I'm holding yours now, and I *promised* her, Claude. I promised her that I would do everything I could to keep you safe. Can you not see what I've sacrificed? The dreams that disappeared for me overnight?'

'I'm not going to stop just because—'

'I'm not asking you to stop,' she said. 'I'm reminding you to be careful. I just need you to look me in the eye and tell me again that you'll make sure none of this comes home with you. We need to protect Adrian, and if you're caught . . .' She paused. 'You need to cover your tracks, Claude. You need to promise me that you'll be vigilant about keeping this from our door, that you'll do whatever it takes to put distance between our home and the work you're doing. Not because I don't believe in you or the work you're doing, but because we need to shield Adrian from it.'

His eyes softened, as if he'd remembered the promise he made when he told her that he was joining the Free French.

'Could you live with yourself if anything happened to him? Because I know that I couldn't.' Tears stung her eyes, but she blinked them away. 'Just promise me that you'll be careful.'

'I promise.'

Chloe sighed in relief and patted his hand. 'Good, now let's go and have some coffee. You must be exhausted.'

He reminded her of a much younger boy then, the way he hurried along beside her and started to whisper all about what they'd done, about what it had been like seeing the explosion tear through the air around them, the truck they'd targeted flipping upside down and being engulfed in flames. But when she sat down beside him, she wished that she could just be his sister. She wished that her father would step up and be the parent in their family, that it was he who sat up late at night worrying instead of leaving everything to her. Because it was exhausting, and even though she trusted Claude, he was only a teenager.

No matter what he said, what he was doing wasn't safe. She trudged back to her bedroom, exhausted but relieved he was home. Only this time she did reach for one of her notebooks. She couldn't bring herself to open it, but she tucked it beneath her pillow and tried to remember what it had felt like to be a young woman with no responsibilities.

A young woman who'd felt like the world was at her feet, with her whole life stretching ahead of her.

Chloe had just started to feel as if some sense of normality had returned to her life, albeit one with the enemy making themselves at home in the city she loved. Adrian was going to school without complaint, Claude hadn't run off on any more adventures as yet, and her father had even thanked her for dinner the night before and asked her about her day. They were small victories, but ones she was happy to claim – these days, she didn't take anything for granted.

As she was about to set the table for dinner, only four nights after Claude had returned home, she heard loud voices and boots shuffling on the other side of their apartment door. Adrian started to complain about his homework, but she silenced him with a finger to her lips and a shake of her head as she strained to listen.

'Go and get Father,' she whispered. 'And tell Claude to stay in his room.'

Her heart began to thunder in her chest, and that was when a loud knock echoed out on their door.

'*Öffne die Tür!*' came a shout. Followed by an even louder 'Open the door!' in heavily accented German.

Fear brushed every inch of Chloe's body as she glanced over her shoulder, seeing that her father was coming down the hall towards her. But his face was blank, not telling her what to do, not giving her any answers. And so she made the decision for herself, knowing that the longer she waited, the more chance they had of their front door being kicked in.

She would have called back that she was coming, only her voice had stuck in her throat. Her hands shook so much that she had to hold on to her right wrist with her left just to steady it enough to unlock the door and turn the handle.

'*Bonjour*,' she said, forcing herself to smile at the two men standing there, even though her legs trembled so violently she had to grasp the door frame just to stay upright. 'Can I help you?'

She knew who they were – she imagined everyone in Europe knew who these men were – that they wore the uniform of the SS and were feared for their cruelty. The man closest to her stepped forward, and when she glanced down, she saw that he'd intentionally placed his foot over the threshold. She couldn't have slammed the door on him even if she'd wanted to and she found it almost impossible to look up from his perfectly polished leather boot.

Chloe quickly glanced behind her, her stomach dropping when she saw Claude standing beside Adrian, his hand on their little brother's shoulder. *Why couldn't you have listened to me, just this once?* But she turned back just as fast, fixing her smile again. Perhaps it wasn't Claude's fault; perhaps this was nothing more than a coincidence.

'Who lives in this apartment?' the closest man asked.

Chloe swallowed. 'Myself, my father and my two brothers,' she said, fighting to keep her voice even. 'They're standing right behind me. It is only us here.'

She knew she was holding her breath, but she couldn't help it. She tried to relax her shoulders, wondering if they were going door to door to look for hidden Jews. That could be why they were here, and if it were for that reason, then there was nothing to fear.

'You,' the SS man said, pointing towards Claude as he pushed past her, almost knocking her over when his shoulder stamped into hers. 'Come forward.'

She stood and watched in horror as Claude stepped forward, his shoulders squared, as if he wasn't scared. And she was angry at him for that, because he should have been *terrified* of the man standing in front of him. He should have quivered just seeing the SS men in their apartment, let alone at being summoned. But what she saw bordered on defiance, not fear, or maybe he was just a better actor than she was.

'This will be easier for your family if you just confess,' said the Nazi. His smile was cold, and Chloe noticed the way her brother's face fell, the terror that finally spread across his features, almost as if he'd finally in that moment realised what was happening and what the man before him was capable of.

She'd asked one thing of him; she'd told him in no uncertain terms that he couldn't leave a trail to their apartment, to their *family*, and yet she knew that her hopes before had been wrong. She knew now there was a reason they were here, just as she knew in that moment that it was up to her. If she wanted to keep her family safe, she couldn't rely on Claude, and she certainly couldn't rely on her father.

'What are you asking my brother to confess to?' she asked, as bravely as she could, even though her voice stuttered.

'Did I ask you a question?' the SS man asked, his lips curling back in a way that made her tremble, that made her wonder if he was going to raise his hand and smack it across her face. Until the man behind him touched his hand to his hip, and she thought that perhaps he might shoot her instead.

She kept her mouth firmly shut from that moment on, pleading with her brother with her eyes, but he still stood silently.

'Search the house!' the first man ordered.

Adrian's cry sent a jolt through Chloe, and she opened her arm, beckoning for him to come to her, tucking him tight to her side when he did.

'It's all right.' She stroked his arm. 'It's going to be just fine.'

'Do you promise?' he whispered back.

'I promise,' she murmured, not wanting to lie to him, but she didn't know what else to say as the Nazi men strode through their house and turned over furniture, as they disappeared down the hall and into the bedrooms. Her father dropped into a chair, his head in his hands, still not saying or doing anything to help his family, falling back into the silence he'd suffered from since her mother had died.

She jumped when she heard glass break, and she stared at Claude as his face turned a deep shade of red, his hands fisted at his sides.

'Don't,' she cautioned, her voice as low as could be. 'Whatever you're thinking, whatever you want to do, just don't.'

He went to reply to her, his mouth open, but he didn't get the chance, and Chloe linked her fingers with Adrian's as one of the men returned and nudged Claude with his gun. She saw him lean in close to speak to him, his mouth near her brother's ear, but he didn't speak in a way that insinuated he wanted their conversation to be private.

'What do you know about a road being blown up?' he asked, smiling when his eyes met Chloe's from across the room.

Claude swallowed, loudly. 'I don't know what you're talking about.'

'What about the truck that exploded, killing innocent German soldiers?'

Innocent. The word made her see red, made her want to scream and launch herself at the men standing in her living room as if it belonged to them. But instead, she balled her fists so tightly that her nails dug into her palms.

'I don't know about any truck,' Claude said.

'Is your name not Claude Boucher?' the man asked. 'Or should I ask them?' He jutted his pistol towards Chloe and Adrian. 'I feel like they will tell me the truth. That they understand the consequences of not being truthful with me.'

Claude nodded, answering quickly. 'You're correct, that is my name.'

Chloe let go of the breath she was holding, but she wasn't any less scared. They knew precisely who her brother was; she felt as if they were cats toying with a mouse, enjoying the hunt.

'Now that you're being so obliging, perhaps I'll tell you something in return,' the SS man said, stroking his moustache and making the other man grin.

Chloe felt as if she might be sick.

'It turns out that some of your friends aren't as loyal as you might think,' he continued. 'One of them started singing like a bird before I'd even tied him to a chair, which of course was highly disappointing for me. I was rather looking forward to working a little harder to extract the information I needed.'

'I don't know who you've been talking to but—'

'Quiet!' the man shouted, silencing her brother before clenching his fists, his eyes making Chloe think of a madman's. A madman who was in her house, mere feet away from Adrian, breathing in their air, threatening the people she loved.

'Please,' she began, but his stare stopped her from saying another word, and she tried to press Adrian behind her. There was nothing she wouldn't do to protect her little brother – she loved him as she would her own child. She'd already given up everything for him – her dreams, her work – and she'd give it all up again, willingly, if she had to.

Chloe glanced around their apartment, at the books strewn on the floor and the overturned vase, the plates swept off the kitchen table. These men had come into her home and damaged their possessions because they could; they'd known who they were looking for and could have arrested her brother on sight, but instead, they were playing some kind of cruel game.

'Your friend gave me the addresses of all those involved,' the man said, his lips tilting up at the corners. 'You can either come with us willingly and tell us all you know, or we can force you. The choice is yours.'

'Never.' The word spilled from Claude with so much hatred, so much venom, that it scared her.

Chloe watched in horror as her brother spat on the ground, as the SS man crossed the short distance between them and smashed Claude's temple with his gun, sending blood trickling down his face as he dropped to his knees.

'I was hoping you'd pick the hard way,' he sneered, kicking him so that he fell to his hands. 'This is going to be fun.'

Adrian began to whimper beside her, clinging tightly to her, and her father began to weep. But Chloe felt as if she were watching from above, as if she wasn't even in the room, while her brother's grunt echoed past her, the man's boot connecting with his stomach before he raised his pistol and aimed it at her brother's head.

'Stop!' she cried, her heart lurching as she met the eyes of the SS man, terror rolling through her. 'Please, stop,' Chloe begged.

The man turned to her, his pistol still in his hands, his hair falling slightly over his forehead, no longer perfectly combed back. But the gun was no longer pointed at her brother, and that was something.

'Please. It wasn't him.' She took a shuddering breath. 'It was me. I'm the one you're looking for.'

Chapter Ten

Chloe

'No!' Claude's guttural cry shuddered through her body and almost shattered her resolve, but Chloe forced herself to keep her head high.

'You?' the SS man spat, stalking towards her, his eyes narrowed. 'You expect me to believe that it was *you*?'

Her lower lip quivered but she fought the tears, the emotion clogging her throat, and nodded.

'Arrest her,' he ordered the man behind him, shrugging as if he didn't care whom he took, so long as he took one of them.

Relief settled over her as she realised they'd believed her, replaced almost immediately by a terror that rolled through her stomach and clutched her around the throat. But if she hadn't said something, Claude would be dead now.

'Chloe,' Claude pleaded from across the room as she was roughly shoved forward, falling to her knees. 'Please . . .'

'Keep him safe,' she said, pleading with her eyes. 'Protect him, Claude. You're all he has now.'

Her father cried, tears silently falling down his cheeks, but he said nothing as she was hauled to her feet.

'Should we take the older boy, too?' asked the other SS man.

'He's innocent,' Chloe cried, as fear threatened to choke her again. 'He knows nothing of what I was involved in. It was only me!'

She looked away from Claude, eyes barely grazing her father's, and turned her head to Adrian. Her darling little brother, with his big brown eyes and even bigger heart.

'I love you,' she whispered, as something sharp prodded her in the back and forced her forward. 'I love you so much.'

He cried and went to bolt towards her, but Claude stopped him, hauling him into his arms, holding him as he cried for her.

What have I done? The thought reverberated through her. *What have I done?*

'Silly bitch,' said the man prodding her, shoving her so sharply out of the door and down the stairs that she was barely able to stop herself from falling. 'Should have let your brother take the blame.'

'You've signed up for a fate worse than death, girl.'

Fear sent goosebumps across her arms and down her legs. She shivered as she was pushed out into the cool night air, wishing for a coat or anything to stop the wind from biting her skin, wishing also that there had been another way.

But she'd promised her mother, she'd promised her she'd keep her brothers safe, that she wouldn't let any harm come to them. She'd sat there and held her hand, on her deathbed, and told her that she'd love them and look after them as if they were her own sons. She'd lost so much of herself after her mother had died; she'd lost her dreams and her writing, but this she could do.

A mother would have sacrificed herself to keep her children safe. A mother would do this.

Chloe had made a promise, and she'd never regret fulfilling it.

'Move!' the man behind her said, his boot connecting with her leg as he kicked her.

She gritted her teeth and forced her feet to keep moving, trying her hardest to ignore the pain shooting like fire down the back of her thigh. But this time, no matter how hard she tried, she was powerless to stop the tears from falling down her cheeks, and they fell as rapidly as rain cascading from the sky.

Chapter Eleven

Aletta

Everything had changed since the occupation, but if there was one thing Aletta was grateful for it was being busy. As curfews had been imposed and soldiers filled coffee shops and loitered on the streets, whistling as girls walked past and scowling at young men, she'd wondered what their life might look like in the weeks and months that followed. Thankfully schools had been allowed to stay open, although there were rumours that whatever Jewish children were left would soon be forced to stay at home, and her school was only opening for half-days now. Every morning after she arrived, she would glance at the desks of her Jewish pupils and wonder where they might be now; some classes had rows of empty desks.

It wasn't long after the occupation before their first proper, covert newspaper needed to be typed, and she'd launched into action with her mother, grateful for the extra time she had in the afternoons. In the beginning, they'd been busy with posters and one-page pamphlets, but there was such a demand for information about what was happening throughout the Netherlands and the rest of Europe, that they needed to put together a proper little paper.

Their secret room transformed from cosy to stifling within a few hours though, and Aletta found herself rolling up her sleeves and fanning her face when they paused to look at what they'd completed so far, trying to focus on the work at hand. It was a Saturday, so they had the entire day to work uninterrupted.

'I think we need to take a break for air,' her mother said, her face beet-red as she leaned back against the wall. 'I knew it was going to be warm in here, but this is almost unbearable.'

'I know,' Aletta replied, grimacing. The back of her neck was damp, and her blouse was clinging to her skin. 'If only the weather was cooler.'

'Then we'd probably freeze in our little box!'

She laughed. They'd started calling their room the little box, although not when her father was within earshot. He was proud of what he'd created, and they'd never let him hear a word other than thanks.

'I'm going to get us a cold drink,' her mother announced. 'I'll be back.'

Aletta was left alone with her thoughts then, sitting with her back to the wall, head tipped back and imagining where Cecilia was and what she was doing. They'd barely gone a day without seeing each other since they were little girls, and she missed her terribly. Their walks home after school and college, the Saturday afternoons spent lying in the sun or meeting her after dinner and talking about the boys they liked. She shut her eyes, imagining her in a field full of grass and wildflowers in the countryside, playing a game of chase with her brothers. In reality, she was probably cooped up inside and trying to convince them to finish their lessons, and the thought of her wrangling her siblings brought a smile to Aletta's face. If that were the case, she'd be hating every moment of it!

'What's making you smile?'

She hadn't even heard her mother return, and looked up to find her holding out a glass of water.

'Thank you,' she said, taking a grateful gulp. 'I was thinking about Cecilia.'

'You must miss her.'

Aletta sighed. 'I do, and I don't know if she'll come back at all now.' She'd wanted to write to tell her about the Resistance, but of course it was too dangerous to mention it now, which meant she'd have to wait until Cecilia came to visit.

'I'd say her mother will want all her children to stay there. If I'd had the chance to send you away to safety, I'd be reluctant to see you come home.'

They both sat in silence as Aletta finished her glass of water before turning back to the work in front of them. Her mother was right – it was unlikely Cecilia's brothers would come back until the war was over, which meant her friend would be stuck there with them.

'Shall we read each other's work?' Aletta asked, wanting to distract herself from thoughts of Cecilia or how long the war might drag on. 'That way we can check for mistakes.'

Her mother nodded and they passed each other their respective papers. They'd taken turns typing and helped each other to form the correct sentences, but she didn't want their first attempt to be anything less than perfect. Some families, she was certain, would still be secretly listening to the wireless, even though the threat of imprisonment or worse was enough to deter most.

They hadn't even heard her father arrive home, but he'd sounded out the knock they'd all agreed on to signal that it was safe to come out.

'Are we done here?' Aletta asked, stretching out her tired limbs.

'We are.' Her mother looked as uncomfortable as she was as she unfolded her legs from beneath her.

Aletta quickly tidied up their papers and prepared what she needed to deliver later, bundling it up and leaving it on her make-shift desk before they eased themselves through the little door and out into the less stifling room. But any happiness Aletta had found at being done for the day vanished when she saw her father at the kitchen table. His leather bag was at his feet, and the deep lines around his eyes and mouth made her think that he'd aged in the handful of hours since she'd last seen him.

'Jan, you're home early,' her mother said, trading a worried glance with Aletta. He'd taken to working a lot during the week-ends, trying to help his clients as best he could.

'I couldn't stay there any longer,' he said, his shoulders falling as he sighed. 'I don't know what to do anymore, how I'm supposed to help them.'

It was obvious who he was referring to. 'Has something happened?'

She knew about the mass round-ups of Jews in Poland and Austria – they'd been tasked with including it in the text they'd been working on all day – and it sent a shudder through her thinking about the same happening on their own usually quiet streets.

'It's almost worse,' he said, shaking his head and meeting her gaze, his mouth opening and closing, as if he couldn't quite bring himself to say the words. 'There are . . . there are Jews taking their own lives. Their fate is so bleak that they can't . . .'

Aletta felt herself burning inside. It wasn't just the tears stinging her eyes, it was a feeling like being set on fire as his words filled her, as anger, no, *fury*, filled her veins. And she couldn't help but think about the children she'd taught who'd disappeared. It was unbearable to think that families just like those might feel it was their only option.

'*Your* clients?' She heard her mother ask the question, and closed her eyes to hear her father's answer.

'Two of my clients, just today, and I heard that yesterday . . .' His voice caught and Aletta opened her eyes, hearing the pain in his words. 'Just yesterday an entire family died. They were found in their bed.' He wiped his eyes, and seeing him cry almost broke her. 'They truly felt that was a better fate than whatever lies ahead. To do that to your children . . .'

Aletta didn't want to know how they'd done it or what it must have felt like for that to have been their only option, and she had to fight the bile rising in her throat as her father failed to finish his sentence.

'I don't know what to do. How I'm supposed to help them. And the Nazis, they emptied an entire Jewish rest home just this morning. There is not one patient left. Not one. They've all disappeared into thin air.'

Aletta sat down at the table beside her father, taking his hand into hers. Her mother kissed his cheek, squeezing his shoulders and then going over to the cupboard where they kept the liquor. If her father had ever been in need of a stiff drink, it was now.

'I just feel so helpless, there must be something more I could be doing,' he said, his eyes seeming to search Aletta's as he spoke. 'There are people pledging to open their homes to Jews, to hide them, but for how long? The punishment is imprisonment or death, and for a family to risk their own lives to help another . . .'

She knew what he was trying to say, the hidden question in his words. Would he be prepared to risk her life and her mother's, to save the life of a Jewish client? Would it be worth the consequences if they were to take in one person or one child or one family? To risk all their lives like that? Her heart said yes, but her mind understood that the decision wasn't so simple, especially not for her father.

'Where exactly do they intend on imprisoning all these people who might help the Jews?' she asked. 'Do you think they would truly—'

'The Nazis don't make idle threats, Aletta,' he said, rubbing his temples before accepting the drink her mother placed on the table in front of him. 'They've established camps, places of horror where they're transporting prisoners to.'

When she swallowed, her mouth was dry. 'They've created these places for the Jews?'

He shrugged. 'That's what we thought. But perhaps they're not just for the Jews, perhaps they're for anyone who stands against them, as well.'

Aletta shuddered, watching as he drank his whisky much faster than she'd ever seen before, and wishing that her mother had poured her a drink, too.

It had been one thing working alongside her mother in their little safe room, but it felt like another thing entirely to leave home after dinner and step out on to the street with the typed papers hidden in her jacket. The weather was still warm, and Aletta hadn't wanted to draw attention by wearing a large coat, so she'd chosen a lightweight jacket that belonged to her mother. She was also carrying a small bowl of food covered in wax paper, which was her cover story. If anyone asked her, she was to say that she was delivering food to a relative who lived alone. There was no tolerance for anyone disobeying the eight o'clock curfew, but up until that point, at least she had a reason for leaving home in the evening.

Aletta knew that she didn't have long. She had to walk as quickly as she could to the drop-off point, and then she would barely have enough time to get home. Her father had almost rubbed through the skin of his jaw at dinner, constantly glancing at the clock and then at her, but there was no point in them working so hard all day if she didn't deliver the material as planned. Scared or not, she had to follow through with what she'd agreed to do.

Just keep walking, she told herself. *Hold your head up high, straight shoulders, and keep walking.*

Which worked, until someone called out to her.

A shiver ran the length of her spine as she slowed, turning her head to see two German soldiers. They were leaning against the side of a building, but one straightened and waved her over. She hesitated, but deep down, she knew there was only one choice she could make. If she didn't obey them . . . she didn't even want to think what they could do to her.

'Hello,' she called back, forcing herself to smile.

The soldiers were young, barely older than she was.

'Where are you going?' one of them asked.

She had learnt languages at school and then at college, so she attempted to speak to them in German, hoping to impress them enough that they might let her be on her way. It was stilted, but from their raised eyebrows, her attempt had surprised them.

'I'm taking dinner to an elderly relative,' she said, trying a small smile again even though it made her stomach turn.

The first soldier grinned at her, his teeth straight and white. The other didn't look quite so taken with her, and glanced at his watch.

'You have thirty minutes until curfew,' he said.

'I promise I'll be home before then,' she said, starting to back away. 'If I could just—'

'Show me your identification papers,' he said.

The first soldier groaned and shook his head, saying something to him in rapid-fire German that was too fast for her to fully understand. But from what she imagined, it was him disagreeing and telling him to stop with his questions.

'We apologise,' the first soldier said. 'You've done nothing wrong, we don't want to hold you up any longer. Please be on your way.'

'Thank you,' she said, making sure to look at each of them and smile as she slowly backed away.

'You'll need those papers if we catch you after curfew!' the other man called out.

She shuddered again, hurrying off and not even wanting to think what might have happened if they'd searched her to see if she was carrying anything. Aletta only wished the plate in her hand would stop trembling.

It was barely fifteen minutes later when Aletta arrived at her destination. She glanced around, pausing to look at her watch and take a moment to quell the unease in her stomach. But no one had followed her, and no one was watching – or at least not that she could see. So she approached the house, lifting her hand and knocking firmly on the door.

The printed pages would go from here to a factory where there was a printing press of sufficient size to copy the number of pages needed, but they'd each been asked to focus on their own part of the process only. No one had explicitly said it, but she knew that it was for the greater good. Even if one of them was tortured, there was very little they could ever divulge, which kept their network protected.

There was no answer, and Aletta went back over her orders, even stepping away to check she was indeed at the correct address. But then the door opened, just enough for her to see a man peering out at her, his eyes narrowed with what she could only imagine was distrust.

She nodded, but something made her nervous. Maybe it was the way he was looking at her, or the fact that she didn't recognise him. He most definitely wasn't who she'd expected, and she didn't recall seeing him at any of their meetings.

'I'm—' she started.

'Follow me,' he mumbled. 'She's, well, just follow me and close the door behind you.'

Aletta hesitated, but when she glanced down she saw a drop of blood on the carpet. And then another. There was a trail of blood leading across the living-room floor.

Her stomach clenched and she had the immediate sense that she should flee, that something dreadful had happened in this house and she needed to put as much space between her and the place as she could. She couldn't stop thinking about the soldiers she'd passed, and what they could do to her if they caught her here, if it was a trap of some kind.

She lifted her gaze and saw the way the man was looking at her, as if he had something to hide, and she balled her fists, refusing to give in to her fear. He was tall and young enough that she knew she'd be no match for him, and she certainly didn't know if she could outrun him, but she wouldn't go down without a fight.

'Where's Heleen?' she asked, standing her ground. 'I was told to meet her here.'

He only gave her a look that she couldn't decipher, and Aletta knew she had a split second to decide what to do. But just as she was about to throw her bowl of supper at his face and run for her life, deciding that the soldiers on the street were less terrifying than whatever was going on in this house, a woman's voice sounded out.

'Did she give you the papers?' she called.

Aletta's heart beat out a rapid staccato as the woman she'd been expecting appeared in the hallway, but her eyes dropped to the bloodied cloth in her hands.

'I—' Aletta began.

Aletta never got her words out as a young man of barely twenty stumbled behind her, groaning as he held his hand to his side.

But it wasn't just the sight of a man covered in blood that made Aletta gasp.

It was the unmistakable cloth of his British uniform.

Chapter Twelve

Aletta

The man in the uniform groaned and slumped against the wall as Aletta gasped, hearing the blood pounding in her ears. She watched in stunned silence as the man and woman before her hurried to his side, helping him back to his feet and holding him upright.

It wasn't often her instincts were wrong, but Aletta was prepared to admit that she'd thought the worst of the man in front of her, and she'd in fact been very, very wrong. His narrowed gaze had been because he was hiding a man whom he could be killed for helping.

'What happened?' Aletta asked.

'We had an unexpected arrival of downed British airmen,' the woman said. 'Some of the other Resistance members managed to get them here after they disposed of the parachutes, but we can't keep them.'

'He's the last of them,' the man said. 'The others weren't as badly injured so they were easier to move, but this one is proving a little more difficult.'

'We thought he was going to bleed out, and the worst thing is that we haven't been able to understand most of what he's said.'

Aletta studied the man in front of her, seeing the discomfort he was in and wishing there was something, *anything*, she could do. Her eyes ran over his face, seeing the brace of pain in his features, and then down his side to where he held his hand.

'How bad is it?' she asked.

'Bad enough that he should have seen a doctor,' the man said with a grunt.

'And will he?' Aletta asked. 'See a doctor?'

The woman sighed. 'We have the local veterinarian coming by shortly. He's going to stitch him up as best he can, and then we have to find somewhere safe to hide him. He's going to need a long time to recuperate before we can attempt to smuggle him out.'

Something about the young man tugged at Aletta's heart strings, and she didn't know if it was because he was young, or looked broken, but all she could think about was what would happen to him if he were found. Her father's words about the awful camps the Nazis were sending people to filled her mind, as she imagined a soldier holding a gun to his head, and she knew she couldn't just walk away. But the truth was that the fate of anyone who helped him would be the same, and that should have scared her more than it did.

'He can come home with me,' she said, before she'd even considered her words. 'We have somewhere safe in our apartment where we can hide him. He'll be safe there, and I can speak English.' Thankfully, her English was much better than her German.

The man and woman before her exchanged glances, and Aletta followed them down the hallway to a bedroom where they carefully laid the British airman on the bed. She could sense that they weren't certain whether they could trust her, and she understood the feeling – she'd felt the same about them only minutes earlier.

'How old are you?' the man asked.

'Twenty,' she said, not understanding why it was relevant.

'You live at home with your parents?' he asked, his eyebrows shooting up in question. 'Because you can't just arrive home with a British airman without their permission.'

Aletta began to answer but the woman spoke for her.

'Her mother's with us,' she said to the man whom Aletta presumed was her husband. 'She's in this as much as her daughter is, so if she says she can take him, she can take him. We need him gone from here, and if she's willing . . .'

'You're worried he'll be discovered here?' Aletta asked.

She looked at Aletta, as if deciding whether or not to tell her any more. Her eventual sigh indicated that she was going to. 'We're distributing the newspaper from here once it's printed, and we can't risk drawing any more attention to the house. We've already had enough comings and goings that it might seem suspicious to the neighbours.'

Aletta nodded. She knew full well that the knowledge of where the newspaper was being distributed from wasn't supposed to pass to her – it was essential that they all knew as little as possible, for the safety of everyone involved. She also knew that the time she would be spending at the house meant she might not get home before curfew.

She glanced at her wristwatch, thinking about the soldiers she'd passed. This time, she was proposing to not only walk the same route home after curfew, but with an Allied airman in tow. But she kept seeing the pained look on his face, and there was no way she could turn her back on him and run home. If he could walk and make it back with her, she would take him.

Every single one of us needs to do our bit. We need to be brave. We cannot collapse before the enemy, we must find a way to stand our ground and fight behind the scenes, to find a different path to victory. The words spoken at the last meeting of the Resistance echoed through her mind, and she knew that she'd made the right decision, however reckless it might feel now.

'Let me clean up and you can give me the papers,' the woman said. 'I'm Heleen by the way. I saw you at the meetings.'

'Aletta,' she replied, her hand over the pocket of her jacket where the papers were carefully folded. But the woman knew her name, just as she'd already known hers.

'Have you lost any friends yet?' the woman asked. 'Is that what's making you want to get involved in all of this?'

Aletta shook her head. 'No. But my father . . .' She hesitated, realising she needed to be careful about saying too much that might give his identity away. 'He has many Jewish friends. Some have taken their own lives. And I have pupils who've disappeared, whom I fear I'll never see again.'

The woman nodded, as if it didn't come as a surprise. 'We lost a son. Our only child. He was killed trying to defend Rotterdam.'

'I'm sorry.' Aletta felt as if the air had been punched from her lungs when she heard that. This is what they'd meant at the last meeting about everyone having their own reason for helping.

'Doing this, helping in any way we can to kill those bastards? It's the only thing we have left, the only way we can honour our son's memory.'

Aletta understood, and it only made her want to help by taking their unexpected house guest all the more.

'What do we do now?' she asked.

'Now?' Heleen repeated. 'Well, we start by you giving me the papers, and then we wait. You can leave as soon as the boy is all stitched up.'

◆ ◆ ◆

It felt like the longest hour of Aletta's life as she waited for the veterinarian to arrive and work on the British airman. She heard deep moans of pain come from the bedroom, but she'd been told to stay out of the way and only move to answer the door if anyone knocked, so that was what she was doing – and trying her best to block out the noise. As well as fretting about her parents, because she could only imagine how worried her father would be by now, and she hated that she'd broken her promise about when she'd come home. She only hoped that he'd understand, and that he didn't risk his own safety by breaching curfew and coming out into the night to search for her.

'He's all patched up,' the veterinarian said, as he walked down the hall.

'How long until he can walk with me?' Aletta asked as she rose. 'He is going to make it, isn't he?'

The older man peered at her over his round spectacles. 'My dear, I work on family pets, cats and dogs and the occasional guinea pig. I have no idea whether the poor boy will make it, or what his internal injuries might be, but I've patched him up, he has painkillers enough to work on a Great Dane, and I've managed to rustle up some antibiotics.' The man frowned at her. 'All I can wish you now is luck.'

Aletta took the bag of supplies thrust at her, and when she peered inside she saw a bottle of tablets, and a supply of bandages. Her stomach churned as she realised that by taking him with her, she was now in charge of caring for him.

'Clean the wound regularly, check him for a temperature, and make sure he's keeping his fluids down. You need to apply pressure to the wound if it starts bleeding and find a way to stem the flow.'

'And if I can't?' she asked, looking up at him. 'What am I supposed to do then?'

The veterinarian shrugged. 'Then start praying, because unless you can find a doctor who'll treat him in secret, there's little anyone will be able to do for him. You just need to stop that blood and hope for the best.'

Aletta didn't exactly like the instructions she'd been given, but she braced herself and took a deep breath. She wished she'd chosen to study nursing instead of teaching; the trouble was she'd never had the strongest stomach, and just the thought of seeing his blood and having to keep his wounds clean was making her feel ill. Heaven help her if she was expected to stitch any wounds that didn't stay closed.

'It's almost dark now,' Heleen said. 'You're going to have to go quietly and carefully, and come up with one hell of a good cover story if you're caught.'

Aletta tucked the bag she'd been given under her arm as the man of the house appeared with the British airman propped up beside him and still looking very much worse for wear, although he'd at least been changed into civilian clothing, even if it was slightly too large for him. There was nothing about him that *didn't* look suspicious, but Aletta didn't waver. It was like finding a stray dog out in the rain – there was no way she could leave him behind, not when there was a chance she could save him.

'What are my chances of him walking all the way there without assistance?' she asked, not really expecting an answer.

'The pain medication I've given him will help, but I don't know how long it will last before it starts to wear off. So I'd make haste if I were you.'

Her charge hissed out a breath of pain as he let go of the man holding him, pushing off from the wall.

'You speak English?' he managed, holding out his hand to shake hers. But he wobbled then, and she turned herself around and clasped it, keeping hold.

Aletta nodded. 'I do. I'm Aletta.'

'Harry,' he said with a grimace.

He wobbled and she tightened her grip, keeping hold of his hand.

'You don't have to—'

'Don't even think about protesting. I'm keeping hold of you and I'm not letting go until we get to where we're going.'

'All right,' he said, punching out another painful-sounding breath. 'All right.'

When they finally stepped outside, with assurances about the newspaper delivery not being behind schedule and her additional contribution to their movement acknowledged, Aletta set off into the dark. Her stomach clenched as she worked out roughly how long it *should* take them to get home, but she knew that Harry wasn't able to move as nimbly as she was. They were just going to have to go as fast as they could, and slow down when they needed to.

'I'm guessing you know what happens to anyone caught out after curfew here,' she whispered, still holding Harry's hand with an iron grip.

'I imagine,' he said, grunting as she tugged him along, 'that it's similar to what they do to downed Allied airmen.'

Her mouth tugged upwards into a grin sensing that, despite his pain, he had a sense of humour.

'I really don't want to find out,' she murmured. 'But I'm thinking you might be right.'

They continued on, hugging the shadows, Aletta scanning the streets constantly, but so far, they were clear. She was surprised by how quickly he was moving, despite his injuries, and she wanted to maintain their pace while he could.

'Whatever that doctor gave me is working,' he mumbled. 'I have the strangest sensation, almost like I can't feel my legs properly.'

Aletta glanced down at his legs. That didn't sound good to her.

'I mean, I know they're working, I'm walking after all, but it's like they're disconnected from me or something.' He made another grunting sound. 'And for some reason, I keep wanting to laugh. That's not normal, is it? To want to laugh when my insides feel like they're falling out?'

She found herself hiding a smile again, although it was even harder not to laugh from nerves. Clearly whatever pain relief he'd been given was doing its job. 'Did no one tell you that your doctor was actually a veterinarian? He may have had to guess the dosage.'

Harry almost stopped walking then, but she tugged him along, not letting him slow down.

'A *veterinarian*?' he asked, sounding horrified. 'So whatever he gave me . . .'

'Was for animals,' she said, finding her way around the English words, pleased that she was able to talk to him.

'Christ almighty,' he swore under his breath.

She did laugh then, not able to help herself. 'I'm sorry.'

'Well, it wasn't you who decided to let a *veterinarian* tend to me.'

'Shhh,' she hissed. 'Keep your voice down. We don't need anyone hearing that British accent, it'll—'

'A veterinarian!' he exclaimed, clearly under the effects of whatever he'd been given.

She clamped her hand over his mouth. This man was going to be the death of her. She should never have offered to take him. But when Aletta glanced at him, she knew that not even a tiny part of her had considered leaving him behind.

'Tell me, Aletta. What exactly are your parents going to say when they see me? Is there a chance . . .' He groaned and she slowed as he pressed his other hand to his side and bent over a little, clearly in pain again. 'Is there a chance they'll turn me out into the street?'

'On to the street?' she asked, hoping she understood his meaning.

'Turn me away, not let me in,' he clarified.

'Oh. No,' she said, truthfully. 'They'll likely be furious, but not with you.'

'Is there a chance they'll turn *you* out into the street then?'

She bit down on her lip and shook her head, already imagining the look on her father's face. 'You let me worry about my parents,' she whispered. 'Now keep walking.'

Aletta pulled him along beside her, feeling him slow down as terror rose inside her. She wanted to run for home, arms pumping and legs covering as much ground as possible, so walking like this was excruciating. But she almost wished he'd go back to talking and joking with her, because she could tell that even if he wanted to, he wouldn't be able to now. His breathing had become more laboured, and he was no longer gripping her hand.

'Harry?' she murmured, once they only had a few blocks left to go.

'Yeah?' It was more of a breath than a word.

'We're almost there, I just need you to stay with me, all right? Keep holding my hand.'

His grip had loosened further and she didn't like it. It felt as if he were getting weaker, and if he staggered now or, heaven help her, fell down, there was no way she'd be able to get him back to her apartment. She simply wasn't strong enough to brace his weight.

'I can feel my legs now.' He grunted again. 'It hurts so fucking bad.'

She didn't react to his language, but she did move closer to him, pressing her shoulder to his, and when he put an arm around her, Aletta didn't move away. His body felt warm against hers through the shirt he was wearing, maybe too warm, and as her apartment block came into view, she tried not to think about just how close he was to her, or how much she liked the feel of his arm around her.

She'd often joked with Cecilia about what it would feel like to have a man so close that she could smell his aftershave, and even though her friend would want every last detail, Aletta would have to report that this particular man smelt of disinfectant, not aftershave. Which only served to remind her of the ordeal he'd been through.

Just keep the man alive, she told herself. She could think about his body being so close to hers later, once they were safe for the night. Because after the evening she'd just had, she'd have plenty of time to think. For it was doubtful that sleep would ever find her, certainly not tonight, anyway.

Aletta steeled herself once their apartment was only two blocks away, feeling Harry lean on her more heavily. She stopped for a moment to catch her breath against a corner wall bathed in shadows, as she looked around them. To get to her place they had to cross the road, when they'd be at their most vulnerable.

And just as she was about to tell Harry they had to go as fast as they possibly could, a shout rang out down the otherwise empty, silent street.

Please not now. Please don't let us get this close only to get caught now.

Her breath caught in her chest as she heard another shout, and she pressed back tightly against the wall, drawing Harry with her, swallowed by the dark silhouette of the building. She could tell that he was barely conscious, his breathing fast and shallow now, but he didn't make a noise as they both waited, their backs pressed to the cool bricks. A young man appeared, being chased by not one but two SS men, and Aletta watched in horror as they ran him down, one of them beating him across the back with a baton as they caught up to him. There was another shout, and he was hauled away, back the same way they'd come, and she turned to Harry, her lips almost touching his ear.

'The moment they disappear, we have to make a run for it.'

His head moved and she took that as a nod.

'We're almost there, and I know it's going to take everything you have, but when I say go, we have to go.'

He turned his face slightly towards her and she felt a shiver run through her that was as much due to how scared she was as his proximity. But she didn't have time to think about that right now – their lives depended upon her getting them across the road while the coast was clear.

She peered out into the street, squinting as she looked both ways. There could easily be soldiers waiting in the shadows, watching the road from some hidden vantage point, but they were going to have to take the chance.

'Now,' she whispered, holding him tight as they ambled as quickly as they could across the road, her arm tight around his waist.

Aletta ignored his muffled cries of pain, her only focus getting them to the entrance to her apartment block, and once they were there, she hurried him inside.

'Keep going, up the stairs,' she said. 'One flight and then we're there.'

All she received from him was a grunt, but bless him, despite the considerable pain he must have been in, Harry managed to keep putting one foot in front of the other until they were finally at her door.

And for the first time in hours, Aletta was able to breathe a steady sigh of relief.

The apartment was silent when they finally got inside, and Aletta finally let go of Harry's hand, seeing how deathly pale his complexion had become, and hearing just how painful the wheeze of his breath sounded. It was as if he'd run ten flights of stairs, except with a slight crackle to each inhale that didn't sound at all right, and the bag she was clutching didn't feel adequate enough to help him. What use were medical supplies if she didn't know how to use them?

'Hello?' she called out, wondering where her parents were. She'd expected her father to be sitting waiting with his eyes trained on the door. 'Mother?'

Within seconds of calling out, both her mother and father came hurrying down the hall, breathless, and dressed as if they were about to leave the house. She knew then they had been preparing to look for her, that they would have risked the consequences of breaching curfew to find her. Which meant that tonight she could have lost them, if they'd been caught.

'Aletta! We were . . .'

Her mother's voice faded away as they stopped and stared.

'Ahh, Mother, Father,' she said, gesturing to the man standing beside her. 'This is, this is, ah, Harry. He's a British pilot.'

But before her father could say a word, his jaw still hanging open in surprise at their unexpected visitor, Harry collapsed to the floor beside her, his legs crumpling as if he'd been shot.

Chapter Thirteen

Aletta

'Aletta, what were you thinking!' Her father rushed forward, dropping to his knees and roughly turning Harry over, lowering close enough to listen for his breath, his eyes wide.

It was then that Aletta saw the blood that was seeping through his shirt and realised just how close she'd been to losing him on the journey home – what a miracle it was that he'd managed to keep moving. If their apartment had been even one more block away, he might not have made it, and she couldn't imagine what it would have felt like to leave him behind. 'He's been stitched up, but—'

'Jan, we need to do something,' her mother said. 'What, Aletta, why—' She shook her head. '*How*?'

'I—' Aletta couldn't say anything. She didn't know *what* to say, other than something deep inside her had refused to turn away from him. That she hadn't been able to even consider leaving him behind.

'Quickly, we need to move him, and we need to stop this blood or we'll have a body on our hands,' her father said. 'We can question our daughter later, Emma, when there's not an Allied airman lying in our living room.'

Aletta hovered, not sure what to do. She'd never heard him so angry before, and she understood. *Of course* she understood. How could she not? They'd made a deal, they were to stay safe, and instead of following those rules she'd brought danger directly to their doorstep. She'd disobeyed his only rule.

When she looked at her father, his face was as white as a sheet, and she wished she hadn't been the cause of it. But her guilt was overridden by imagining what might have happened to Harry if she hadn't agreed to take him.

'I have supplies,' Aletta said, finding her voice and looking up at both her parents. 'We have to stop the bleeding, and I have fresh bandages in here. I don't care if I have to hold my hand to his side all night, I'm not giving up on him.' She took a breath, her heart pounding. 'We have to save him.'

Her mother met her gaze, her nostrils slightly flared, her anger perhaps giving way to a shared determination to save the man lying on their carpet. Because her mother was one of the most compassionate people she knew, and there was no way she could have turned her back on an injured young man either. As angry as she might be in the moment with her daughter, Aletta knew her mother would forgive her.

'I'll get some towels and warm water to clean him up,' her mother said. 'You check the wound and see how bad it is. Jan, get some bedding together and put it in the secret room for him. We need to keep him warm and comfortable if he's going to survive the night, and one way or another, we're going to have to get him in there.'

Aletta swallowed and caught her mother's wrist as she rose. 'I'm sorry, I just couldn't—'

'We'll save him first, Aletta, and talk later,' she said, her voice terse. 'Right now, we need to focus on keeping this young man alive.'

She let go of her mother and looked at the man lying in front of her instead. Her father left her alone with Harry, and she lifted his shirt, her stomach turning when she saw how much blood had soaked through his bandage. He might have been stitched closed, but there was still blood leaking everywhere and she was starting to wonder just how skilled the veterinarian had been. Shouldn't the stitches have stopped the blood? She didn't know much about nursing, but if the wound had been stitched correctly, he wouldn't be leaking like that.

'Harry.' She fought tears as she studied his face. 'Harry, if you can hear me, you have to fight. This can't be it. You have to keep fighting.'

'Aletta?'

She shifted her weight when her mother spoke and glanced up at her, not having heard her come back into the room.

'I have about as much experience at nursing as you do, but we're smart women. There's no reason we can't help this man, do you hear? There's no reason we can't make sure he survives until morning.'

Aletta nodded, biting down on her bottom lip to stop from crying. She barely knew him, but to think that a young man who'd only a short time earlier been talking and walking beside her, might die? She couldn't even make sense of it, and something inside her wanted to break.

'I'm going to cut this bandage off him, and then you're going to press this to his wound and hold it firmly, until the bleeding stops,' her mother instructed. 'Then we're going to apply this towel over the top of it.'

Aletta did as she was told, fighting nausea as the blood stained her fingers red. She couldn't stop staring at the way it seeped into her skin.

'Talk to your young man, Aletta. When he wakes up, he's going to be in a world of pain, and I'd say your face and your voice is what'll get him through this ordeal.'

'But he barely knows me,' she said, looking down at Harry's face as she pressed firmly on his wound. He had thick, dark eyebrows with black eyelashes dusting his cheekbones, full lips that were just parted. She'd have been lying if she said she hadn't noticed how handsome he was, but it didn't change the fact that they were essentially strangers.

'Trust me, Aletta, you being the first thing he sees when he opens his eyes will help, whether you realise that now or not.'

It felt like forever until they had the bleeding under control, but Aletta had no concept of whether it was seconds, minutes or hours. All she knew was that her hands were now stained entirely red, but that red was drying and there was no longer blood seeping from Harry. Her breath was shaky as she let it go and met her father's gaze as he knelt beside her, seeing the worry in his eyes.

'We're going to move him now, Aletta,' he said, gently. 'We're all going to help lift him.'

'My hands,' she managed, staring down at her right one in particular. 'I need to—'

'Sweetheart, you can wash your hands once he's safely moved.'

'Jan, I think she's in shock.' Aletta heard her mother speak but didn't turn, her focus firmly back on Harry.

'All of us need to lift him,' her father said. 'On three.'

Aletta scrambled to her feet and cupped her hands beneath Harry's shoulders, using all her strength to heft him up, her mother and father both groaning as they lifted him above the carpet.

'Let's go, just little steps,' her father said, as she began to shuffle backwards, her fingers digging into Harry's warm shoulders.

They managed to get him into the room, but from there it was more difficult. They set him down and her father took the position by Harry's head, dragging him backwards into the hidden space, and when Aletta crawled through, she helped to move him a little more. Her mother appeared behind her with two pillows, and they propped them beneath his head, covering him with the blankets, and when they were finished, they stood and stared down at him.

'Do you think he's going to make it?' Aletta asked, the words thick in her throat.

She saw her mother and father exchange glances. Their guess was probably as good as hers, but their silence worried her.

'I certainly hope so,' her father finally said, rubbing at his face, and she wished that she hadn't been the one to heap even more worry on his shoulders.

'I'm sorry,' she said, her shoulders beginning to shake as she noticed her blood-stained hands again. 'I just couldn't, when I saw him, when I—'

'Shhhh,' her mother murmured, holding out her arms and folding Aletta into her body. 'You didn't do anything wrong.'

'She's right, Aletta,' her father said. 'You didn't do anything wrong. The only wrong is that this young man needs someone like us to hide him, just to keep him alive.'

She stayed in her mother's arms, eyes shut as she inhaled the familiar, sweet, floral smell of her perfume.

'It's time for you to get cleaned up,' her mother eventually said, pressing a kiss to her brow.

'I can't leave him,' Aletta said, letting go of her and looking down at Harry.

'You don't have to leave him, you just have to go and wash up,' she said. 'I'll stay with him until you return, I promise.'

Aletta hesitated. She didn't want to leave the room, but she also felt as if her skin were crawling with the blood drying all over it, and when she moved her fingers it almost felt as if the blood were cracking across her skin.

'You promise?'

Her mother nodded and reached out to stroke her hair. 'I promise. Take all the time you need to wash up, and I'll be here until you get back.'

Aletta moved past her father, who stayed silent but softly touched her shoulder, and she padded through the house, not stopping until she slumped forward over the washbasin. As the water ran over her skin, so did her tears glide down her cheeks, thick, gulping tears that had her entire body shaking as she scrubbed at her hands and wrists.

This is war. For the very first time, she'd seen a glimpse of what war did to the men fighting for them, and she didn't know if she had the stomach for it, if she could live with the thoughts that would now haunt her, especially if Harry didn't wake up.

She took a deep, shuddering breath, and once her hands were finally clean, her nails scrubbed, she splashed her face until her eyes no longer stung from crying. She knew they would be swollen and red still, and a quick glance at the mirror confirmed it, but at least she was clean.

Aletta dried herself and then made her way to her bedroom, finding something warm to wear and a pair of wool socks. The house was warm, but she couldn't stop shivering, and the winter clothing at least made her feel better. But she still had to wrap her arms around herself as she walked back down the short hallway to the sewing room, ducking into the secret room to find both her parents still there. They were speaking in hushed voices, but they stopped talking when she entered.

'I'm going to stay with him,' she said, looking up at her parents, prepared to fight them on it if she needed to. Because she *needed* to stay with him, and she wasn't prepared to back down. 'I know he's a young man and it might seem inappropriate, but—'

'We're not going to stop you, Aletta,' her mother said. 'He needs someone to watch over him.'

She couldn't have been more surprised. 'Thank you.'

Aletta watched them shuffle through the little door, listening to them talk about cleaning the carpet where they'd tended to Harry earlier, and she positioned herself beside him, tucking the blanket up a little higher to keep him warm. There was a lamp on in the room, and it cast shadows over his skin as she studied his face.

'You're going to make it, Harry, do you hear me? I'm not letting you die on my watch.'

And so, Aletta settled in, drawing one of the blankets over her lower legs as she leaned against the wall and fixed her gaze on the steady rise and fall of his chest, intending to watch every breath he took until he finally stirred.

Aletta wasn't sure exactly when she'd fallen asleep or how many hours she'd sat guard beside Harry, but when she woke, she was immediately aware of how hot she was. *Boiling hot.*

She pushed the hair back from her face and swallowed, her mouth dry as she realised that she'd slumped down beside Harry, and that she wasn't so ridiculously warm because of the extra layers she'd put on, or the fact they were in an airless room. Harry was burning up, and the heat had radiated from him through to her.

'Harry,' she said, giving his shoulder a gentle shake before placing her hand to his forehead.

He didn't respond, but his skin was clammy and hot, and she knew that he had a fever. If she hadn't fallen asleep, she would have seen the sheen on his skin.

Aletta leapt up, pulling the blankets from his body and hurrying out of the room. She filled a bowl with cold water and found a cloth and a towel, hurrying back to him while trying not to slosh the water everywhere.

Through still-bleary eyes she unbuttoned his shirt and left it open, dipping the small towel into the water and then wringing it out a little before placing it over his skin. Then she used the cloth to wipe cool, damp circles over his face, squeezing a little over his lips.

You can't die on me, Harry. Please don't die. Please. She knew she'd never be able to forgive herself if he did.

She kept bathing his burning skin, stopping only to refill her bowl with colder water before tending to him again. And finally, when her back had begun to ache and her fingers were sore, she realised that he was no longer on fire.

She placed her hand over his forehead, then against his cheek, and eventually she put her palm to his chest and held it there. It felt wrong to touch him so intimately when he was asleep, and it made Aletta's heart race to have her skin against his like that, the closest she'd ever been to a young man before. But it also healed her heart to know that his fever had broken.

'We're not out of the woods yet,' she whispered, letting her hand linger there for a few moments longer than necessary before checking his bandage, pleased to see that only a small amount of blood had stained the fresh fabric.

Aletta discarded her bowl of water and the towels, placing it all in the corner of the room, before going back to Harry and tucking the blanket up to his chin. He was cool now, and she certainly didn't want him to get any colder.

She only wished that she could sleep as soundly as he was for a few hours before dawn.

◆ ◆ ◆

When Aletta woke, she'd forgotten where she was. Something soft, although a little bit scratchy, was beneath her cheek, and when she pushed up, whatever she was leaning against most definitely wasn't the floor.

And then her cheeks set alight.

The soft thing she'd been sleeping on was Harry.

'Morning,' he said, his voice gravely from pain or sleep or maybe both.

'Ah, good morning,' she said, quickly sitting up and running a hand through her hair and a tongue over her teeth. She imagined she looked a fright. 'How are you feeling?'

He grunted. 'Like I've been hit by a bus.'

It took her a moment to understand the joke, but when she did, she smiled. She couldn't help it. Despite the slight clench of his teeth when he shifted position, and the bandage on the side of his abdomen, he actually looked pretty good.

'I haven't been able to stretch my legs for a while.'

Aletta was about to ask why, when she saw the side of his mouth kick up into a smile, and then she realised. He hadn't been able to move because of *her* tucked up asleep on him. She shuffled even further away from him.

'Sorry about that. It was a long night.'

His eyes softened and she felt her cheeks heat again, even though all she saw in his gaze was kindness. But that gaze was still fixed on her, which was embarrassing, given that they were alone.

'You stayed in here and looked after me all night?' he asked.

Aletta nodded. 'I did. You had a fever and . . .' She glanced over at the bowl of water and towels she'd left in the corner. 'Anyway, I'm just happy you're awake.'

He smiled again, and she found herself thinking that it was one of the nicest smiles she'd ever seen. Heat rushed into her face again and she tried her best to ignore it.

'You must have family who're worried about you,' she said, shuffling back a little and stretching her own legs out.

'I do. But they'll be grateful to you for keeping me alive.'

I'm grateful that you're alive, she thought, which she knew sounded silly when she barely knew him, but still. If he'd not survived the night, she'd never have forgiven herself.

A knock sounded out then, and Aletta looked up as her mother's head appeared.

'Thank goodness the patient is awake,' her mother said with a sigh of relief, ducking down to come through and then crouching beside Harry, switching to heavily accented English. 'I'm Emma, Aletta's mother. I speak a little English.'

Harry held out his hand, but Aletta didn't miss his wince when he leaned a little too far forward.

'It's a pleasure to meet you,' Harry said, his breath huffing a little as he adjusted his position again. 'Thank you for taking me in.'

'Well, Aletta didn't give us much choice on the taking you in part, but I'm very happy to see you upright this morning. You had us all worried there.'

'Thank you, Aletta,' Harry said. 'Your bravery is something else.'

She imagined that it was stupidity more than bravery, but she didn't say anything as her mother gestured to Harry's wound.

'May I take a look?'

He nodded and Aletta leaned in too. It was a relief not to see any more bleeding, and she hoped the worst of it was behind them.

'You need to be fastidious about those antibiotics and keeping the wound clean, Aletta,' her mother said, switching back to Dutch. 'Make sure he has them morning and night so that we don't have an infection on our hands.'

Aletta glanced over at the bowl and decided not to say anything about the temperature he'd had through the night. The fever had broken quite quickly, and he seemed well enough now, so she would keep that as her own little secret so that her mother didn't have that to worry about, too.

'Harry, do you think you can move? Or should we bring breakfast to you?'

He immediately went to push himself up and hissed out a breath.

'Let me get you something for the pain,' Aletta said, trying to remember what was in the bag she'd been given.

'I'll be fine if you just give me a minute,' he said.

'Or you can just stay here and—'

He shook his head, and her mother inclined her head that they should leave him. When they were in the other room, her mother leaned in close: 'The poor man probably needs to relieve himself, and he certainly won't want any help with that.'

Aletta's cheeks, she was certain, were stained a deep red all over again, but she simply nodded and went to find the bag of supplies. She would take it back to him with a glass of water and then tell him to find his way to the kitchen for breakfast, while she changed and made herself look a little more presentable.

When Aletta stepped in to the kitchen, she heard her father speaking and knew that Harry was already there. She didn't know how he'd found the strength to get all the way through the apartment, let alone through the little door in the wardrobe of the sewing room, and she was pleased to see him sitting there at her kitchen table.

'Good morning,' she said to her father, touching his shoulder as she passed and joining her mother in the kitchen.

'*Je verbergt jezelf*,' her father was saying, making all sorts of signs and gestures that made Aletta bite her lip to stop from laughing. '*Je verbergt jezelf*,' he said again, pretending to duck under the table.

She nodded and glanced at Harry. 'Do you have any idea what he's trying to tell you?'

He shook his head, but had the good grace to keep smiling.

She sighed and turned to her father, telling him that she would translate. He spoke quickly, and she told Harry what her father wanted him to know.

'He's saying that he's trusting you to be under his roof with his daughter, and he wants you to stay hidden at all times. That is the rule for allowing you to stay here, that you must stay in the room at all times when we're not here.'

'Yes sir,' Harry said, his voice lowering a little when he said: 'I owe your daughter my life.'

Their eyes met and Aletta felt an unfamiliar flutter deep in her stomach as she translated. Her parents began to talk then, and she was vaguely aware of her mother mentioning going to the shops to see what food was available and her father to work, but her focus was on Harry. Thankfully she was able to busy herself with spreading fruit preserve on her slice of bread and stirring her coffee.

'Aletta?'

She turned when her father said her name, looking up as he stood behind her, his hand on her shoulder.

'I want you to know that any anger I felt towards you last night was born of fear,' he said, softly, as if he didn't quite trust his own voice, but speaking English so that Harry could understand.

'I would have brought this young man home, too, and I wanted you to know that.'

Aletta smiled up at her father. 'I know you would have,' she replied. And it was true – she'd seen her father's struggles, the empathy he felt towards others from the very beginning of this war. It was the reason she'd chosen to bring Harry home with her, knowing that he wouldn't turn him away, no matter how worried or upset he might be with her in the moment.

She said goodbye to him and turned to Harry, spreading his second piece of bread for him. It was clear that even the act of leaning forward and trying to do it himself was enough to cause him pain.

'He's a good man, your father,' Harry said. 'You're lucky to have him.'

The way he said it made her wonder if his own father wouldn't have done the same. 'Your father—'

'Would be the kind of man to close his door to another, not open it, no matter how much my mother might protest.' His jaw seemed to harden as she watched him. 'Which only makes me all the more grateful for yours.'

They sat across from each other, both eating, and Aletta was grateful she had something to keep her occupied. It was one thing to care for Harry when he was unconscious and injured, but it was another entirely to sit across from him and try not to stare when he was awake.

Because one she'd excelled at, and the latter she was finding very, very difficult indeed.

Chapter Fourteen

Chloe

Chloe forced her chin up, determined to hold her head high as she stepped out of the wagon on to the platform. Dogs barked, and as she blinked and looked around her, she saw the vicious-looking canines were being held on short leather leashes by guards – male and female guards – who were yelling at those who'd exited their wagons ahead of her. The dogs wore the same military-grey coats as the guards holding them, complete with SS pin badges, and although she'd never been afraid of dogs before, the sight of the Alsatians sent a shiver of fear through her.

She surveyed the area beyond the platform – in the distance there were tall walls made of concrete, higher than anything she'd ever seen before. As she swallowed, her throat so dry it made her cough, she realised that the wall was to stop anyone from leaving.

Chloe had no concept of how long it had been since she'd left her apartment. Hours, days, possibly a week? She didn't know. The cattle wagon she'd been transported in had been dark and airless; a dank place of death and misery, with people jammed against one another, huddled together against the biting wind. But she was certain it had been days, at least four if she were to guess.

But she had an inkling where she was now, and nothing could be worse than here. This was one of the Nazi camps, the places of death and misery that she'd heard whispers about, the SS men up ahead hitting the new arrivals with sticks.

Other women shuffled along beside her as they were instructed to keep moving, and she wondered at the oddity, that there were no men in their transport group or among any of the other new arrivals she could see. Her mind drifted to Claude, finding it impossible not to see the gun pointed at his head, knowing he had been only seconds away from being executed in front of her, and wondering how she'd managed not to be killed herself. She could only imagine it might have been because she was a woman, but she couldn't be sure.

Claude. Her eyes prickled with tears. Her brave, fearless brother, who'd unintentionally done the one thing she'd begged of him not to do. And Adrian; her darling Adrian. She only hoped that her father would wake from his stupor and care for him in the way the boy needed to be parented now that she was gone, or that Claude would step up and nurture the little brother that they both so adored.

But it wasn't just her brothers she mourned as she slowly moved, marched forward by the guards and their dogs; it was the memory of her mother, and the sister she'd buried alongside her. It was grief for the life she'd once had, the life that had been so suddenly stolen from her.

She focused on putting one foot in front of the other as they walked from the train through the entrance, past even more guards who leered at them and laughed, down a main street of sorts, past a large house. Their destination appeared to be a tent, and as she looked down, she couldn't help but wonder what was beneath her feet, because it seemed to be a thick layer of ash.

A dog barked, frightening a young woman in front of her. The guard holding it laughed, letting it lunge and intimidate her, not stopping even when the girl tripped and fell to the ground, the dog's teeth snapping close to her face and eliciting even more laughter as other guards turned to watch.

Chloe wanted to scream at them to stop, but her cry died, as she knew that the dog would only be turned on her if she dared to say a word.

And that was why she'd given her life in exchange for Claude's. Because she hadn't been able to save her sister or her mother, but she would be damned if she wouldn't do everything in her power to save her remaining siblings and keep them from harm. She could be angry with him later, and she knew she would be, but for now all she could think about was that she'd kept them safe, and she'd led the enemy away from the people she loved. Who were safe in their apartment because of her.

I will survive this, she told herself, murmuring as she continued moving. *I will survive this, and no one will stop me from returning to my family. There is nothing here that will break me, I won't let it.*

I can't.

A shout made some of the women ahead of her cower, and Chloe quickly averted her gaze, looking down as more shouts echoed out and someone was hit with a baton, the woman's legs buckling as she fell into the line. Other guards brandished whips, cracking them in the air before slicing them against the bare skin of one of the trembling, terrified women. Surviving meant being smart, figuring out how to stay out of trouble, and if that involved keeping her head down, then so be it.

Chloe balled her hands into fists and forced her breath in and out, focused on every shuffle forward of her feet, trying not to shiver despite the harsh lash of cold in the air that sank into her bones and threatened to steal the very breath she was focusing on.

She couldn't imagine what it would be like in the middle of winter, when snow brushed the ground.

When she looked up, she did so cautiously, realising that there were no SS men patrolling around them anymore. The men who'd been in charge of their transportation had disappeared, replaced only by women in uniform who walked up and down the slow-moving line of prisoners. But the smirks on their faces, the cruelty that seemed to hover over their expressions, told her that just because they were women didn't mean they would be any kinder.

'*Schnell, schnell! Heraus, heraus!*' the guards shouted.

Quick, quick. Chloe knew the meaning of the first word, and even if she hadn't, the intent was clear. The women were to keep moving as quickly as possible and go where they were directed, and she heard someone mutter about being checked for lice and having to take their clothes off, as other women emerged outside the tent, wearing strange grey striped dresses, some with their hair shaved off to make them look like men.

'Where are we?' one of the women behind Chloe asked.

'Ravensbrück,' barked a female guard.

But it was the next words, said in a thick German accent, that Chloe knew she'd never forget. The snicker was so evil, it made her want to wrap her arms around herself and pray for home.

'The last place any of you will ever see.'

Chapter Fifteen

Aletta

Harry had been with them for two weeks now, and although not a day passed when Aletta wasn't terrified of him being discovered, she had started to believe that they could keep him hidden indefinitely without being caught. There was no reason that she knew of for anyone to come looking for him, but it didn't stop her parents from being on tenterhooks.

She knew that every morning her father left with fear in his bones, although that may have been as much to do with what he had to face each day. Her mother was more pragmatic, but Aletta noticed the weight she'd lost from worrying, and the way she jumped whenever there was an unexpected noise.

Aletta wished she could write to Cecilia about their unexpected house guest. Harry was . . . she didn't even know how to describe him, but he'd brought with him a lightness that Aletta hadn't realised how much she'd missed since Cecilia had left.

'Morning,' Aletta said, sounding out a little knock on the wardrobe door.

'Morning.'

Harry's hair was dishevelled from sleep, and she found herself glancing at his bare chest as he reached for his shirt.

'I, ah, I can—'

'It's fine,' he said, grinning as he pulled the shirt on. 'It's like a furnace in here at night, that's all.'

'A *furnace*?' she asked, trying to identify the English word.

He fanned at his face, and she realised he was trying to tell her how warm it was.

'Ahh, like *verwarming*?' she asked, trying not to laugh at his attempt to act out the word to her. She nodded to indicate she understood, because if she were honest, she too was finding it rather hot right now. Her throat was dry and she cleared it as her eyes dipped to glance at the buttons he was doing up. *Stop staring at him!* she scolded herself, but still found it almost impossible to tear her gaze away.

'I just wanted to bring you some breakfast and check your wound.'

Harry gave her an easy smile and held up his shirt at the side, and Aletta dropped to her knees and carefully took off the bandage, checking beneath it.

'It's looking good,' she said. The skin was pink, the stitches had held well, and she was nervously optimistic that he was going to be fine. 'It's healed very nicely.'

'I'd say it has something to do with the nurse I've had doting on me,' he said with a grin.

Aletta pushed back, putting a little distance between them, but Harry reached for her anyway. His fingers closed softly around her wrist before releasing and coming to rest on her hand. She wasn't sure what the word *doting* meant, but she could infer that it was meant to flatter her.

'I mean it, Aletta,' he said, his eyes searching hers. 'I would never have survived without you. I won't ever forget what you did for me.'

She glanced at his hand over hers before looking up at him and seeing the earnest expression in his eyes.

'I just did what anyone would have done.'

'You and I both know that's not true,' he said, his voice husky. 'Let's not pretend that just anyone would have dragged me home and convinced their parents to take me in.'

His mouth kicked up at one side and it made her smile straight back at him. She tentatively moved her fingers just the slightest lift upwards.

'Well, I did what any *good* person would have done,' she clarified. 'But honestly, Harry, I keep thinking about the way I found you, what would have happened if—'

His fingers tightened over hers. 'But they didn't, because you saved me,' he said. 'It's not worth thinking about what might have been. I'm here and I'm safe.' Harry's voice dropped. 'Because of you.'

Aletta's heart started to beat too fast then, and her breath caught in her throat, as she glanced down at her hand which was still covered by Harry's.

'Aletta? Are you in there?'

She withdrew and clasped her hands together at her mother's call, her cheeks burning as Harry buttoned the rest of his shirt.

'I'm just checking Harry,' she called back, as her mother's head appeared in the doorway.

'Why don't you come out for breakfast, Harry?' her mother asked. 'I'm sure you could do with a little air, it's very stuffy in here.'

He smiled and thanked her mother, and Aletta excused herself and went to her bedroom, needing a moment on her own. She leaned against the wall, head back, eyes shut, remembering the feel of Harry's fingers. And she wondered what might have happened if her mother hadn't interrupted.

Or maybe he's just being nice to you. She sighed, wishing for the hundredth time that week that Cecilia was there to confide in, and decided that she was going to have to write her friend and tell her about Harry after all. She wouldn't give anything away, but she had to tell someone about him, otherwise she was going to burst.

◆ ◆ ◆

A short time later, she found Harry sitting at their kitchen table, being fussed over by her mother, and Aletta poured herself a coffee and sat across from him. They were laughing about something he'd said, and Aletta was happy to just listen to him, liking how at ease he was with her mother. For someone deeply worried about the war, there were moments like this that made her believe the world wasn't imploding around them. She was only grateful that they all spoke English, which wasn't common in many households. Her father had learnt it at university and her mother had always had an excellent ear for languages.

'Do you both have work to do today?' Harry asked.

Aletta realised he was looking at her, and she nodded. 'After school, I have some typing to do,' she said. 'Sorry, you must hate it when we have to squeeze in there with you.'

'I wish I could come to see you teaching,' he said. 'I bet the children love you.'

Her cheeks heated again. 'Well, I try to make it as fun as possible for them. Although I don't have many children left now. More than half the class has left for the countryside, or their parents are keeping them home.'

'Teach me something in Dutch,' he said. 'Give me something to practise.'

She laughed. 'Like what?'

'How about something helpful, in case I'm asked what happened to me,' he said, before grinning. 'Teach me, I was saved by a beautiful Dutch girl.'

She shook her head, her cheeks positively igniting now. But she wouldn't give him the satisfaction of seeing her embarrassment.

'*Ik werd gered door een mooi Nederlands meisje*,' she said, with a grin.

Her mother came into the kitchen then, her eyebrows raised, and she just shook her head at Harry's terrible attempt at repeating the phrase, which made both Aletta and Harry laugh.

'Your mother is brave, helping with the Resistance,' Harry said, once her mother had said goodbye and left the apartment. 'Has she always been like that?'

Aletta shook her head, keeping her voice low when she replied. 'If you'd asked me before the occupation, I'd have said there's no way she'd be involved in something like that. But something changed in her when the Nazis arrived here. She just, I don't know, she just decided she wanted to step up.'

'It's amazing,' he said, and Aletta felt him watching her as she lifted her coffee cup. 'I can't imagine my mother doing anything like that.'

'What's she like?' Aletta asked. 'Your mother, I mean.'

Harry didn't reply straight away, and she wondered whether she shouldn't have asked him. But when he did answer, she was pleased that she had.

'My mother would love you,' he said, his eyes softening the moment he spoke. 'I'm the oldest of four boys, and she's spent my whole life feeding us, tending to our skinned knees and showering us with kisses.'

Aletta felt she could almost see his mother in her mind. 'And your father? You mentioned once before that he's very different from your mother.'

Harry's face hardened then. 'He's everything my mother is not.'

'I'm sorry, I—'

'You have nothing to apologise for,' he said, finishing his toast. 'Thankfully my brothers all take after my mother, and he's hardly ever home anyway. I suppose you can't miss what you don't have.'

They sat for a moment longer before Aletta rose to clear the dishes. But when she glanced back, she saw that Harry was looking at their bookshelf.

'Do you want me to find you some books?'

He laughed. 'Well, that would be great if I could read Dutch.'

Aletta felt so foolish. Why hadn't she thought of that!

'But maybe you could translate and read to me tonight?' he said. 'If it's not too much trouble.'

Aletta imagined lying there at night beside Harry, their heads propped up on pillows as she read aloud, and it sent a very unexpected thrill through her body. She quickly cleared her throat and pushed the thoughts away.

'Of course. Any requests?' she asked.

'An adventure novel,' he said with a grin.

Aletta laughed and turned back to her dishes. 'All right, an adventure novel it is.'

And just like that, she suddenly couldn't wait until nightfall.

Aletta had found herself looking forward to dinner each night, now that her father had relaxed the rules around Harry being allowed to join them. In the beginning, he'd barely been allowed out of the little room, except to stretch his legs in the morning and use the bathroom, but now her father had asked if he'd like to join them for dinner. She wasn't sure if his relaxing of the rules was to do with the length of time Harry had been with them, and perhaps that he no longer expected anyone to be looking for him, but regardless, she was just happy to spend more time with him.

There was something about Harry too, a cheerfulness despite what had happened to him that seemed to lift everyone's spirits, and Aletta had noticed how often her mother was smiling now, as if Harry had somehow eased some of her worries. Or maybe he was simply providing a welcome distraction for them with his presence.

Aletta closed the last of the blinds just as Harry came to the doorway of the living room, and she felt a now familiar rush of anticipation at the prospect of having dinner with him.

'Is the coast clear?' he asked.

'It is,' she replied, catching his eye as she went into the kitchen to help her mother.

Her father was already seated at the table, a whisky in hand when Aletta brought the first two bowls of soup out, her mother following with a loaf of bread that she placed in the middle of the table.

'Tell us, Harry, what would you be doing now if we weren't at war?' her father asked. 'What had you hoped to do?'

'Well, I was actually intending on being an architect,' he said, smiling at Aletta across the table before turning his attention back to her father. 'I've been interested in buildings from a very young age, and I'd just finished my first year at university before everything changed.'

'I see.' She noticed the way her father was nodding, as if he were impressed. 'Well, let's hope that you get to return to your studies once all this is over.'

'I certainly hope so, sir,' Harry said, holding out his plate for her mother to pass him a slice of bread. 'Aletta, you must feel the same about your teacher training?'

She nodded. 'I do. As soon as the war is over, I'll go back and finish my studies.'

'It's all of you young people I feel most for,' her mother said as they began to eat. 'These should be the most wonderful years of your life, and instead you've all been forced to put your lives on hold for this war.'

Her mother wasn't wrong, and Aletta wasn't naive enough to think that war wouldn't touch them personally, but without the war, she would never have had the good fortune to cross paths with Harry.

'Aletta, have you heard from Cecilia lately?' her mother asked, her soup spoon hovering. 'She must be so bored stuck in the countryside.'

'I—'

Aletta's reply was cut short by three short knocks on the door. The thumps were loud enough to reverberate through the room.

She met her mother's frightened gaze across the table as her father leapt to his feet, yanking Harry's chair out so fast he almost fell off it.

'Hide him! Quickly!'

Neither she nor Harry needed to be told twice. They both ran across the room and down the hall, and Harry practically dived through the little door to get into the safe room. She reached out to him and he grabbed her hand, holding it tightly for a second before letting go so she could shut the door. Aletta quickly arranged the coats hanging in the wardrobe and threw two pairs of shoes in, making it look as messy as possible, as if no one had so much as looked in there recently, before hurrying back out to the kitchen as three more knocks echoed out.

Her mother was frozen in fear as Aletta went to stand beside her at the living-room table, their hands interlinking while her father stepped into the hallway to open the door. They could see the front door to the apartment through the living room, and Aletta heard her mother's little gasp.

Two SS men stood there, and Aletta felt as if her heart might actually stop beating.

'Can I help you?' her father asked, politely, in the same voice she'd heard him use when addressing his clients.

She saw the way one of the men stared at her father, but the other was staring past him into the apartment, and Aletta looked away. She felt nauseous, and all she could think about was Harry hidden so close that he would be able to hear the commotion.

'We're searching homes,' the man said in a thick accent.

It was then that Aletta glanced down at their interrupted dinner and realised there were four plates on the table. Her stomach lurched, but she quickly slid one bowl on top of the other and placed one set of cutlery on to the chair. Even if they came closer, the tablecloth covered that part of the chair. They would only discover what she'd hidden if they moved it out to sit on.

She looked up, forcing her face into a neutral expression as the SS man looked at her again from the hallway before stepping around her father and coming into the living room.

'Who lives in this house?'

'Myself, my wife and my daughter,' her father said, and she was impressed that his voice didn't falter.

'Are you the only people in this house now?'

'Yes,' he said. 'Please, you may look around if you wish. We have nothing to hide.'

Her father stood back and gestured with his arm, and Aletta grimaced as the man pushed roughly past him. Clearly, he had every intention of looking around, whether her father permitted it or not.

'May I ask what, or who, you are looking for?' her father asked.

'We're looking for Allied soldiers and hidden Jews,' said the man still standing by the door. 'If you have anyone in this house who shouldn't be here, or you've heard of any neighbours who are hiding anyone, now is the time to tell us.'

Her father just slowly shook his head, calm in the face of an approaching storm. 'We have nothing to hide,' he repeated.

Aletta watched in silence as the man walked slowly through their living room, looking around. When he came closer to the table, she shuffled forward a step, pressing the front of her legs into the chair and reminding herself to breathe. She realised then that their wireless wasn't hidden, but there was nothing she could do about that now.

The man who'd disappeared returned, and she listened to them converse in German, not understanding what they were saying. The only thing she was certain about was that they hadn't found Harry.

'May I offer you a plate of food?' her father asked. 'We have just eaten, but my wife could—'

'*Nein.*' The response was sharp, and the men both turned on their heels to leave, although one did stop at the door.

'What is your name?' he asked, as Aletta heard the sharp inhale of her mother's breath beside her.

Her mother's knuckles were white now, tightening on the back of the chair where she held it.

'Jan,' he said. 'Jan Visser.'

The SS man smirked. 'Well, Jan, if you value this little family of yours' – he gestured to Aletta and her mother – 'you will keep your eyes open for the people we seek. We don't give second chances to those who betray us.'

When they left, her father shut the door and locked it, and she took hold of her mother as she cried into Aletta's shoulder. Her father's arms came around both of them and they stood together in the kitchen for what felt like forever. When he finally let them go, she saw tears in his eyes.

'We were lucky tonight,' he said, his voice low. 'But next time, we might not be so fortunate.'

Aletta looked to her mother, as fear rose inside of her. 'You're not suggesting that we—'

'I'm not suggesting anything,' he said. 'Other than we need to be careful, Aletta. Very, very careful. The risk we're taking . . .'

They stared at one another, until her mother cleared her throat. 'It's been quite the night and I think we all know what's at stake,' she said.

She nodded and began to clear the table, not even trying to listen to what her parents were saying, and by the time they'd finished talking she'd almost done the dishes.

'Goodnight, Aletta,' her father said, kissing her cheek as his hand brushed her arm.

'Goodnight,' she murmured, nodding to her mother who also came to press a kiss to her cheek.

'Goodnight, Mama,' she said, dropping her head to her mother's shoulder for a moment.

'I know you care for him, Aletta, but you do know that he won't be able to stay here forever, don't you? There will come a time when he'll have to move on.'

Tears immediately burned her eyes. 'I know.'

Her mother said goodnight to her, and she quickly finished the dishes, hearing her parents talking behind the closed door to their bedroom before going to her own room to change into her nightgown.

But she didn't get into her own bed.

Instead, she pulled on her warm dressing gown and padded quietly down the hallway, knocking gently on the secret door in the wardrobe before letting herself in. She could just make out Harry's features in the candlelight.

'Is everything all right?' he asked, his eyebrows drawn together in what she could only imagine was worry.

'No,' she whispered, barely trusting her own voice. 'No, I don't think it is.'

'Come here.'

He shifted over, holding up the blanket that was covering him, and she scooted in beside him, tucking into his side and laying her head on his chest as his arms went around her, intimate in a way she'd only dreamed of until now. Harry held her as she trembled, even though it was he who should be scared. But she couldn't stop thinking about what would happen to him if he was found; where they might take him or what they might do to him. Couldn't help but think that she might never see him again when he left the apartment.

His arms tightened around her as his mouth brushed her hair, his heart beating loudly beneath her cheek. 'Everything's going to be fine, Aletta. I promise.'

Aletta wished she could believe him, but nothing about tonight had been fine.

They were only ever one search away from Harry being found, and no promise was ever going to change that, no matter how earnestly it might have been spoken.

Chapter Sixteen

Aletta

Aletta sat cross-legged across from Harry, holding her cards close to her chest. She'd already completed her lesson plan for the next day and come up with some fun activities for the rest of the week, but now Harry had her undivided attention.

'Stop trying to peek!' she laughed as Harry made a dramatic move to stretch and lean around her.

'Hey, if you can't keep them hidden . . .'

Aletta shook her head and bit her lip to stop herself from laughing again. 'Just play your card, come on.'

He'd taught her a game called Gin Rummy, and even though she should have been bored silly from playing so many card games after work and late into the evenings, somehow playing them with Harry made it fun. Although she was starting to wonder if they couldn't just be out in the living room rather than cooped up in the secret room. No one had knocked on their door again; as far as she was aware no one was looking for him, and maybe they were being a little bit too cautious. Although her father's warning still echoed in her mind. *You never know when someone could come, Aletta. Or who will betray us if it's a choice between their family and ours. You heard what those SS men said, how convincing they sounded. We can't trust anyone, not anymore.*

'Harry, I've never asked you what happened to the other men you were with.'

He glanced up at her, and even though his smile barely faltered, she saw the pain etched around his eyes. She'd been in such close quarters with him for days now that she imagined he'd notice every small change in her, too.

'Honestly? I don't know,' he said. 'I try so hard not to think about that day, it would drive me mad otherwise.'

She nodded, torn between wishing she hadn't said anything and knowing that it had been time for her to ask.

'Is there anything I can do?' she said. 'To try to find out for you?'

'You've already done enough, Aletta,' he said, and he set his cards down then, their game clearly forgotten. 'I don't want you putting yourself in danger any more than you already have.'

He swallowed and she reached for his hand, touching his fingers.

'I was unconscious when I was dragged from where I'd landed,' Harry said, his voice low. 'I don't remember a lot, but the men I was with, they were like brothers to me.'

'I'm sorry,' Aletta said, and she meant it, with all her heart.

Harry's smile was sweet. 'I suppose it's easier to pretend they're each cooped up in a warm little room with a beautiful girl, like I am.'

Aletta's breath stalled as Harry leaned in closer. He hesitated, as if he were giving her time to pull away and change the course of what was about to happen.

But she didn't.

Instead, she closed the distance between them. Their lips touched, and then there was an awkward moment when her teeth bumped into Harry's before his hand lifted and gently cupped the back of her head. He kissed her so softly it stole her breath, his mouth moving over hers. And when he finally pulled away, she still felt as if she couldn't breathe.

'I think I saw your cards,' he whispered.

Aletta laughed. Her cheeks were on fire, and she had no idea what to do next, but somehow, Harry had known how to make her smile and stop the moment from being awkward between them.

She touched her fingers to her lips and cleared her throat.

'I think I'll go and make us a coffee,' she said, needing a moment to gather herself.

Harry grinned. 'I'll shuffle the cards.'

But when she went to stand, Harry still had his fingers linked with hers, and he lifted them, gently kissing her hand before letting her go.

Aletta stood and glanced at him one last time, shaking her head before leaving the little room. But she'd barely had time to process the fact she'd had her first kiss when her mother called out.

'Aletta, you have a visitor.'

A visitor? She wandered out into the living room, wondering who it could be – she hadn't even heard anyone knock – and she gasped when she saw a familiar face. She stopped dead when she saw who was standing there, the biggest smile on her face that Aletta had ever seen.

'Cecilia!' she cried, throwing her arms around her friend. 'What are you doing here? Why didn't you write and tell me you were coming! When did you get back to the city?'

'I did write,' Cecilia said, hugging her back just as fiercely. 'But I'm guessing the post is a little slower than it used to be.'

Aletta found herself glancing at the wall that separated Harry from the kitchen, hoping that he wouldn't come looking for her when she didn't reappear.

'Come and sit, let me make us coffee,' she said, linking her arm through Cecilia's and steering her towards the kitchen.

'I want to hear all about this mystery man of yours,' Cecilia said, leaning against Aletta's shoulder for a moment. 'I'm so jealous of you still being in the city. I'm bored out of mind in the country stuck with my brothers.'

'Mystery man?' Aletta's mother asked as she appeared in the doorway.

Aletta knew that her mother would have been checking the door to Harry's room, but now she stood with a hand on her hip and her eyebrows raised in question.

'I wrote to Cecilia about a young man I met where I was volunteering,' Aletta said, surprised at how easily the lie ran off her tongue. That was exactly what she'd told Cecilia in her letter, but still, saying it aloud felt wrong.

'Well, I'll let you two catch up then,' her mother said with a warning glance. 'I'm going back to the butcher to see if he hasn't had any more meat arrive.'

Aletta immediately wished that she hadn't told Cecilia about Harry at all, because omitting a large part of the truth had seemed easy in a letter, but face to face? Cecilia was her best friend and Harry was hidden only metres away from where they were standing; nothing about lying to her seemed right. Especially when her lips could still feel the soft imprint of his kiss.

'So come on, tell me everything,' Cecilia said, grabbing her arm and laughing. 'But we'll have to make do with sitting in your kitchen, because I'm not going anywhere those damn soldiers can ogle us.'

'Cecilia, swearing?' Aletta giggled. 'What would your mother say?'

'My mother chose to send me to the middle of nowhere,' Cecilia grumbled. 'You'd be swearing too if you were stuck with my little brothers. They've gone from cute to downright painful. It's as if they've been tasked with driving me crazy.'

Aletta turned and set to making the coffee as a knot settled in her stomach. She was desperate to go and get Harry so that her friend could meet him, but she'd made a promise to her father to keep him hidden. No matter how much she trusted Cecilia, telling anyone about Harry could compromise them all.

'So, tell me about him, come on!' Cecilia said as she sat at the table and Aletta brought two steaming mugs of coffee over.

'Hopefully it tastes all right,' Aletta said. 'We're mixing in a little of the good stuff each time to make it drinkable.'

Cecilia grabbed her hand then and she looked up into the trusting, beautiful eyes of her friend. Her friend that she'd never, ever told a lie to before Harry, which was why she felt so unbearably uncomfortable.

'Aletta.' Cecilia raised her brows.

She sighed. 'He's wonderful.' Her voice sounded breathy and nothing at all like her. 'He's handsome and sweet, he's just . . .'

Aletta was grateful that Harry didn't understand Dutch, and he'd have needed his ear pressed to the wall to hear them anyway. As far as he was concerned, she was just off making them coffee, not talking to a friend about him. Unless her mother had told him that someone was in the house and to stay quiet, which, now that she thought about it, was very likely.

'So why the sad face?' Cecilia asked. 'Don't tell me, he already has a sweetheart? Gosh he isn't married, is he? You look so sad talking about him!'

'I just wish we'd met before the war, that's all,' she said. 'He's, well . . .' Tears welled in Aletta's eyes as she tried to think of what to say, as she tried to explain whatever was developing between her and Harry without giving it all away. 'He's involved with the Resistance,' she said finally. 'That's why I'm being so elusive about him, because he's sworn me to secrecy and I wasn't even supposed to write to you about him. But I just, well, I couldn't keep him from you. We've always told each other everything.'

Cecilia's face softened, which made Aletta feel even worse about lying to her. 'I understand. Don't worry, your secret is safe with me. But just tell me what he looks like. I need to picture this man in my mind, you lucky thing. Has he kissed you?'

'Cecilia!'

'Well, has he?'

Aletta grinned, she couldn't help it. 'Once,' she said, knowing that she was blushing. 'He's kissed me once and it was, it was . . .' She groaned. 'It was everything I thought a first kiss would be.'

'Are you in love with him?'

Aletta glanced at the wall, grateful that Harry wouldn't be able to understand what they were saying, even if he was listening. 'Maybe. I mean . . .' Her skin felt like it was on fire. 'I don't know, but I think it could turn into that, if we had longer to spend together.' At least now she was telling the truth.

Cecilia clamped her hands together. 'Well, it sounds to me like you're smitten with this boy and I cannot *wait* to meet him.' She grinned. 'It certainly sounds a lot better than wandering around fields and talking to any animals that I find. The most interesting gentleman I spoke to last week was an old horse, and trust me when I say he didn't have a lot to say back!'

They both laughed and Cecilia's hand touched hers, catching her fingers for a second. Aletta had missed her even more than she'd realised.

'It's so good to see you again,' Cecilia said. 'Life's been so boring without you.'

Aletta smiled. 'Same here. Every little thing that's happened, I've wished you were here to talk to. I've hated every second without you.'

'But teaching is going well? Your class are all . . .'

Aletta shook her head, knowing what her friend was asking. 'I've lost all my Jewish children now. Some of them disappeared even before the occupation, and no one has ever heard from them or their families again.'

'I'm sorry, Aletta, truly I am. I know how much you adore all those children.'

They sat for a moment, holding hands, and Aletta had never been more grateful for her friend.

Cecilia sighed then, and drained what was left in her coffee cup. 'On that note, I have to go. My mother said I was to go to the shop and then come straight home, so she's going to be furious with me for taking so long.'

'How long are you back for?'

'Only two days, and then I'm back to the country again.' Cecilia paused. 'I know I sound dreadful complaining so much, but I just hate being there. I miss you, I miss college, I miss my old life. I just want this war to be over with.' She laughed. 'To think that I moaned about studying months ago. I'd give anything to go back.'

They stood and hugged, and Aletta fretted all over again about whether she should just confess to Cecilia and drag her through to meet Harry, but something stopped her. Maybe it was the promise she'd made to her father, but perhaps she wasn't ready to share Harry with the world yet, anyway.

'It was so good to see you,' Aletta said as she hugged her friend goodbye.

'You too,' Cecilia said, hugging her back just as fiercely. 'You know, I half expected you to say that you'd joined the Resistance after I left. I kept thinking about that look on your face when I told you about it all.'

Aletta laughed. 'You think I'm far braver than I am,' she said, feeling as if she were committing a sin by lying to her yet again.

Cecilia turned to leave, and Aletta waved goodbye from the door, calling out to her as she left. But when she closed the door and locked it, she stood with her back to the wall for a long minute before sliding all the way down to the floor, tears flooding her eyes.

She wanted to run after Cecilia and confess it all to her, to tell her she was sorry for lying, but she couldn't. So instead, she gathered her thoughts, wiped away her tears and decided to make coffee and return to Harry. But when she looked up, he was standing there in the hallway, watching her.

'Is everything all right?' he asked, his eyebrows drawn together.

Aletta brushed her cheeks with her fingertips again and quickly rose, not wanting him to see her upset.

'Everything's fine,' she said. 'I'll make you a coffee and bring it in. Maybe we could play cards again?'

Harry watched her for a long moment before nodding. 'You're certain everything's all right?'

Aletta fixed a smile and fought the tremble of her bottom lip as she tried not to think about Cecilia and the lies she'd told. 'Nothing that a game of cards can't fix. I'll be in soon.'

Aletta whistled as she ran up the stairs, smiling to herself as she thought about what she'd just done. This had been a good week. She'd taught each day and worked on not one but two papers for the Resistance in the evenings, and her heart was full from spending so much time with Harry – she only wished that she'd been able to introduce him to Cecilia, because she knew her friend would have loved him. Tonight, she'd dashed out to make her delivery, relieved when nothing had been mentioned about exactly how the Resistance was planning to smuggle Harry back to England, which she knew was selfish. But still, she couldn't imagine her life without him in it. The occupation was terrifying, but if she were honest, she'd been scared ever since Cecilia had left. But Harry . . . Harry had changed everything.

But as Aletta took the last couple of steps, still smiling to herself, she suddenly froze. The door to her apartment was open. Wide open.

Waiting for a moment, she listened, her heart hammering away so loudly she could barely hear a thing. But then came the unmistakable, thick German accent that she'd dreaded.

Aletta knew she had two options; she could either run back down the stairs and disappear into the night, knowing in her heart that her parents would want her to keep safe at all costs. But doing that would mean potentially hiding until after curfew, which could lead to her arrest, and it would also mean abandoning her parents, and Harry, when they needed her the most. Her other option was to walk calmly into the apartment as if nothing were amiss.

She chose the latter.

Aletta took a deep breath and then another, and walked to the door. She softly cleared her throat and stepped into the apartment, seeing the alarmed look on her mother's face that told her she would most definitely have wanted Aletta to pick the other option. But she was here now, where she was supposed to be, and she smiled as sweetly as she could at the two SS men standing in her living room even though her heart felt as if it were going to beat straight out of her chest.

Unfortunately, the men didn't return her smile.

Whatever she'd just walked into wasn't the type of discussion they'd had last time, and that steady breath she'd just taken was long forgotten as she suddenly felt as if she couldn't breathe. Because she realised that both of her parents were silent, and both of the men were predator-like in the way they were positioned, while her mother's eyes silently pleaded with her.

And then her father dropped to his knees.

One of the SS men stepped forward, taking hold of her father's chin. She didn't have to move closer to see the tightness of his hold, the cruelty of his grip.

'Tell me where they're hiding or I'll shoot you,' he said. 'We know you're helping them.'

Her father closed his eyes, and she wanted to scream at him to fight, to tell him to look that bastard Nazi in the eyes and refuse to yield.

The SS man spat in her father's face before screaming: 'Tell me where they are!'

They don't know about Harry. This was something else, this was to do with her father's work, it had to be. *They think my father's hiding Jews.*

'I know nothing. Nothing!' he cried, as the grip on his chin appeared to tighten.

'Tell me!' the man screamed.

Everything from that moment on felt as if it were happening in slow motion.

Aletta glanced at the wall. She didn't even think as she looked up, her eyes flitting over to the space that hid Harry, and by the time she realised her mistake, it was too late.

She hadn't realised the other SS man had been watching her as his colleague screamed at her father, but she did see the satisfied snarl cross his lips when she looked over at him, the flash of his eyes that told her she'd made a terrible mistake.

Because just like that, she'd given Harry away.

He said something in German to the other man, and there was a laugh, a moment of silence as if in slow motion as Aletta's horrified gaze met the pleading, terrified eyes of her mother. As the reality of what she'd done sunk in.

And then there was the sickening sound of the pistol firing, of the moment the bullet pierced her father's head. There was the sound of screaming that she didn't even realise had come from her own mouth as she watched her mother fall, her pale-yellow dress spattered with spots of red, her arms catching her husband as he tipped over, slumping on the carpet.

Aletta was still screaming when the SS man turned around and the butt of his gun smacked against the side of her head, causing her to fall. The room spun, and she could no longer hear screaming, but now everything was spinning, bright colours a kaleidoscope around her as she tried to crawl on all fours and failed.

She was powerless to do anything as one of the men used a baton to smash at the wall, the space that she'd given away by glancing at it. She watched as they kicked their way through, her heart breaking as Harry charged them, armed only with a lamp, as he tried to wind the flex around the throat of one of the men and failed. He collapsed to the floor, so close yet so far away, trying so hard to save himself as one of them stomped on his stomach and the other kicked his legs.

Her mother scuttled across the carpet to her then, holding her tight, as orders were screamed at them and Aletta was hauled to her feet, still dizzy.

'Harry!' she cried. 'Harry!'

She heard him call back to her as she was hauled, half dragged down the stairs, her mother holding her hand in a vice-like grip that not even the SS man had been able to break.

But the worst part was listening for a second gunshot; seeing her father slumped on the floor in her mind, imagining the same fate coming for Harry as she cried out for him once more, forced away from him.

'Harry,' she whispered, blinking through her tears, twisting around to look back at the apartment to see if he was coming too.

But Harry never appeared, and when she shut her eyes, all she could see was her father. Her handsome, kind father, dead. Lifeless and discarded on the floor.

Chapter Seventeen

30 April 2015

After they left the train, it was as if her breath left her lungs in a whoosh of air as she lifted her head and looked up. Aletta gripped the arms of the wheelchair while that familiar feeling of fear ran through her body, from the tips of her fingers to her toes. Her knuckles hurt from the tight grip, but she couldn't let go, even as the pain ricocheted through her bones.

Her daughter placed her hand on her shoulder, as people slowly began to move around them. She looked at the gates, at the wall, at the guard tower stretching well above the wall, and took a deep breath. She wondered how, after all these years, she could still remember what it had felt like to pass through that gate for the first time; she could still imagine her own mother by her side, could still taste the fear that permeated the very air they had all breathed that day.

Aletta nodded her head then, and her daughter began to push the wheelchair. This time, she didn't see anyone who looked like her. They were all young people, well, young to her, anyway.

It's because they've all gone. There's barely a soul left alive anymore who survived this place. I am one of the last.

'Stop,' she said, surprised by the strength of her own voice.

Her daughter did so, leaning forward, her soft hair brushing Aletta's cheek.

'Are you okay?' she asked.

Aletta gripped the arms of the chair more tightly as she pushed herself up, still holding on as she steadied her grip, determined to find enough strength to stand.

'I need to walk,' she said, hearing how raspy her own voice sounded.

There was no arguing about her decision, and she would thank her daughter for that later. But her daughter did take her arm, leaving the wheelchair and guiding her towards the gate. Their pace was only a shuffle, and she knew that many wouldn't understand, but she needed to hold her head up and walk through those gates herself, even if her legs felt as if they might give out from under her.

Aletta was vaguely aware that a young woman was pushing her wheelchair, but she couldn't turn to thank her. She had to focus on the placement of each foot, her gaze fixed ahead of her, finding a strength she hadn't even known she still had.

'You're so brave,' her daughter murmured beside her, and Aletta could hear the emotion in her voice. 'I'm so proud of you, Mum.'

Her words gave her the final push she needed, and Aletta held her head high as they passed through the steel gates.

Once they were through the entrance, she saw her daughter move from the corner of her eye, letting go of her arm for a moment, but Aletta didn't need her. Not then. She barely even wobbled as she stared at the scene before her, at what was left. Years ago, she'd been angry they hadn't torn it all down, set fire to the camps that haunted all those who'd survived, and razed it to the ground, but now she understood. As she looked at the people arriving, young and old, men and women, their heads bowed in silence, she understood.

Without these camps, without the evidence of what had been, maybe it would be impossible to believe it had ever happened. Maybe no one would accept that atrocities had occurred in her lifetime, without seeing the crematoriums, without placing their own hands on the cold, haunted walls of the gas chambers, seeing it for themselves.

They all need to see to make sure nothing like this ever happens again.

'Mum?'

She turned slowly and saw that her daughter had the wheelchair ready for her, and she was grateful to sit down now, and even more grateful for the soft blanket that her daughter tucked around her knees. There were many awful things that had happened to her in her lifetime, but her daughter had made everything worth it from the moment she'd arrived.

'Aletta Visser?' a young man asked.

She looked up, blinking at the smiling man who was standing before her, holding a name tag.

Aletta nodded, and her daughter spoke for her, thanking the man and taking the name tag, pinning it to Aletta's coat.

'I'm John, and I'll be your guide today,' he said. 'We have some other family members here, relatives of survivors, and they'll be joining us on the tour.'

She looked up and saw a handful of friendly faces, their smiles kind as they moved closer. They all said hello and she watched as her daughter greeted them all, her own voice temporarily lost to her as she kept looking around, trying to take it all in.

Remembering.

'Welcome everyone, to Ravensbrück memorial camp,' John said. 'Today is a very special day as we commemorate the seventieth anniversary of the liberation.'

She sucked in a breath. Seventy years. *Seventy* years had passed.

'This camp was built as a women's camp by the Nazis,' John began. 'During its operation, one hundred and thirty-two thousand prisoners were held here, and at its peak, there were around forty-five thousand prisoners held.'

She closed her eyes, listening to his words, knowing them to be true.

'When the women arrived, they were all processed immediately by passing through—'

'Oh no,' Aletta said, her voice clearer than she'd heard it in years. 'That's not what happened.'

John turned to her, as did the rest of the group.

'I'm sorry, I was just—'

'Please, tell us,' one of the women in the group said. 'What happened when you arrived?'

'Well,' Aletta began, glancing back at her daughter before clearing her throat and continuing. 'When we arrived, we weren't all processed immediately. We were made to stand out here for what felt like hours in our flimsy clothes. It was so cold, it was as if the wind had teeth. We were shaking so hard that it was almost impossible to stay standing, so we all pushed into each other, trying not to fall.'

'We've been told that most prisoners knew the fate that awaited them,' John said, his tone kind, his voice low. 'Is that your understanding?'

Aletta took a deep, shaky breath, aware that everyone in their small group had now turned to face her, that they were waiting to hear her answer.

'The truth is that we didn't know where we were or what was happening to us, not in the beginning. And then we realised that those camps we'd heard whispers about, the camps that they said were just for the Jews . . .' She paused, struggling to say the words. 'We learnt that they were for people like us, too.'

Chapter Eighteen

1940

Aletta

Aletta drifted in and out of sleep. Or maybe it wasn't sleep. All she knew was that one minute she was numb and everything was black, and the next her eyes would open and the pain of what had happened gripped her like an iron fist around her throat.

Her stomach ached as if she'd been punched; her body trembled, and she was cold. So cold that her skin was covered in goose pimples and her breath rasped from her throat as she shuddered violently against her mother.

She shut her eyes again drawing comfort from her mother's arm around her, holding her tight. Keeping her safe. It might have been hours or days since they'd been stuffed into the cart, but her mother had held her the entire time. Whenever she'd opened her eyes, whenever she shifted, whenever she cried, her mother's grip on her shoulders had remained constant.

The cart rattled then, going too fast over a bump on the train track, and Aletta felt her stomach lurch. Burning-hot bile rose in her throat as she bent forward, vomiting all over the ground and her shoes along with it.

'Stay strong, Aletta. We're not going to let them break us, do you hear me?'

Aletta cried; she couldn't help it. Tears ran down her cheeks as she tried frantically to shut out the memories of the crack of gunshot; of her father collapsing to the ground; the sound of the baton smashing through the newly constructed wall and then the sickening thwack of the weapon hitting flesh and bone when they'd found Harry; his desperate shouts for her.

They've already broken me. I'm not whole anymore, and I never will be again.

'Aletta, stand strong,' her mother commanded, as she felt the train slow down and all of them toppled forward, legs unsteady after being transported for so long. Her knees were like jelly, barely able to keep her upright.

Aletta felt dampness seeping through her shoes, her toes already wet, and she knew without looking, and from the vile smell in the wagon, that she wasn't the only one who'd heaved up the contents of her stomach. But where that might have revolted her once, now it seemed like the least of her worries. She barely even thought about it as her mother transferred her grip to her hand.

'No matter what, we keep our heads down, we walk tall, and we stay strong,' her mother whispered. 'Do you hear me?'

Aletta nodded numbly, as light filtered through gaps in the wooden sides of their wagon. She thought at first that they were torches being pressed to the gaps, but then she realised it was the sunrise.

'Aletta, do you hear me?'

'Yes,' she managed, her voice barely a crack of sound.

She had no idea how her mother could sound so strong and assertive. Aletta wanted to scream at her that she couldn't be strong, that her father had just been murdered before her eyes and Harry may well have suffered the same fate. That nothing was ever going to be the same again. That she had nothing left to be strong for. Even the thought of her pupils not knowing why she'd disappeared was enough to break her. But as her breath came in rapid gasps, her chest feeling as if there were a hammer inside of it, her mother squeezed her hand, telling her that she was there.

'For your father, and for Harry,' she said quietly, as the door was hauled open, leaving them squinting in the light, hands raised to cover their eyes. 'We do this for them, Aletta. Every step we take from now on, it's for your father, to honour his memory.'

Aletta lowered her arm and looked around her, realising as they were urged forward that she was surrounded by other women. Some were younger girls and some much older, but they were all female. A few she was certain she recognised from the Resistance meetings she'd been to, but they kept their eyes averted, looking at their feet as they shuffled.

Each of them looked as pained and desperate as she felt inside; it was as if they'd been broken. They were all silently terrified of the fate that awaited them, of what might happen once they stepped out of this cart.

'Where are we?' Aletta whispered.

But no one answered her as she stepped out on to the platform, something sharp digging into her back and roughly pushing her as she heard the horrifying growl of dogs, who sounded as if they'd been ordered to rip out the throats of anyone who didn't obey orders. They were divided into two groups, and as rain began to fall and soak through their clothes, leaving them to shiver, their teeth chattering, they waited.

Chapter Nineteen

Aletta

'We're alive, Aletta. That's all that matters.'

Aletta heard her mother's words once they'd finally been processed. They ran through her like shivers, her voice brushing across her skin but barely acknowledged. When she looked down, she couldn't stop staring at the oversized, striped dress she was wearing – it felt like it was swallowing her. It was so baggy that it did nothing to stave off the cold that whipped up her legs, and she yearned for the warm coat hanging in her wardrobe at home, for the soft woollen socks her father had given her at Christmas.

Papa.

A gasp passed her lips as she saw him in her mind, as the memories of him made her forget everything else.

'Aletta!' her mother hissed, her fingers digging into Aletta's arm.

She didn't even bother to yank away. Everything else was numb, but at least she could feel the sharp press of her mother's nails. They hurt enough to pull her from her thoughts. Aletta squinted against the sunlight. Her eyes were sore and scratchy, dry from shedding so many tears, and her throat felt the same. But her mother's hold was tight and unrelenting, forcing her to listen, to answer her.

'Listen to me, Aletta. We cannot show any signs of weakness, do you hear me?'

She nodded. It was barely a move of her head, but her mother released her. She kept walking close to her, their shoulders almost brushing with every step. Her mother, whom she'd expected to be as broken as she was, was somehow, *miraculously*, holding it together and being strong enough for both of them. Aletta wanted to hate her for her strength, but she couldn't.

They were walking with a never-ending line of other women, all of whom had arrived by train and been processed together – deloused as if they were nothing more than animals, stripped naked for an invasive medical examination by a female doctor with rough fingers and a smile that had made her shudder – all wearing the same striped dress as Aletta. Some had been split into another group, but almost all had been shoved and prodded and sent in the same direction. Aletta swallowed, her throat like sandpaper, wondering how long it had been since she'd last gulped down water. At their apartment? Had it been before . . . a pain akin to a blade being plunged into her chest at the memory of her father slumping forward pierced her thoughts; of the desperation in Harry's voice as he'd screamed her name.

It didn't matter how hard she tried to push them away, the memories just kept on crashing back into her thoughts, wave after wave reminding her of what had happened, what their final moments as a family had been like.

Aletta stumbled, barely catching herself with her hands as dust rose to greet her and made her cough. Something hard smacked her around the back of her legs then, and she almost fell down as she turned to look.

A guard, a *female guard*, smirked and held her baton up again, as if taunting her to do something, *anything* so that she could use it again. But her mother's steady hand grasped hers, tugging her along, not letting her stumble once more as they were marched towards a long wooden building. There were so many of them, row after row stretching out across the grounds; it was like nothing she'd ever seen before. Was this to be where they would live now? Were there truly enough women, enough *prisoners*, to fill so many houses?

It took everything Aletta had not to vomit again, even though she doubted there was anything left inside her. The door to a barracks was flung open then and shouts followed, and Aletta found herself being roughly shoved inside, forgetting about her stomach as she blinked in the dimly lit room. There were rows of bunk-style beds, only there were no sheets or pillows, just filthy mattresses that she couldn't have even imagined would be fit for a dog to sleep on, let alone a human. And to describe the quarters as cramped would have been a gross understatement – there appeared to be three times as many women as the space was designed for, and she saw some straw bedding on the floor in one corner, quickly realising that someone slept down there on the cold floor.

I want to go home. A sob erupted in her chest then, and her mother's hand found hers once more, holding tightly, reminding her that she wasn't alone.

The guard who'd hit her earlier barked orders at them, and Aletta shuffled forward again, being pulled by her mother who was the only thing stopping her from collapsing to the floor. And once they were on the too-hard bed, her mother curled Aletta to her body, holding her so tightly it was as if she were a child again, needing to be cuddled after a nightmare.

Only this was no nightmare, and the worst thing was that she didn't know when it would end.

'We're going to survive this, Aletta,' her mother whispered against her hair. 'Do you hear me? We're going to survive.'

Aletta nodded, even though she wasn't sure whether to believe her or not.

'Say it, Aletta,' her mother urged. 'I need to hear you say it.'

'We're going to survive,' she whispered back.

We have to survive. This can't be the last place I see. This cannot be my final memory. This cannot be the end of my story, of my mother's story.

Her skin itched immediately from the bedding, as if there were bugs biting at her flesh, and the cries of women felt like they were engulfing her, almost impossible to drown out. Aletta burrowed against her mother as more women climbed in beside them. There was barely room for the two of them in the wooden bunk, let alone more, and there was a cry from someone near that she'd found a cockroach. But Aletta blocked it all out, caring only for her mother's embrace, not wanting to let go of her.

'We're going to survive. Say it again, Aletta. Say it now and every time you start to doubt yourself.'

'We're going to survive,' she murmured, her voice barely audible.

She couldn't say it any louder. Because the truth was she simply didn't believe it.

And the worst thing was, she'd heard the rumours. She'd heard her father talk about the camps, she'd known they existed, but she'd never thought that they could end up here, that anyone other than the Jews could be imprisoned in one.

How wrong she'd been. Because of all the women she'd seen so far, only a handful had worn the yellow star, most of them wearing the red triangle just as she did, which meant that the Nazis were not just imprisoning Jews. They were imprisoning those who helped them too, just as her father had thought. Political prisoners, they called them.

I miss you, Papa. I miss you so much.

And when she began to cry again, she needn't have bothered to smother her sobs, because cries echoed all around her, the only noise in the otherwise silent bunkroom from hell as every woman there remembered what she'd lost.

◆ ◆ ◆

Aletta had never known how cold rain could be in summer. She remembered not so long ago running down the street with Cecilia, holding hands as they laughed and raindrops drenched their hair, but within minutes they'd been inside towelling off and making coffee. Here, the rain seeped through her thin clothes and left her hair hanging in wet sheets, her body beginning to shiver violently as she gritted her teeth and tried to stop it, with nowhere to shelter from the cold. They stood in rows of ten, all trying to stand tall when their instinct was to huddle together and fold their bodies inwards in an impossible attempt to stay warm.

It was also impossible to know just how long they'd been standing for, because it felt like hours, and every time the guards lost count of how many prisoners were there, they started again. When they were finally yelled at to move, Aletta's toes painfully curled as she tried to force them to obey. She was barefoot, and the mud sunk around her toes as she turned, her skin numb. She longed for the shoes they'd taken from her when they'd arrived, and she silently wondered how some of the women had boots or mismatched shoes.

Just when she thought they were done with standing, as they started to walk in a group, two women in the front were singled out and ordered to do something. Aletta stood, shaking violently now, her arms wrapped tightly around her middle, wondering what they'd been sent to do, when they returned with a wooden barrel.

It was then she remembered that a tin mug dangled from her fingers – they were so cold she'd forgotten she was even clasping it, the one thing they were given other than their striped clothes. She was curious about what was happening as they slowly edged forward and were told to dip their cups inside the barrel, which Aletta did, following the lead of the others in front of her.

'What is this?' she heard her mother ask no one in particular, her nose wrinkling as she smelt whatever the cup contained.

'Breakfast,' came one lonely whisper.

It turned out it was a watery substitute for coffee – it tasted putrid, but Aletta still swallowed it, forcing it down her throat. She saw her mother doing the same, her eyes meeting Aletta's in quiet horror, and she knew that her mother's stomach would be growling just as desperately from hunger as her own was. But right now, she was so hungry, her throat so dry, that she would have eaten or drunk almost anything.

'*Beeil dich! Beweg dich!*'

Hurry! Move!

A woman near her cried out in pain as a female guard with her blonde hair pinned back from her face smacked her with her baton. Aletta looked away, not wanting to draw attention to herself or let them see her staring, but she found it almost impossible to believe that another woman, that other *women*, could be so cruel. But it seemed that breakfast was over; clearly there was to be no actual food.

A dog barked, and she glanced past her mother, seeing yet another female guard, but this time one holding the leash of a dog with its teeth bared. Aletta shuddered, and this time it had nothing to do with the cold.

'Where do you think they're taking us?' Aletta whispered.

'Work detail.'

Aletta looked over her shoulder to see who'd spoken. A young woman a similar age to her with light brown, wet hair plastered to her scalp, raised a brow. Even in the rain, she was pretty. She must have slowed a little, because the woman spoke again.

'Keep walking, don't slow down,' the woman said. 'If you fall, they'll shoot you. If they don't think you're strong enough to work . . .'

'They'll shoot me,' Aletta finished for her, whispering back, swallowing and realising just how precarious their situation was. And how right her mother had been to say they had to at least appear strong.

She'd foolishly thought the Nazis wouldn't want to be caught killing a non-Jew, but when she looked around at the barren camp, she realised that no one would ever know whom the guards killed. They were just a number now; a number that could be eliminated without any consequences. Was this the type of horrid place her father's clients had ended up? Where some of her beloved families from school had been sent?

'What type of work is expected of us?' Aletta's mother murmured as they marched.

'Our group goes to the Siemens & Halske factory to work on munitions. It's almost two kilometres from here, up that hill, and we start work at six o'clock sharp. But we're the lucky ones, so no one likes to hear us complain.'

Two kilometres? Aletta braced herself, concentrating on putting one foot in front of the other and wondering how many steps it would take to complete a two-kilometre walk without shoes.

'Why are we lucky?' her mother asked.

'Because the others are on farm work and construction,' the woman said. 'They're the ones more likely to break and not come back. We at least get to work inside.'

The woman behind them didn't speak again, but Aletta's mother reached out her hand, touching her little finger to Aletta's as they trudged on.

If this isn't hell, then I don't know what is.

It turned out that Aletta was soon to discover what hell truly was. The factory was hot inside, made even worse by the rising steam coming off all the women. They were like a group of damp dogs brought in from the rain and forced to work until their hands bled, and the damp, warm conditions were making Aletta feel as if she were going to vomit – something other girls around her had already done, and been lashed for. She wasn't sure if it was the foul, watery slop in their stomachs or the conditions, or perhaps a combination of both, but she couldn't recall a time when she had felt so queasy.

But she kept her hands moving regardless, trying to master soldering the fine metallic threads she'd been tasked with after her abilities had been tested, even as she fumbled. Her fingers felt bruised, her wrists ached, still so numb from the cold seeping into her bones, and the pain in her heart was making everything seem impossible. Not to mention how afraid she was of the guards watching them, waiting for them to make a mistake, that she didn't dare to stop no matter how hard the task felt.

'How long are we expected to work for without a break?' someone near Aletta whispered.

'Until nightfall,' a woman on the other side of her murmured back. 'Unless Herr Weber is on our shift, and he will insist on breaks. He's the only one who cares.'

'If it's not him, you work until you collapse,' said another. 'Twelve hours straight, ten if we're lucky.'

Aletta tried not to show her terror, glancing across at her mother and seeing how pinched her mouth looked, how tired her eyes. Her mother had always been so quick to smile, her cheeks always pink, and seeing her like this almost broke Aletta all over again. Her father's heart would have broken to see them both like this.

'They have families here, you know. The guards.'

Aletta looked over her shoulder and saw the young brunette from earlier in the line standing behind her. She quickly looked back down at her work as she listened.

'I've heard them talk about how it's the best place they've ever worked. There's a lake they take their children to, and they live in pretty cabins away from the camp.'

'It's our living hell, and their living paradise,' someone else muttered. 'The worse they treat us, the more they're rewarded.'

Aletta's body suddenly felt as if it were on fire at the thought – that these women, capable of such cruelty and watching them with smiles that said they were waiting and watching for them to step out of line – were living such normal lives with their families. That the camp was a place of happiness to them, that they couldn't even see the prisoners in front of them as women, just the same as them.

'Evil bitches,' another woman hissed.

The metal slipped from between Aletta's fingers then, and she dropped to her knees to find it, fingers sweeping across the ground to locate the missing thread. She rose the moment she found it, too distracted to hear the boots that had crossed the floor towards her.

The guard gave her a look that said she was going to enjoy what came next.

Aletta opened her mouth to protest, to explain that she'd found what she'd dropped, but she didn't get the chance. The only noise that came out of her mouth was a cry of pain as a baton was slammed into her back with enough force to tip her over the work bench; it made her feel as if every bone in her spine had shattered.

'Get back to work!'

The words were said in thickly accented English, and as Aletta bit down on her lip to stave off the pain, she saw tears falling silently down her mother's cheeks. It had already been the worst day of her life, and Aletta knew that this was only the beginning – for both of them.

'The days when Herr Weber is here are the ones when you can relax, he's the manager; but the others are right,' said one of the women from earlier. 'When he's not here, this place is a living hell.'

◆ ◆ ◆

Later that night, after working for almost ten hours straight with no break before the gruelling walk home, Aletta felt as if her body was going to break. Her stomach cried out for food, her back still ached, and even curling up in bed didn't ease any of her pain. It was like nothing she could have imagined before; none of this seemed real. Not what had happened at their apartment, not arriving at the camp.

'Hold on to the good, Aletta. Hold something beautiful in your mind and keep it there, don't let go of it.'

She held her mother's hand, curling into her as they shivered against the cold in the room, as they tried not to wriggle against the scratchy mattress. But her words had worked, because Aletta held Harry in her mind just as she'd suggested, as if he were right there beside her.

Her body ached, and her stomach growled so loudly it hurt, but no one could stop her from closing her eyes and pretending she was somewhere else – it was the one thing nobody could take from her.

Aletta looked up shyly at Harry as his fingers traced lazy circles on her skin. His smile was ever so slightly lopsided, and something about the way he looked at her warmed her from the inside.

'This little room must be driving you mad,' she said. 'Are you going crazy yet?'

His mouth tilted into a wider smile. 'Well, I would be, if it weren't for the very pretty visitor who keeps calling by.'

Aletta laughed. 'Truly though, you must be bored out of your mind being stuck in here.'

He leaned forward and touched her hair, brushing it gently from her face, his fingers lingering. It was the first time he'd touched her so casually, almost without thinking, and she liked it.

'I'm not,' he said, his voice low. 'I'm safe, I'm warm, I'm well fed, and I have you. What more could a man ask for?'

Her breath caught as he leaned in a little further. He didn't kiss her straight away, he never did, always giving her the choice, but this time he didn't hesitate for long.

When Harry kissed her, she forgot everything else. She forgot where they were, what time it was, the fact that one of her parents could walk into the room at any time. All she could think about was the gentle, warm brush of his lips against hers as she tried to remember to breathe, as his mouth kept moving so softly against hers.

And when it was over, when Harry touched his forehead to hers, his fingers resuming their gentle circles against the bare skin of her arm, she had a feeling that he'd meant it. That he didn't mind being stuck in their little hidden room at all.

Aletta closed her eyes then, as if by shutting them, she could shut out the memory too. But all she did was create a more vivid picture in her mind, one that she couldn't erase, no matter how hard she tried.

Chapter Twenty

Chloe

Chloe sat in the dirt, her knees drawn up and her back against the side of the barracks wall. She knew she'd be reprimanded soon and told to go inside, but sometimes, just sitting and turning her face up to the sun let her imagination take hold. She could believe, even if just for one minute, that she was anywhere but there, even if the feeling only ever did last a short time. That she was at home; that her mother was still alive; that she was about to embark upon her first year of university studying literature, that her sister was only one call away. That her entire life hadn't been turned upside down – twice.

The sound of footfall made her open her eyes, and she lifted a hand, half expecting the thwack of a baton. But instead, she saw one of the women who'd arrived a few weeks earlier.

'Hello,' the woman said, coming closer and holding out her hand. 'I'm Emma.'

Chloe glanced at her, but she didn't lift her hand.

'Do you have any paper?' Chloe asked.

The woman let out a sudden laugh that sounded more like a cry. Tears began to slip down her cheeks, and Chloe noticed that she didn't bother to wipe them away as she stood there.

'I have nothing,' Emma finally said. 'The only thing I have here is my daughter, they've taken everything else. So no, I don't even have a piece of damn paper.'

She lowered herself to sit beside Chloe in the dirt, close enough that they could talk in low voices, but far enough away that they weren't touching. She watched as the woman named Emma tipped her head against the wall for a moment. Chloe asked everyone for paper, she never had enough, but no one had ever cried when she'd asked them before.

'I don't know why hearing you ask that upset me so much,' Emma said with a raspy sigh. 'Just the thought of not having even the most basic provisions I suppose. It's beyond demeaning, isn't it?'

'I understand, you don't have to explain yourself to me,' Chloe said, folding the piece of paper she was holding in her hand. 'How did you end up here? What did you and your daughter do?'

Emma sighed, and Chloe watched as she cradled her hands, palms facing up. She knew the pain she was in – she remembered too well how raw and red her hands had been when she'd first started working in the factory. At home, she would have had a basic salve to help soothe her skin, but here they were given nothing. It was as if they wanted them to suffer, to experience all the pain possible just to see how far they could push a person before they broke.

'I suppose there's no point in keeping secrets in here,' Emma said. 'It can't get any worse than it already is.'

Chloe nodded, but the truth was that it could get worse. She'd seen what they could do to women they didn't like, or women who got sick or couldn't work anymore, but she kept her thoughts to herself. When she'd first arrived, she'd refused to talk to anyone, not wanting to get close to someone and face losing them, but lately, something inside her had changed. She still didn't want close personal relationships, but she did want to know the stories of the women in here.

'My daughter and I were part of the Dutch Resistance,' Emma said. 'We were so careful not to be caught, but my husband was known to work for many Jewish clients, so I suppose that was enough to make them suspect us. Maybe it put us on a watch list of sorts.'

Chloe met Emma's gaze. 'You were part of the Resistance?' she asked. 'Is that why they arrested you and your daughter?'

'They arrested us because they found the British airman we were hiding in our house,' Emma said sadly. 'My daughter went to deliver papers one night and came home with him, and we thought we'd got away with it. But in the end, it was having him in our home that sent us here.'

'Your husband?' Chloe asked.

She knew the moment the other woman swallowed roughly and looked away, not answering straight, what the answer was. But Chloe gave her time, sitting in silence beside her.

'My husband is dead,' Emma said. 'Killed the night we were arrested.'

Chloe wasn't sure why, but there was something about Emma that she was drawn to. Perhaps it was because she'd been in the Resistance, which reminded her of her brother Claude, or that Emma was of a similar age to her mother, but she found herself holding out her hand. Or maybe she just, finally, needed a friend.

'I'm Chloe,' she said, surprised at how warm Emma's hand felt in hers when they touched.

'It's nice to meet you, Chloe,' Emma said. 'Were you in the Resistance too?'

'My brother was, *is*,' she said, praying that it was indeed present tense, but not wanting to get her hopes up. 'It's the reason I'm here.'

'I've noticed you distance yourself from the other women,' Emma eventually said. 'Do we have to be careful who we trust?'

Chloe shook her head. 'Not really. Everyone here is just doing their best to survive.'

They were silent again for a long moment, but it was Chloe who broke the silence this time. She found herself taking some of the papers she kept hidden in her clothes out and showing them to Emma.

'Before the war, before all of this, I wanted to be a writer,' she said. 'Well, a poet if I'm honest.'

'This is your poetry?' Emma asked, gesturing at the papers Chloe held close to her chest. 'That's why you asked me for paper?'

'I haven't written a poem since my mother died, the words just aren't there anymore, but I take down other people's words. Their poems, their recipes, their memories,' she said. 'If I ever get out of here, I want something I can share, of the women who were here. The mothers, the daughters, the sisters. All of them.' Chloe took a breath, her shoulders moving up and down. 'I'd always hoped to publish a collection of poetry, but now this seems more important than anything I've ever wanted to write before. The women smuggle me any paper they can from their work detail if they're on office or clothes sorting detail.'

She watched as Emma went still, and Chloe's fingers tightened on the papers as she looked down at them. Part of her wanted to show this kind woman what she'd been working on, but another part was still cautious about who to trust.

'How long have you been here?' Emma whispered.

'Too long,' Chloe murmured back. But the truth was, she no longer knew how long it had been. The days had turned into weeks, until she barely remembered what date it even was. 'Every day here is the same. More women arrive, more women are killed, more women are marched out to work. The days all blur into the next. But this keeps me going, it gives me something to believe in, something to work on.'

'What would happen to you, if you were found with this?'

Chloe just shook her head, and she could see from Emma's stare that she understood.

Emma handed her back the papers. 'I'll do my best to find more paper for you,' she said. 'What you're doing, it will matter greatly to the families of those who've died.'

Chloe nodded; it was why she was doing it after all, but she wondered if anyone else would ever see it, whether she'd even survive long enough to give it to anyone who could share it.

But something happened then that made her forget all about her work. Emma reached out and took her hand again, her fingers light and warm as she held Chloe's palm. They didn't say anything else, but the feel of Emma's skin against hers, after so long of not having another human touch her with kindness, brought tears to her eyes. It was the simplest act, but in that moment, it meant the world to her.

'We'd better go back inside soon,' Chloe said, clearing her throat when she heard how raspy her voice sounded.

Emma just nodded, standing first and offering her hand again. Chloe grasped it, letting her help her up, knowing that it wouldn't be long before this kind woman was as weak as the rest of them, and unable to lend a hand to anyone. But it wasn't just that thought that made Chloe tearful, it was that somehow, in that moment, Emma reminded her so much of her own mother.

'At work tomorrow,' Chloe said, feeling as if she needed to do or say something to help Emma navigate camp life, to give her some kind of advice. 'Rip off the lowest part of your dress to tie over your mouth and nose. It helps with the fumes. You'll get used to the smell eventually, but for now, that will help.'

Emma nodded her thanks and they walked inside, and Chloe found herself staying close to her as they climbed into their beds, just before the *Blockälteste* came down yelling and swearing at them, and looking for someone to beat. She would make sure in the morning to warn Emma to steer clear of the *Älteste* and her assistants.

The sadism of the guards and those they appointed to run the barracks for them knew no boundaries, but for the first time since she'd arrived, Chloe had the strangest feeling that she might have met a true friend inside the camp walls. That she might have someone to survive with.

Don't get too close. She'll only be taken from you.

The warning sounded in her mind even as she tried to force it away. She'd been reluctant to befriend anyone, too scared of losing someone she cared about after seeing how many women were killed for little more than breathing the wrong way. But Chloe was tired of being alone. She was tired of being lonely. She was tired of all the death and the sadness and the silence. And she missed her mother almost more now than when she'd first lost her.

She felt for the papers, tucked up her sleeve, a familiar comfort to her, an obsession that she could no more stop working on than she could stop breathing. But then her thoughts turned to home, as they always did after lights out, and she forgot all about Emma and her papers and the camp, as she lost herself to the tears that always found her before sleep as she cried for home.

Chapter Twenty-One

Chloe

Chloe positioned herself close to Emma at roll call the following morning, walking nearby on their way to the factory. Her heart simply couldn't take another loss – which was why her attachment to Emma had surprised her.

Up until now, her way of showing the other women in the camp she cared was by writing for them, rather than herself. When her mother had passed away, she'd abandoned her university plans and her writing, as if her creativity had been extinguished the day her life turned upside down, and it had never come back. And although she still couldn't write poetry, what she could do was write the stories of others. They'd sit and talk to her, and she would write as much as she could, and even though they weren't her own words, it was enough.

She found herself increasingly curious about Emma and her daughter, although she'd barely heard the latter speak. Observing them as they worked, she could see that Emma was fiercely protective of her daughter, who seemed to be working almost robotically, going through the motions without any feeling, as if she had nothing left to give. And it made Chloe want to yell at her, to tell her what happened to those who looked too weak to work.

It wasn't until later that night, when they had some free time after dinner, that she had the chance to speak to Emma again. They met in the same way they had the night before, with Chloe sitting on the ground, and Emma walking out of the barracks to find her. A joint moment of calm during an otherwise insufferable day.

'I hope someone found more paper for you today.' Emma's voice was soft, her words spoken with care, as she joined her.

Chloe sighed. 'Not today. But I still have a little more room on my last piece.'

'What do you like writing most?' Emma asked.

Chloe thought about her question before answering. 'Whatever it is that's most important to the woman I'm talking to. Oftentimes it's a recipe, because it's a reminder of home, of the family they once had. I find those the hardest though, not the easiest, but I think that perhaps they imagine a relative surviving and the recipe finding its way back to them.'

They sat for a while in comfortable silence, until Emma spoke again.

'I'm so hungry that my stomach feels as if it's eating itself alive. Does the pain get any better? Do our bodies ever get used to this?'

Chloe shook her head. 'Sometimes I find myself staring at a blade of grass and wanting to eat it, just to chew something. I think about food more than anything else some days.'

'If you could eat anything right now, what would it be?'

'Roast chicken,' Chloe said. 'And a fresh slice of bread with a thick piece of cheese on top.'

Emma groaned. 'I want my mother's beef stew with mashed potatoes. Sometimes I think about it so often, I can almost taste it.'

They were both lost in their own thoughts before Chloe spoke again.

'I've heard that they might be building sleeping rooms for those of us that work at the Siemens factory, so we don't have so far to walk each day. Maybe we won't be as hungry if we don't have to use so much energy, although it's probably nothing more than a rumour.'

'Maybe.'

Emma certainly didn't sound convinced, and Chloe glanced at her, deciding to ask the question she'd been thinking about all day.

'Your daughter. Is she all right? I've hardly seen her speak since you arrived.'

Emma's face told a story of heartbreak, and Chloe almost wished she hadn't asked. But there was something about the women that made her want to know more, and her daughter reminded her a little of herself. She imagined she'd appeared just as withdrawn when she'd arrived, until she'd decided to write again.

'My husband, her father, was killed in front of her. And she lost someone else she loved the night we were taken, too. I think she's trying to come to terms with her entire life being snatched away from her, that's all.'

Chloe nodded. Her own memories were hard enough to bear, the image of her younger brother crying for her, of the anguish on his face, haunting her every night since she left. But as hard as it had been to be dragged away from the people she loved, she was grateful her last memory of them was when they were alive, even if most days she felt as if she wasn't. At least she could imagine them going about their lives still.

'I'm sorry you lost your husband,' Chloe said. 'I don't know if I said that the other night, but I should have.'

Emma's eyes shone with tears. 'Thank you. I still can't believe it, if I'm honest. In my mind I keep imagining him being at home waiting for us, which is stupid, I know. As if we're away for the week instead of imprisoned indefinitely.'

'It's not stupid. Thoughts like that are what keep us alive in here, they give us a reason to keep rising every morning instead of giving up.'

Emma sighed, and Chloe could see tears welling in her eyes.

'My daughter, Aletta, I think she blames herself for the way we were caught. It's why she's so quiet,' Emma told her. 'During the occupation, she kept busy with teaching and the work we did with the underground movement, but it was she who brought the Allied airman home. I don't think she'll ever forgive herself.'

'I understand,' Chloe said. 'More than you could imagine. We all have to live with the guilt and what-ifs of how we ended up here.'

They'd barely finishing speaking when Emma's daughter appeared, her hair hanging limply, her eyes so wide they seemed to take up most of her face. But before Emma could introduce them, her daughter spoke, her voice barely a whisper as she stared across at the barracks on the other side of the road.

'There are children here.' Her voice was raspy, as if it hadn't been used in a long time.

Chloe silently followed her gaze, seeing a handful of children walking quietly from a bunk room. The younger children were left behind when the women left for work duty; left to fend for themselves and stay silent in the barracks, too afraid not to follow the orders given to them. But after dinner they were allowed free time like the adult prisoners, appearing in their oversized clothes, their hair scraggly and their skin dirty.

'They're children who need a teacher,' Chloe finally said, glancing at Emma as she turned to face Aletta. 'And I hear that's what you did before you came here.'

'Me?' Aletta's eyes grew even wider as she shook her head, wrapping her arms around her body. 'No. I can't be their teacher.'

'I'm Chloe,' she said, rising so that she could stand beside Emma's daughter.

'Aletta.' The word was barely a whisper, but Chloe heard it.

'I know it's a lot to process, you've only just arrived and you've been through a lot, but these children need a teacher, Aletta. Some of the others have been trying their best, but . . .' Chloe sighed. 'They need someone with training, someone who knows what they're doing. They need a proper teacher.'

'I . . .' Aletta's voice trailed off, but her gaze never wavered, focused on the children who now had a stick and were drawing something in the dirt. It was as if she couldn't tear her eyes away from them.

'If we ever leave this place, they need to have had an education, at least the basics,' Chloe said. 'We need to keep their minds active, they need to learn.' She took a breath. 'We all need to believe that there's a chance they'll one day have a life away from this camp.'

She watched as Aletta swallowed, almost as if she had a large lump in her throat. She did it again and again, and Chloe saw her tears begin to fall as her mother wrapped an arm around her shoulders.

'Tell me,' Aletta said. 'About the children. Tell me more about them.'

Chloe moved closer, so that all three stood facing the playing kids, her words soft as she began to share with Aletta what she'd learnt about them. She hadn't thought about searching the barracks for teachers until now, but hearing that Aletta had been training to be one made her realise that it might be possible to find some time each day for the younger children who wanted to learn. All they needed was someone willing to help.

'They have to stay hidden while their mothers are away working, and they are many different nationalities. Some of them are Jewish, but others are here because their parents are political prisoners,' Chloe said, her eyes following one little boy in particular, who reminded her of her brother when he was younger. He had slightly too-long hair and a smile that seemed to light up his face, despite his surroundings. 'They do awful, brutal things to the children who don't obey the rules, and the babies . . .' Chloe swallowed and blinked away the burn in her eyes.

'What?' Aletta croaked. 'What do they do to the babies?'

Chloe swallowed and balled her fists so tightly that her nails dug viciously into her palms. 'The babies aren't allowed to survive.' She didn't tell her what they did; Chloe never wanted to speak of it.

Aletta was silent then, and Chloe wished she hadn't told her. But she needed her to see how desperate these children were for comfort, for anything that distracted them from the cruelty and uncertainty of the place they lived in and the probable fate that awaited them. Their mothers needed it, too.

'Do they at least get more to eat than we did tonight?' Aletta asked.

'No.' Chloe shook her head. 'It's the same watery cup of soup and sorry excuse for a piece of bread for everyone, and sometimes they get even less because they don't work. They don't think it's worth feeding them.'

Chloe's throat burned just saying the words aloud, hating that there was nothing they could do to fight what was happening to them. But perhaps in telling Aletta the truth, she could spur her into action.

'The papers you have,' Emma said, and Chloe looked up, distracted from staring at the children. 'They are records?'

Chloe nodded. 'I record whatever is most important to each of the women who come to me. I suppose it's my little act of defiance, so that maybe one day I have proof of at least some of the women who were killed here. I can't bear the thought of them being forgotten.'

'What happens when the boys come of age?' Emma asked, still staring at the children.

'The boys are sent away when they turn twelve,' Chloe told them. 'They have to go to a men's camp.' She breathed out a pained sigh, remembering the last group of boys ripped from their mothers' arms. Just children still, terrified to leave their mothers for the unknown, forced into wagons to be transported somewhere even worse than the brutal camp they already knew. It made her sick to the stomach thinking about it, knowing what it would have been like for her if Adrian had been transported to the camp with her, how she'd have wanted to die herself if she'd seen him taken from her, not knowing what his fate would be. 'But the worst is saved for the prettiest of the teenage girls. They're young enough to be bribed with the promise of milk and extra food, but old enough for the men to find them attractive.' She swallowed, thinking of the fifteen-year-old who'd been taken only the week before.

'What happens to them?' Emma asked, her voice hoarse, as if perhaps she didn't really want to know.

'They're taken to a brothel for the SS men and guards,' she said.

Chloe looked at Aletta, and something about her expression made it seem as if she'd suddenly come to life, her eyes widening.

'Any little thing means a lot here. If you were to teach them, to give them a glimmer of hope . . .' Chloe let her voice trail away, surprised when Aletta spoke up, her voice louder than before, more confident. It was the reason Chloe had forced herself to start writing, after all. She'd wanted to give herself and those around her hope, hope they wouldn't all be forgotten.

'I'll do it,' Aletta said. 'I'll be their teacher.'

'I have to warn you though that if we're caught with drawings or writings . . .' Chloe met her gaze, needing her to understand the risk. Chloe reached for her hand, not letting go when Aletta jumped, as if surprised that someone had touched her.

'I don't care. I'll do it.'

'Thank you,' Chloe said.

Aletta just nodded, but Chloe felt her hand soften, and she kept hold for a little longer. Because it wasn't just Aletta's hold that had softened, it was something inside her, too. Perhaps it was because her own mother had been a teacher, or knowing that someone else wanted to help the children. Maybe it was because of the kind, open way Emma looked at her when she smiled and mouthed *thank you.*

Whatever it was, Chloe felt her guard lower just a little, and for the first time since she'd arrived, she didn't try to raise it again.

Chapter Twenty-Two

Aletta

After a month at the camp, Aletta had moments of wondering how she was supposed to put one foot in front of the other, and hours when the gnawing hunger in her stomach was so overwhelming she would have dropped to the ground and eaten grass if she'd seen any. But the one thing that made her feel anything beyond pain and sadness was the children. And for that, she knew she had Chloe to thank – Chloe who was the closest person she now had to a friend, who'd made what had happened to her and her mother just a little bit more bearable.

Tonight, in the little time they had before dark, her mother and Chloe were sitting watching as Aletta knelt before a small group of children and traced circles in the dirt. There were women all around them keeping a lookout, ready to alert her if any of the guards came near, as she had all the youngest children whisper their alphabet in English and take turns tracing it into the dirt. It wasn't ideal, but it was better than nothing, and other than when she'd met Harry, she'd never been so grateful for her decision to learn other languages.

'Well done!' she praised one little boy, who had bright blue eyes as round as saucers.

'Miss Aletta,' said an older girl who already knew her letters. 'I want to practise my writing.'

'Then how about we trace the words with our fingers,' Aletta said. 'You can draw the words on each other's backs in your bed when you're bored, or even draw them in the air during the day.'

There were little nods of encouragement, and Aletta smiled down at them all.

'If you trace on each other's backs, perhaps you could take turns and guess what the other is writing?' she said, grinning when she saw their little faces brighten at the challenge.

She waited for a moment until their chattering had stopped, before clearing her throat and leaning towards them all again.

'I'd also like everyone to make up a little poem,' Aletta instructed. 'At the end of the week, we can all share. I thought it might be fun.'

'What's a poem?' asked another girl.

'A poem is like a little rhyme,' Aletta told them. 'I'd like everyone to think of something happy, something that makes you smile. Like . . .' She thought for a moment, then smiled. 'Roses are red, violets are blue, sugar is sweet, and so are you!'

That made them all laugh, and Aletta's heart felt as if it had been cracked open in a completely different way. It made her remember why she'd wanted to be a teacher in the first place, why she *still* wanted to be one. She hadn't smiled since the night everything was taken from her, but today, her happiness came naturally, even if it was only for a short time. But it made her want to feel again, *to live.* Even if it was hard not to think of the children she'd left behind, whom she might never teach or see ever again.

'My tummy is hungry, my tummy is loud,' one boy said, making the other children giggle. 'Is that a poem?'

Aletta grinned. 'I think it's a very good start,' she said, before leaning forward and lowering her voice. 'Speaking of food, I have a very special treat for you all. I have a pocket full of bread pieces.'

Their eyes went so wide with excitement at her words that it almost broke her heart.

'Do you see all the women keeping guard?' she asked, watching as they turned to look. 'All of them saved a piece of bread for you, which means everyone gets a little mouthful more, and maybe next time there will be something else, too.'

Aletta's own mouth was salivating as she made the children form a little queue, each holding out a hand for her to put a piece of bread into. In truth, it tasted more like what she imagined lightly baked floor sweepings would, but it was the best they had, and the children's faces had lit up as if she'd offered them a wrapped gift.

'Place it on your tongue and chew it slowly, to make it last,' she told them as they dispersed and went back to their mothers, as her own mother stood and came over to her.

'You did a lot of good tonight, Aletta.'

She touched her mother's arm, their gazes meeting. 'It felt good,' she said, honestly. 'It's the first time I've felt alive since . . .' Aletta didn't need to say it; they both knew what she was referring to.

'These children need you as much as you need them,' her mother said. 'You've given them something to look forward to, and you've given their mothers something to believe in.'

Aletta hoped she was right, but she was also worried. What they were doing wasn't allowed, and if they were caught . . . she swallowed and watched them disappear and join their mothers. She hoped that it would only be she who was punished, and not they, because she'd never forgive herself if anything happened to those innocent, trusting children.

'If we ever get home, I want to teach again,' Aletta said, turning to her mother as they walked slowly over to join Chloe. 'I want to spend the rest of my life making children smile. I've never wanted to be a teacher more than I do right now.'

Her mother placed an arm around her and Aletta dropped her head to her shoulder.

'We all need something to aim for,' her mother said. 'That's the only way we'll survive this place.'

Aletta turned to her. 'What are you looking forward to?' she asked.

'Being with my daughter and seeing her smile every day. That's all I need to imagine, Aletta, is you happy and safe, and me watching over you.'

Aletta wished there was more that could bring her mother joy, but before they could talk any longer the guards began to shout and their *Älteste* yelled at them to get inside. So they linked arms, her mother extending a hand to help Chloe to her feet, and they headed inside for another night of being eaten alive by the bed bugs. But tonight, at least, Aletta had something other than old memories to make her smile.

'Chloe, I hope you didn't mind me suggesting poetry tonight,' she said. 'It's just that ever since I heard you were a poet . . .'

'I haven't been a poet in a very long time, Aletta,' Chloe said. 'But it's fine. So long as the children are smiling, that's all that matters to me.'

As they stood up the next day after her little class was finished, Aletta shuffled even closer to her mother and Chloe. They were all huddled together, bracing themselves against the icy cold wind, which had made teaching almost impossible as the children couldn't stop their teeth from chattering. At one point she'd wondered if some of their teeth might actually fall clean from their jaws while she'd sat with them on the ground, tucked up so close that their shoulders touched.

'Chloe, what will we do if the rumours are true? If they move us to the Siemens factory and we can't stay here?' Aletta asked. 'How will we continue to teach them?'

Chloe sighed. 'I don't know. Perhaps they'll let some of the children come with us? At least the older ones who are close to working age?'

'Surely they won't expect women to leave their children here without them.' But even as Chloe said the words, she knew that there was no limit to the cruelty of those who'd imprisoned them. Of course they would do that.

'Then we find someone to continue our work, and we teach the ones we can,' Chloe said, wrapping her arms around herself as the cold wind bit at their exposed arms and hands. 'Maybe some of the other women arriving are teachers? Maybe your work will make others offer to help? And there are always Sundays.'

'I suppose I could leave a lesson plan for each week,' she said, thinking it through. 'Or perhaps small homework tasks, something that follows on from their Sunday lesson? Something the other women can do with them?'

One of the Czech prisoners came up to Aletta then, making her jump when she touched her arm. They largely kept to themselves, a tight-knit group of women who'd been in the camp since the very beginning, and Aletta barely saw them talk to anyone else. But today, this woman's eyes were bright as she gripped Aletta's arm.

She spoke English, but her thick accent made it difficult for Aletta to understand her.

'Karolina,' the woman said, tapping her chest.

'Aletta,' she replied with a small smile as she shivered, envying Karolina's thick, padded coat. When she glanced down, she saw that she also wore thick wool socks and leather boots.

'You go to the *Bekleidungskammer* and ask for Anna,' she said, pressing her fingers even more tightly into Aletta's arm. 'You are cold, but she will look after you.'

Aletta knew what that word meant; it was the stockroom, where all the confiscated clothes were taken and sorted through.

'The Czech women work in there, they have the best jobs,' Chloe whispered. 'She doesn't want you to be cold. They're the ones making sure the children have extra clothes where they can.'

The woman kept staring into her eyes, repeating what she'd already said as if Aletta hadn't heard it.

'You want to give me warm clothes?' Aletta asked.

Karolina nodded. 'Yes, yes. You stay warm. Keep helping children, we need you here. And you, the writer,' she said, pointing to Chloe. 'You get more clothes too.'

Aletta nodded and thanked her, turning to Chloe who was shaking now in her thin dress, her eyes suddenly looking more alive as she nodded her thanks, too.

'Perhaps we will survive this place after all,' Chloe said through her shivers. 'If we can stay warm, if they'll help us to find some clothes without being caught . . .'

'Will those clothes have been taken from prisoners?' Aletta shuddered, thinking that they could have been taken from women who'd been sent straight to their death. 'Will other women in the camp recognise their belongings if I suddenly appear in them?'

Chloe took her hand. 'This is a place of death, Aletta. If you get the chance to eat one more piece of bread or feel the warmth of a coat, you take it, you don't worry about upsetting someone else. We all have to do what we have to do to stay alive.'

Aletta blinked away tears, wishing she was stronger, that she didn't have such a conscience.

'You're teaching their children, Aletta, and these women want to find a way to thank you,' Chloe said. 'So let them. Besides, have you seen what the new women are doing? They get someone to hold their things when they arrive, and they hold them and exchange them when they come out of the delousing chamber. It's why some of them have more than just the striped dress.'

She knew Chloe was right, but it still didn't ease her conscience.

'Just be careful, going down there,' Chloe said.

'Why?' Aletta asked.

'Just be careful. There's nowhere in this place that isn't dangerous. Sometimes . . .'

'Sometimes what?'

'It's nothing. I'm just nervous of going anywhere other than my bunk or the factory in this place. I've seen too many women be sent away and not come back, that's all. Looking at some of the words I've written each day makes me nervous.'

Aletta shivered again, this time from fear rather than cold, but she knew that if she wanted to survive the winter, if she wanted her mother to survive and now Chloe too, she would have to do this. By the time the snow settled, and the temperatures plummeted for days in a row, there would be no chance of survival without something better to cover their skinny, malnourished bodies.

But that would have to wait for another day, because everyone was back from work now, slowly making their way outside to stretch their legs after their meal. If she hadn't known better, she'd have expected all the women to want to stay inside, out of the cold, but the hut filled with bunks had a pungent smell that was almost impossible to stand. The smell of so many unwashed bodies, of mattresses that were beyond saving, the overcrowding, the relentless bite of lice – it was not somewhere anyone usually wanted to linger. Even if outside was as cold and unrelenting as she imagined it might be in Siberia, it was still preferable to those cabins.

Aletta watched Chloe as a steady line of women dropped by to call on her. It seemed that her new friend was becoming even more in demand for her collection of writings, and it made Aletta anxious that one of the guards might discover her act of defiance, that Chloe could be hauled away and punished for what she'd done. But she was also heartened to see how many women were smuggling stolen paper to her, and the protective huddles they made around her so that no one could see her writing. She was recording little snippets of love and life from these women, writing in tiny words to make use of every inch of paper, and Aletta could see that it meant the world to them, even if it did seem to take a toll on Chloe.

When the women finally dispersed, Aletta wandered over. She was so tired she wanted nothing more than to collapse and sleep, but the idea of lying down on the lice-infested mattress inside made her shudder. It was bad enough they had to sit on them to eat their dinner, if that was what it could even be called.

'Soon you're going to find it hard to hide all those papers on you,' Aletta said as she approached, sitting down beside Chloe. 'I think you should give some of them to me, to hide for you.'

Chloe shook her head. 'Absolutely not. I can't let you risk that.'

'I will hide some, and my mother has already told me she wants to take some, too,' Aletta said. 'You don't need to do this alone, especially now that we have more clothes to wear. Look at all the pockets I have.'

Chloe didn't look convinced, but she eventually nodded.

'I'm certain there are many women who'd love to help you if you needed them to, Chloe. You're more widely loved than I think you realise. We're not the only ones who appreciate you.'

'Thank you. I don't think you know how much that means to me.'

Aletta sensed Chloe was going to say something else, so she waited, her hands folded in her lap and her knees drawn up. Her bottom hurt sitting on the dirt as she'd already lost a significant amount of weight, and it felt like she barely had any padding over her bones anymore.

'Some days there are women who die at the hands of a vicious guard or dog, other times they die from exhaustion or starvation, or even typhoid,' Chloe said. 'But I always think that at least I have something of theirs, the ones who have shared with me. I tell myself that when they disappear, at least I have something, but you're right, I can't keep hiding them on my own. There are so many papers now.'

Aletta blinked back at her, looking at the papers as Chloe sorted through them, at recipes that made her stomach growl in hunger, at the names printed in the corners.

After a long moment of silence, she spoke. 'Chloe, how did you end up here?' Aletta asked, her voice soft. 'I know no one likes talking about how, but—'

'You can ask me,' she said. 'I don't like sharing my story, but I've told your mother, and I'll tell you.'

Aletta watched her face, not wanting to make her uncomfortable and wondering whether she should have asked the question in the first place.

'Sometimes it feels like not talking about home keeps the people I love safe, but I know that's not true,' said Chloe.

'That makes perfect sense to me.' And it did. Aletta imagined that everyone in the camp would understand in their own way – they all had someone who'd been taken from them or someone they'd been forced to leave behind. 'You don't have to tell me, truly you don't.'

Aletta stretched her legs out, sore from the hours of standing in the factory, surprised when Chloe reached out and touched her legs.

'Do you want me to massage them for a bit?' Chloe asked.

Aletta groaned as she started to press into her calf muscles with her fingers. 'I'll do yours after.'

'You know, I was too scared to get close to anyone before you and your mother arrived,' Chloe said as she kneaded Aletta's lower legs. 'I just, I suppose I wanted to keep to myself and not get close to anyone. I couldn't stand the thought of getting to know someone and then losing them. Facing each day was hard enough without grieving anyone else, and staying quieter felt easier than talking, which is why I was happier to write, but not to share myself with anyone.'

Aletta nodded. 'I understand. It's the same reason I don't like talking about Harry. I just want to keep the memory of him in my mind, like if I hold him there and don't tell anyone what happened, it won't be true.'

'He was the man you were hiding? Your mother told me a little of what happened.'

Aletta nodded, closing her eyes for a second and squeezing away the memory of her last moments with him, still hearing the way he'd screamed her name as she was dragged away. She didn't want to keep remembering him like that, but the nicer memories were becoming harder and harder to hold on to.

'You're the only member of your family in here? In any of the camps?' Aletta asked.

'As far as I know. I gave myself up.'

Aletta saw the pain cross Chloe's face. 'Your parents?'

'My father is still alive, but after my mother died he just . . .' Chloe's fingers stalled against Aletta's skin. 'I suppose part of him died that day, too. He just lost himself I suppose, like he'd retreated into a shell and couldn't find his way out. Even when I was arrested, he just stood there and watched.'

Aletta sensed the anger burning inside of Chloe as she spoke. 'Do you blame him?'

'For me ending up in here?' Chloe asked. 'No, it wasn't his fault, but I keep thinking that it should have been him standing up to protect our family, sacrificing himself to keep us safe, but it's like he was numb to everything going on around us. I thought it might have been enough to make him fight for us, for *me*, but even with the SS standing in our apartment . . .'

Aletta shifted so that she could massage Chloe's legs instead, knowing they would be every inch as sore as hers, wanting her to know she was happy to sit and listen, that she wouldn't judge her. Chloe's legs were thinner than hers though, her bones prominent, and Aletta knew that it would only be so long before she lost the last of her body fat, too. She was convinced that the green floating in their soup each night wasn't even a vegetable but grass, picked and thrown into the pot.

'Did you take the fall for someone else?' Aletta asked, sensing that there was more to Chloe's story. 'Is that why you thought your father might have spared you? That's what you mean when you say you gave yourself up?'

She watched as Chloe tipped her head back and closed her eyes, and when she finally met her gaze again, they were filled with unshed tears.

'I pretended I was the Resistance member instead of my brother, when they came looking for him,' she whispered. 'I gave myself up so that my brothers could be safe. That's why I'm here.'

Chapter Twenty-Three

Chloe

Chloe watched as Aletta blinked away visible tears. She understood why hearing it upset her, because Chloe had felt the same when Emma had shared their story – they'd both endured so much, knew so intimately the pain of loss.

'Do you regret it?' Aletta asked. 'If you'd known where you'd end up, if you'd known you would be suffering like this . . .'

Chloe shook her head, her answer honest. 'No, I don't. Because I knew I'd be able to survive whatever my fate was, that I'd be strong enough, but my brothers . . .' Chloe swallowed as Aletta kept rubbing her legs, and she found herself wishing it would never end. She hadn't been touched by someone who cared about her in a very long time. 'I made a promise to my mother before she died that I'd do anything to protect my brothers, that I'd look after them, and the only thing I couldn't live with would be having lied to her.'

Aletta's fingers stopped moving as tears fell fast down Chloe's cheeks. They were unexpected, which was why they had slipped past her defences, and Chloe steeled her jaw to stop them.

'I would rather die than break my promise to her.'

They sat in silence and Aletta moved closer, shuffling on the dirt until she could slide her arm around Chloe's shoulders, holding her as her body trembled with emotion.

'How did your mother die?'

Chloe shuddered, wishing she didn't have to relive her pain but wanting to share her story with Aletta. 'A lorry crashed into our car. My father had taken my mother and sister to a dance, and I was at home with my brothers, and he was the only one to survive.'

Aletta's eyes widened as she turned to her. 'They both died that night? Your mother and your sister?'

'My sister died instantly, she didn't stand a chance, but the doctors operated on my mother, and they told us she had a good chance of survival. I sat beside her hospital bed every hour that she was in there, praying for her to make it, but she knew that she was dying. She never believed she was going to recover.'

'That's when she asked you to make her a promise?'

Chloe nodded. 'She looked me in the eye and even though she was weak, she held my hand so tightly, and she begged me to look after them. To do anything I had to, to keep them safe.'

Aletta continued to hold her as if she were taking her time to digest what Chloe had told her. And then she softly spoke, changing the subject and taking Chloe by surprise.

'If there was no war, if none of this had happened, what would you be doing right now?' And then more softly. 'What did you give up to care for them, Chloe?'

Chloe found herself leaning into Aletta as she considered her question. It had been a long time since she'd let herself dream about what might have been without the war.

The *Blockälteste* and her assistants began yelling then and Aletta pushed to her feet and held out her hand to help Chloe up.

'I gave up university. I would have been the first in my family to go, and my dream was to be a poet or write a novel,' Chloe said, quickly, before they were silenced. 'Since I was a little girl, all I've ever wanted was to be a writer.'

'The memories and recipes you're keeping, that's your way of honouring your dream? Of doing good but keeping that dream alive?'

Chloe closed her eyes for a beat, remembering how excited she'd been, the new notebooks she'd bought for university, the sense of anticipation about her life finally beginning, of being in charge of her future.

'Yes. I suppose you're right, it does keep my dream alive. It keeps *me* alive, and stops me from giving up.' *Just. Only just.*

She saw Aletta hesitate as they stood on tired legs. Chloe quickly tucked the papers into her top, grateful that she'd found a brassiere to wear beneath her shirt. Her breasts had shrunk down to almost nothing, but it was the perfect place to hide a lot of the papers. She only hoped they'd be undamaged and still legible if she ever escaped the camp.

'I heard you reciting a poem to the children today. Was it one you wrote yourself?' Aletta asked.

Chloe laughed, cringing when the movement hurt her ribs, but she never got to answer Aletta, because their *Älteste* came and hurried them on, sending them scurrying after the other women who were still outside.

But this time when Chloe lay down beside Aletta, her legs curled up because there wasn't enough space to stretch out. Grateful for the warmth of her friend's body, she couldn't stop thinking about her mother and her sister, wanting to talk about them. Aletta had reached out to hold her hands as they lay in the dark. When they were finally alone, the guards and *Älteste* gone, Chloe whispered in a voice so low, it was barely audible.

'You remind me of my sister, and your mother, she reminds me of my own.' Chloe nearly added, *I've almost started to think that she is my mother, she's shown me so much love and kindness.*

Chloe moved her hands so that it was her holding Aletta's fingers warm in her palms. If Chloe closed her eyes and tried hard enough, she could almost imagine she was lying with her sister in the big bed they'd shared since they were little.

'Ever since I arrived here, I've woken to the same memory, before my sister died,' she told Aletta. 'It's like I've been taken back in time, as if my mind wants to keep returning to my last truly happy memory.'

'Perhaps it's our mind's way of keeping us alive,' Aletta murmured back. 'Mine is the same, but I can't stop wondering if remembering is harder than forgetting. It makes the pain of being here seem so much worse, that desperation to get back to what you left behind.' They were silent for a long moment, and it was Aletta who finally whispered again.

'Tell me about your sister,' she said. 'What was she like?'

Chloe smiled at the memory, closing her eyes. Part of her was grateful that Julia wasn't here with her. She'd been so pretty, and Chloe knew that her time at any of the camps would have gone one of two ways – she'd have had her beautiful long hair shaved off and been treated even worse than the other girls, or she would have been taken to service the men at one of those awful brothels. The thought of either made her want to be sick.

'Julia wanted to be a teacher, just like you,' Chloe eventually said. 'She wanted a brood of her own children one day, but while she waited to meet her future husband, she wanted to teach the youngest pupils.' Chloe smiled at the memory. 'She always said that she wanted to make them love school, that she'd wipe their tears and make them smile, that she could think of nothing better than reading them stories and seeing their little imaginations come to life with excitement.'

'It sounds like you could have run the school here well enough without me. I'm sure you learnt a lot from her.'

Chloe closed her eyes, the memory of Julia so bright and clear in her mind. She only hoped it would always stay that way – the idea of it fading was too much to bear.

'Chloe, you act as if they're all little devils rather than darling little children,' Julia teased as they lay in the sun, stretching out their oil-covered legs as they tried, rather unsuccessfully, to get a tan.

'They do sound like little devils to me,' Chloe said with a sigh.

'We might need more teachers once the war begins,' Julia said. 'So many men will be off to war and—'

'I'm not going to suddenly become a teacher if there's a war,' Chloe said, exasperated with her sister. 'Can't you imagine me doing something like coding poems for our soldiers? I've heard talk of a home-front type of resistance being formed, a network that will be set up in case France falls so that we can still fight. If I can't attend university, then I'll find a way to turn my words into weapons to help France.'

'Chloe, you can't be serious! Do you have any idea how dangerous that would be? Mother would never allow it.'

Chloe sighed. She supposed Julia was right. 'What she doesn't find out won't hurt . . .'

Julia groaned and turned over to sun her back. 'Let's just hope this maybe-war is over soon enough so that we can both marry and get on with our lives. If there is a war? It'll take all the young men away, and we'll be left old maids.'

Chloe laughed. 'I might be left an old maid, but you'll find a husband even if half the male population is depleted, Ju.'

'You truly think so?'

'I truly think so,' Chloe said, shutting her eyes and lying back in the sun. 'Who knows? You might meet a husband tonight while I'm left at home looking after the boys.'

Julia sighed. 'It does seem unfair that you can't come. I mean, you're already eighteen, it's not like—'

'It's fine,' Chloe interrupted. 'We both know that I'm being punished for what I said the other night. I'm happy to stay home, anyway.'

She still groaned when she thought of how upset her mother had become when she'd told her she wasn't certain she wanted to get married – that she'd rather be alone than feel she had to marry someone she wasn't in love with.

'We'll survive this war and both fall in love,' Julia said with a grin. 'Just you wait and see.'

Chloe opened her eyes and felt Aletta's warm arm shift to cover her. She leaned into it, crying silently as she wished the memories away. To think that less than seven hours after that her sister had gone and her mother soon after.

And just like that, Chloe had gone from being so fiercely ambitious to the mother of their family. Cooking, cleaning and doing laundry and caring for her brothers and father, the role she'd never seen for herself thrust upon her anyway. Her dreams had fallen by the wayside, no longer important to her, not compared to keeping Adrian safe.

I'm staying alive for them.

She brushed her tears away with her knuckles and gritted her teeth as she thought about what she'd left behind. Because she was going to survive to see them again, if it was the last thing she did.

The walk to the factory each day was always brutal, but as more and more women had fallen unwell over the months and years they'd now been at the camp, it was becoming ever harder. Until now, all three of them had been spared the worst of every passing illness. But today, Aletta had become sick so quickly, and there was so little that anyone could do to help her or any of the other women who were struggling. Today, too, they were to relocate to the new wooden barracks that had been built beside the Siemens factory. They wouldn't be coming back until Sunday to their old ones, and Chloe doubted there would be any room for them on Sunday when they returned, anyway.

'We're going to have to walk her between us,' Emma said. 'Can you help me to keep her upright?'

Chloe placed her hand against Aletta's hip, alarmed at the bone that protruded out. She was certain hers felt the same, but still, it was a shock to see it in another woman.

'Just keep walking,' she said. 'You know the way, we just have to keep putting one foot in front of the other.' She gave Emma a look over Aletta's head to indicate that nothing would stop Chloe from keeping her upright.

Thankfully roll call had been much faster than usual, with only the women assigned to the munitions factory told to line up. There hadn't been time to think about the children being left behind or the women they might not see again. Chloe knew that if they'd been forced to stand for two hours at roll call, as often happened, Aletta would have collapsed and been left behind.

'Why don't you tell me about your Harry while we walk,' Chloe said, as she supported Aletta. She wasn't as strong as she'd thought.

'Harry?' Aletta asked, and when she turned her head, Chloe saw how pale she was.

'Harry was a lovely young man,' Emma said. 'I imagine he's somewhere as horrid as this right now, fighting to stay alive just to see you again, Aletta. So, you're going to have to fight, too.'

Chloe laughed, but it quickly turned into a cough. 'You wouldn't want to disappoint the young man, so you'd better keep walking,' she teased once she caught her breath.

'What about the children?' Aletta asked. 'I didn't get to listen to all their poems, I—'

'You can listen to them on Sunday,' Chloe said, knowing she was lying, that not all those children would even be there when they returned. Typhus was passing through the camp like wildfire, and they all knew that going to the infirmary was a death sentence.

'Did you see that girl?' Aletta suddenly cried, turning so fast that Chloe almost lost the grip she had on her arm.

'What girl?' Chloe muttered, struggling to keep hold.

'She was one of my pupils! Else, her name was Else.'

Aletta was frantically looking at the group of new arrivals, but Chloe hissed at her as one of the guards started to walk down the line towards them.

'Stop turning and stay quiet,' she whispered, ducking her head and looking to the ground.

Aletta did as she was told, but it was Emma who whispered next, despite the attention focused on them.

'The little girl who disappeared from your class?' Emma asked. 'You're sure?'

'I'm certain.' Aletta's legs seemed to give way and it took all Chloe's strength to haul her back up, with Emma doing the same on the other side.

'Don't stop, Aletta. Don't you dare stop putting one foot in front of the other,' Emma ordered.

'But Else . . .'

'If that was your Else, then we'll find her on Sunday,' Emma said, grunting as they half dragged Aletta. 'But that'll be no use if we can't get you up this hill.'

'Just one step after the other,' Chloe repeated, tears filling her eyes as she thought of her own mother, heard her voice echoed in the desperation of Emma's as they both fought their own exhaustion to keep her moving.

◆ ◆ ◆

When they finally reached the factory, they were shown to their new sleeping quarters, and although Chloe had hoped for something better than where they'd come from, her hopes were quickly dashed at the sight of the hard wooden bunks.

'I need to sit,' Aletta whispered, and Chloe helped her down, even as the *Älteste* barked at them.

'You will work the day shift and sleep here,' said the woman charged with overseeing them. 'When you rise, the night shift will take your bunks.'

These beds are never going to have an hour of not being slept in. They're going to work us to death.

'Get her up,' the *Älteste* said. 'If she's sick, she goes.'

'Aletta,' Emma urged, as Chloe took hold of her arm to help her, hearing the panic in Emma's voice. 'You have to get up.'

'You go to work, or you go back down there to the infirmary,' the *Älteste* stated. 'It's your choice.'

'She'll work, she's fine,' Chloe snapped, keeping hold of Aletta's arm. But inside, fear rose like a hand trying to choke her around the neck, because she knew that there was no way Aletta was going to manage a ten- or twelve-hour shift any longer without collapsing in a heap.

She exchanged glances with Emma, neither of them saying a word as they half dragged her to work between them.

'Are you sick?' Herr Weber asked, as he came around to inspect their work.

Chloe heard him ask Aletta the question and inwardly cringed as she waited to hear her answer, although they all knew that he would be more understanding than anyone else charged with supervising them. They'd barely been working for an hour, and it was clear that Aletta was struggling to stand upright, sweat sheening her forehead as she swayed on her feet.

'Yes.' Aletta's voice was raspy. 'I am.'

'You don't need to come to work if you're unwell,' he said. 'You may go and lie down.'

'Herr Weber,' Chloe said, knowing she was taking a risk by speaking to him directly. 'If I may?'

He turned to her, and she smiled politely.

'My friend, Aletta, she needs extra food,' Chloe told him. 'If there's anything else you have to spare . . .'

'You can't get extra for her at the camp shop for dinner?'

Chloe grimaced as she tried to find the words. She wanted to tell him the truth, but she also knew how careful she had to be. 'Herr Weber, we don't have a camp shop. We're fed very little, just a cup of watery soup and bread for dinner, and Aletta is becoming weak.' She hesitated. 'We all are. It's why we're so thin.'

She watched as he stroked his moustache, considering her and then looking at Aletta, who was shivering now, her skin appearing even paler than before, her lips cracked. She hoped she hadn't read the situation wrong, that he was a decent man as she suspected he might be. Because if he wasn't, she might have just made a decision that could cost her her life. But at the same time, she couldn't understand how this man could look at them all and not see how skeletal and unwell they were, how much they were all suffering.

'I had every intention of rewarding you all with a voucher for the camp shop, for your hard work these past months,' he said, his brows drawing close together. 'But you're telling me that you would have nowhere to spend it, if I were to give it to you? Why did none of the women tell me this last month when I issued them?'

The women around her were silent, listening, and Chloe bravely met his stare and nodded. 'The intention is very kind, sir, but you are correct there would be nowhere to spend it. And as for the women, I would say they were too scared to tell you the truth. Our guards might have punished them if they did.'

'There is nowhere at all for you to buy any provisions?'

She shook her head. 'We also have no choice about coming to work. We might, well . . .' Chloe paused, considering her words, wondering if he truly knew why they were there, if he knew that they were forced to work. She chose to be more careful with her words. 'We'd be in terrible trouble if we didn't turn up for our shift. Even when we're unwell, we're expected to be here, otherwise we can get in a lot of trouble.'

'You are prisoners though?' he asked. 'I don't know what all you women have done to end up here, but this is part of your punishment for your crimes, is it not?'

Chloe glanced at Emma, who had turned a ghostly shade of white, fear written all over her face. She knew she'd said enough, that to say more could land her in more trouble than it was worth if the conversation was repeated to one of the guards, but she couldn't not continue. Not now.

'Yes sir, it is,' Chloe said. She wanted to scream at him that they had done nothing wrong, that there were no crimes to be punished for, but she forced the words down. Yelling at him would be the end of her, and although he was as much to blame as anyone, he was a factory manager, not a guard or a soldier. She needed to know when to stop.

He gave Chloe a curt nod and turned back to Aletta, and she watched as he bent closer and said something to her before he walked away. But he wasn't gone for long and she noticed that when he returned, he pressed something into Aletta's hand.

'If anyone questions you, you tell them that Herr Weber told you to take the afternoon off,' he said, before lowering his voice and turning to include Chloe in the conversation. 'And now that I know how little you're fed, and that there is nowhere for you to obtain extras, I'll try to get some more for you to share between you all. Now that I understand the situation, I will distribute food as a reward each week instead of vouchers. How does that sound?'

Chloe wanted to throw her arms around him, her fear at having disclosed too much replaced with joy, but instead she offered him a warm smile. 'Thank you, Herr Weber. Your kindness will never be forgotten.'

'Nor taken for granted,' Emma whispered beside her.

Emma's wide-eyed stare when he left told Chloe that she couldn't believe what had just happened, that someone in this hellhole was capable of showing them any degree of kindness, and she only hoped that Aletta had the strength to make it back to the bunkroom without collapsing. That she could enjoy whatever morsel he'd given her. And it wasn't lost on her that one man's generosity with food could be the only thing that kept all of the Siemens workers alive.

After their shift ended, she and Emma hurried to look for Aletta. It was only after finding her safe in bed and with her hand still clasped around whatever she'd been eating, that Chloe was able to relax. Continuing to work while knowing how unwell Aletta was had been like worrying about her brothers all over again.

'Saved this. For you both.'

When she opened her palm, Chloe watched as Emma took two small pieces of sausage from the wrapping. Despite being starving hungry herself, Aletta had kept something for them.

'Aletta, you need to—'

'No, I ate most of it,' she murmured. 'I'm already feeling a little better. I'm not eating it all without sharing. Please, take it.'

Chloe wanted to argue with her, but her stomach disobeyed and let out a long growl, giving away just how desperately hungry she was, and so she took her piece as Emma took hers and placed it in her mouth. She held it under her tongue for a moment, savouring the flavour before slowly, very slowly, beginning to chew.

It was the best-tasting piece of food of Chloe's life.

'I've been meaning to ask, if you'd like to look at some of the papers?' she said.

Aletta's eyes brightened a little, and Emma smiled before she spoke.

'I think we'd both love that, Chloe.'

Which was how she ended up sharing what she'd recorded with the two women who'd come to mean the most to her in the world, as they pored over recipes that made their mouths water and little descriptions of beautiful places and snippets of memories, all with the first name of each woman printed in the bottom right-hand corner.

Chloe didn't often let herself re-read what she'd written, but tonight, for once, it was worth it, to relive the emotions of each woman who'd come to her. Soon they might all be gone, but maybe someone would find this, and at least it would be something.

Chapter Twenty-Four

Chloe

Chloe fought a laugh as they made their way back from the factory on Sunday. Aletta walked close behind, and when Chloe glanced at her she saw the smirk on her face, too, for Aletta clearly understood French.

'What's so funny?' Emma asked.

'The French girls are singing a song they made up about the guards,' Chloe whispered. 'They're calling it their opera, and they say they're going to perform it once we leave this place.'

She noticed the way Aletta smiled; it was almost like it hurt. Her lips were cracked, and her eyes looked pained, but she'd refused to let them help her, insisting she could make the walk herself without their assistance. The extra bits of food had helped, despite the *Aufseherin* exploding when she'd found Aletta sleeping instead of working for the first two days at the new barracks. Even the guard hadn't been brave enough to go against Herr Weber's orders.

'Are you all right?' Chloe asked. 'And tell me the truth, you have nothing to hide from me.'

'I'm fine, truly I am. Just hungry and tired, like always.'

Chloe nodded, glancing back at Emma who still looked concerned, even though there was little either of them could do about it.

'You know, I heard that one of the girls went to the doctor last week with diarrhoea, and she was given mashed potato,' Emma whispered from behind. 'Maybe if we all pretend to have dysentery, they'll let us have some food.'

Chloe almost closed her eyes at the thought of mashed potato – food was all most of them talked about or thought about in the camp. It was also why so many of the women wanted Chloe to record their favourite recipes – all they wanted was the chance to cook something for their families again.

'Maybe in time we can tell Herr Weber about the children down here. Maybe he'll help us with some extra food for them, too,' Chloe said. She was inclined not to push her luck, but she also knew that if she hadn't been brave enough to speak up, Aletta might not be walking beside her today.

'Maybe.' Aletta's voice was quiet; too quiet.

'Aletta?' Chloe didn't like the look on her face, or the way she was swaying as she walked. 'Aletta, what's wrong?'

'I don't feel so well again.'

Emma stepped closer and pressed a hand to her back, keeping her upright.

Chloe had seen plenty of sadness in her time at Ravensbrück. She'd witnessed death and illness, but she'd never lost anyone she loved in the camp. Seeing Aletta look like this made her think that she had been right to stay away from the other inmates. But there was nothing she could do now, no distance she could create, because she already loved her like a sister.

'I'm just cold,' Aletta mumbled. 'I'm sure I'll be fine.'

Chloe pursed her lips and kept a tight grip on Aletta's arm. They were all wearing woollen jumpers now and thick socks, but it wasn't enough for her too-thin friend while she was so unwell.

Chloe steeled herself, knowing what she needed to do. Once they got back to the main camp, she'd have time to find the Czechs and beg for something else for Aletta to wear. These women owed Aletta for everything she was doing for their children – the least they could do was find her another pair of wool socks and a warm hat, perhaps even a coat. The food they'd secretly saved for the children to have at their lesson would be a good bargaining chip, too.

'I can't stop thinking about the little girl I saw when we were coming up here,' Aletta said as they walked. 'I know I had a fever, and I might have been imagining it, but I was so sure it was Else.'

'Well,' said Chloe, 'if it was her, you'll be sure to come across her. Maybe it was?'

She swapped glances with Emma, who didn't look convinced, but Chloe wasn't about to say anything to the contrary. And who knew? Maybe the little Jewish girl was at the camp.

The weeks at Ravensbrück all rolled together, day after gruelling day feeling no different from the one before, except for Sundays, which had become Chloe's favourite day. Once she'd dreaded the final day of the week, because they were forced to clean and do other menial jobs around the camp, locked outside no matter what the weather, but now Aletta was also teaching the children. And somehow Aletta had convinced her and Emma to teach, too, insisting that she could no longer do the job on her own, so they could divide the children into age groups. So many more children had arrived over the past month.

'Chloe, you're taking the older ones. We'll split up and sit behind the barracks,' Aletta said, directing her to the group of mainly girls who were eleven or twelve. 'I thought you could try to think of books you've read to discuss, and maybe talk about writing with them.' She gave her a little smile. 'But only if that's something you feel comfortable with.'

Chloe looked up at Aletta, the words catching in her throat. 'I thought I might talk about poetry,' she said.

Aletta's smile widened. 'That's perfect, Chloe.'

'I haven't written a poem since, well, before everything, but I want to share poetry with them. Maybe if I'd kept writing, I wouldn't have kept everything so bottled up inside.'

Aletta touched her arm. 'Then you teach them about poetry. I love it.'

'I just wish I could write home. Just one letter to let my family know I'm alive,' Chloe said. 'If I had the chance, I'd write my little brother a poem, so he knew it was me. One he loved when I used to read from my notebook to him.'

Aletta hugged her. 'I wish you could write to them, too.'

Chloe took a big breath as Aletta stepped away, telling her she was fine and that they needed to get on with what they were there to do. But she listened as Aletta told her mother to take the middle band of children, instructing her to have them practise maths and finish by telling them a story.

'And I shall take the little ones and continue to teach them their letters—' Aletta gasped.

'What—' Chloe started.

'Else!' Aletta cried, dropping to her knees beside Chloe as a little girl with the biggest, bluest eyes Chloe had ever seen stood blinking back at her. 'I can't believe it! I was so certain I saw you weeks ago, but then I never saw you again!'

Chloe laughed. She actually laughed, because the only alternative would have been to cry. She'd thought Aletta had hallucinated her former pupil when she'd been feverish, but clearly she should never have doubted her.

'So this is your little Else, huh?' she asked, watching as Aletta seemed to examine every inch of her. She'd never seen her friend so happy.

'Who are you here with, Else?' Aletta asked. 'Are your family . . .'

'My aunt and my sister,' Else said, her eyes filling with tears.

'Well, I look forward to meeting them,' Aletta said, giving a little cough that did nothing to disguise the emotion in her voice. 'It's so good to have you back in my class.'

Chloe placed a hand on Aletta's shoulder, waiting for her friend to sit down with the youngest children before she faced the group waiting for her. Some of them looked unsure, with big eyes, arms wrapped tightly around themselves, but some were more curious and took a step towards her.

'Well, I suppose you should all follow me,' she said. 'My name is Chloe, and I'm going to do my best to teach you each Sunday. I'm Aletta's friend, so that means you're in very good hands, I promise.'

There were a few hellos and a handful of smiles, and Chloe sat down and beckoned for them to sit around her. Even though she felt completely out of her depth, there was something about being surrounded by younger people that made her want to fight, to stay alive, to do anything she could to make their lives a little better in the short time she had with them.

'What do you teach?' one of the boys asked.

Chloe tried not to think about how much longer he would have at the camp as she turned and smiled at him. 'Well, I've never actually taught anyone before, but today I thought we'd talk about poetry and maybe books. We don't have paper to use, so maybe we could all share some favourites that we remember, and try to compose something of our own?'

One of the girls looked particularly excited, her smile lighting up her face. 'I love poetry.'

Chloe smiled, even though she wanted to cry. 'So do I.'

'Are you the lady who takes down the recipes?' one of the girls asked.

That question almost broke her, especially the innocent way it was asked.

'Yes, I do. But we must be very careful not to speak of that in front of the guards. I keep those recipes and memories for safekeeping, for many of the women here.'

'Can you share them with us?' a boy asked. 'I'm so hungry, I'd like to listen to them.'

'One day I will share some of them with you,' she replied, trying not to see her brother in the bright-eyed boy. 'But today, we're going to talk about poetry.'

The children continued to look at her expectantly, and she took a deep breath and forced herself to go on. She could wallow in her memories later, when she was alone, when so many young minds weren't depending on her.

'Would anyone like to go first?' she asked.

They just blinked back at her, suddenly silent, and Chloe knew that she was going to have to share part of herself, no matter how uncomfortable it might be.

'Perhaps I could share a poem I wrote for my little brother one day, although I might not remember it perfectly.'

Chloe cleared her throat, ignoring the dampness in her eyes as she tried not to think of home, of the last time she'd whispered the little verse. The night she'd put Adrian to bed, in the hours before everything had changed.

'Feathers brown, soft and damp, the little bird searches. Beak full, stealing sticks, the little bird perches.' Chloe stopped then, her voice catching, the rest of the poem slipping from her mind. She quickly cleared her throat, unable to continue on. 'Sorry, I, well, it seems I can't remember it as well as I thought. But perhaps you could all come up with some more lines for me?'

'Are poems always supposed to rhyme?' asked a girl.

Chloe smiled and nodded. 'Well yes, it is nice to have rhyme, it makes it easier to listen to, but it doesn't have to.'

'Do you mean it doesn't have to rhyme if I like the way the words sound together?'

The innocence of her question, the way she was looking at Chloe with such trust, almost broke her. But instead of letting it, she lifted her hand and touched the girl's shoulder, smiling as she looked her directly in the eye.

'If you like the way the words sound together, then it's a poem. That's the beautiful thing about poetry, it can be anything you want it to be.'

Chloe felt new eyes upon her and she looked over to see Aletta watching her. Aletta's mouth turned up at the corners, and Chloe knew that she'd done the right thing in helping. And she could see just how much it meant to Aletta to meet the little girl Else.

Chloe's heart was open to breaking now, and it hurt just looking at the beautiful children around them and knowing how few of them might survive this hellish place, but at least she was trying instead of hiding away on her own. At least she was doing *something*.

Maybe she'd been wrong to close herself off in the beginning. Perhaps it was better to care and to love – and then lose – rather than be alone.

All she knew was it felt good in that moment to feel needed and wanted, to have something other than sadness and misery surround her. She glanced over at Emma, watching as the children smiled at her, and the last edge of hardness around her heart, the iron-clad hold that had held her in its grip for so long, finally began to melt.

Because something was humming between them all. They might all be beaten, but today had proven to Chloe that they most definitely were not broken.

No one can break us, not so long as we're still breathing.

These children were the bond connecting her to so many other women; to Emma and to Aletta; and the only thing she'd look forward to more than teaching them again was seeing their faces light up once they gave them the extra rations from the factory.

Chapter Twenty-Five

Two months later

Aletta

Aletta watched Chloe, noticing the way she stared so angrily at the papers she clutched in her hand, as if she wanted to rip them into pieces. But she knew Chloe would never do that – those papers had come to mean everything to her. And as the volume of papers had grown, so had the network of women tasked with hiding them.

'Can I sit with you?' Aletta asked.

Chloe looked up. Her eyes were red-rimmed, her skin blotchy. 'Always.'

Aletta slowly lowered herself to the ground, her knees aching and her back sore. In the time she'd been at the camp, she felt as if she'd aged three decades or more; she felt more like an old lady than a young woman in her early twenties.

'Can I tell you something?'

Chloe nodded before resting her head on Aletta's shoulder. Aletta took her hand, linking their fingers and looking at the smudged list on her friend's lap. But she forced herself to look away as she spoke, staring out at the trees in the far distance.

'I think today is my birthday.'

Chloe's head lifted. 'Today? How do you—'

'I had to go into the office yesterday, Herr Weber asked me to get some documents for him, and I saw a letter that had just been typed with a date at the top.'

Aletta's throat bobbed as she swallowed, and she fought against her emotions.

'February the twenty-sixth,' she said, as Chloe squeezed her hand.

'Happy birthday, Aletta,' Chloe whispered, sliding an arm around her as Aletta tucked into her, the cold wind stinging her cheeks. 'I wish we could be anywhere else but here.'

'I wish that too,' Aletta murmured back.

They sat in silence, the only noise the wind picking up speed around them and making a howling sound that sent shivers straight through Aletta.

'How many birthdays and anniversaries have been missed in this godforsaken place?' Chloe muttered. 'How many lives have to be lost until it's enough?'

Aletta didn't answer, because she didn't know how to. Nothing about what was happening to them, about where they were or the pain they saw every day, made sense.

'It feels like yesterday we were sitting over there, with all those kids around us. It felt like we were doing something good, that it mattered.'

Aletta couldn't stop her tears then. 'It did matter, Chloe, and it still does.' She refused to think about Else and the other children; she couldn't. It was too much, the pain too great.

Chloe turned to her, her face streaked with tears. 'Almost all of them have gone.'

Aletta bit hard on her lip, trying not to think about all the beautiful children who were no longer with them. The boys who'd been sent away; the little ones who'd perished; those that had become sick and not been strong enough to survive.

'It matters because some of them are still here, and because more have filled their places. It matters because we provide something for them to hold on to while they *are* here.'

She inhaled a sharp, big breath.

'It matters because *we're* here, and *we* need to keep going, Chloe. Because no matter what happens, we are going to survive this place. This is not going to be the last place I see before I die.'

Chloe's tears dried, and Aletta watched as she tucked a piece of paper away before standing up.

'You're right,' Chloe eventually said, helping her to her feet. 'We are going to survive this place.'

Aletta stood, her chest still rising and falling from her impassioned little speech.

'I was going to ask you to just let me hate the world for one day, but it's your birthday.'

Despite it all, Aletta grinned. 'It *is* my birthday.'

'And since I have no gift to give you or cake to bake you, I'm going to have to at least give you a smile.

They both laughed, and Chloe gave her a hug.

'Happy birthday, Aletta,' she whispered, kissing her cheek. 'One day we will celebrate with the biggest cake and champagne, and we'll sing and drink until our voices are hoarse from all the fun. I promise.'

Aletta sighed, closing her eyes and imagining it, knowing what fun she and Chloe would have if they could just survive long enough. She could see them both with Cecilia, laughing as they sat in the park, and maybe Harry would be there, too. She could almost hear the giggles and shrieks of laughter; the fun and merriment that would come from her two best friends meeting each other.

'Maybe next year,' she said, as Chloe pulled back, her hands still on Aletta's shoulders. 'Perhaps next year the war will be over, and we'll be celebrating our freedom.'

They both smiled, but even as she said the words, even as she tried to believe in them, Aletta wondered if she would ever see another birthday that wasn't behind the wire of this dreadful camp. Because no one had escaped in all the time she'd been here, no one had been released.

This will not be the last place I see, Aletta told herself, as she linked her arm with Chloe's and they went in search of her mother. *I'm going to survive this place, and no one is going to take that dream away from me.*

'Chloe, I actually have something for you,' Aletta said, reaching into her pocket.

'For me?' Chloe frowned. 'It's *your* birthday, not mine.'

She took out the few sheets of paper, as well as a small pencil and an envelope. 'When I was in Herr Weber's office, he caught me taking a sheet of paper.'

'Aletta! Why would you take such a risk!'

'Because I believe in what you're doing, and I know how long it's been since you've had any paper to write anything new,' she said.

'And what happened? What did he say? Did he just let you take it?'

'I explained to him that we weren't allowed to write, that paper and pencils were forbidden to us, and that even if I couldn't send it, I wished to write a letter to someone I loved.' Some inmates had been allowed to write heavily censored letters at times, but mostly they'd been completely cut off from the families they'd left behind.

'To Harry?' Chloe asked.

'No, Chloe. The paper and envelope are so that you can write to your brothers. Herr Weber said that he would post the letter for me.'

Chloe's tears came fast and furiously, and Aletta held her as she mumbled against her chest, making the front of Aletta's dress damp.

'You could have been killed for this,' Chloe grumbled.

'Well I wasn't, and it was worth the risk. He told me that he couldn't spare much, but he let me take a little extra paper, just in case.'

'How is he such a good man among such evil?' Chloe asked, wiping away her tears.

'He told me that his wife is a compassionate woman, and that she'd never forgive him if he didn't show us a little kindness,' Aletta recounted. 'Whatever the reason, I'm just grateful.'

'Thank you, Aletta,' Chloe said, shaking her head. 'You're the best friend I ever had.'

Now it was Aletta's turn to cry, as they wrapped their arms around each other once more. Aletta couldn't imagine surviving the camp without Chloe; she only hoped she never had to.

Chapter Twenty-Six

30 April 2015

Tears slipped down Aletta's cheek, and she lifted a shaky hand to wipe them away. She held her chin high as they stood outside the barracks, a shiver running through her body that had nothing to do with the cold.

I used to live here.

She remembered the cold nights, huddled beside her mother and Chloe, taking turns to be in the middle for the tiny bit of warmth it created. Not that any of them had enough body fat to offer much comfort to the others. They'd been little more than bones by the end, the only constant that they'd always had each other. But it hadn't just been about the three of them. The children who'd gathered around them every Sunday had bound them to many of the women in the camp, and as heartbreaking as it had been to see so many children come and go, it had also given all three of them a reason to live. The presence of Else alone had made Aletta determined to survive.

Aletta looked over her shoulder when she heard her daughter's voice. For a moment she thought it was her calling to her own mother against the wind after roll call. But, of course, Emma was long gone.

She'd listened to everyone talk about the beauty of the grounds beyond the camp as they'd moved through the first part, and it was true. On one side it had been a barren place of torture and misery, and on the other, an idyllic paradise for those who lived and worked there. The more she'd heard about the guards who'd treated them with such derision, the more she'd learnt about what the conditions had been like for them. It had almost seemed like a cruel joke at the time.

'Mum, you don't have to do the full tour. If it's too much—'

Aletta was silent as she turned, as she looked at the group gathered, and then past them, to the endless stream of people walking through the gates of the camp that had once held her captive. It was heartening when she thought about it, to see how many people still cared about what had happened in the past, that they'd chosen to see the camp for themselves, to pay their respects.

'Mum?'

Their group was silent as Aletta blinked, swallowing that now-familiar lump in her throat as she refocused on her daughter, as she tried to subdue the memories.

This was once my home. This was the place that kept me captive.

This was where I met Chloe.

'My teenage son,' one of the men in their group said, his eyes shining with tears, 'he asked me how I knew that the Holocaust was real. He said that he and his friends don't believe that so many people could have been killed.' The man shook his head. 'My son, he's a good boy, but I don't think they can believe that such cruelty ever existed.'

'They get all their news from YouTube, that's why,' a woman near Aletta said. 'If they don't see it on there, they don't think it's real.'

As the people around her murmured, Aletta found a strength growing within her that she hadn't felt in years, as she began to nod. She found it in the group gathered around her, in the hundreds and thousands of people who'd cared enough to visit the camp and commemorate history. It made her believe in humanity again; it made her believe that her story was worth telling, that she'd been right in coming.

'Then you must bring him here,' she said, as everyone fell silent to listen to her speak. 'You tell him to place his hand on the walls of the crematorium. You tell him to feel the truth in those walls. And you tell him to listen. To people like me, before we're all gone.'

Chapter Twenty-Seven

1945

Aletta

Aletta swayed on her feet and prayed that she wouldn't fall over in front of the guards. They'd been standing out in the cold for much longer than usual, and now it was starting to rain as they waited for roll call to be completed. She'd spent so many mornings like this now that she should have been used to it, but she wondered if anyone could get used to anything so brutal. Five years of roll calls and punishment, starvation and pain.

She wrapped her bone-thin arms around herself and closed her eyes, thinking about some of the children she'd been teaching as recently as a few weeks ago. So many of them were gone – their little lives extinguished far too soon – but as hard as it had been to keep going, she'd refused to give in. The children who were left needed her as much as she needed them, and even if she did only have Sundays with them, it was her favourite day of the week, and likely theirs, too. The day that gave her something to look forward to.

But today was harder than most, and when she opened her eyes, it was to glance over at two of the boys who'd now turned twelve. She'd been certain that today they would be sent to the men's camp, had presumed that was the reason for the constant re-counting and the guards pacing up and down. But now, she wasn't so sure.

She looked around then, when the guards had turned away and were standing huddled over their lists, first at her mother, and then at Chloe. They were like her – almost doubled over from the cold, even though they wore more clothing than many. She'd sometimes wondered if that was what had saved them, why so many others had perished but somehow, miraculously, they were still alive after all this time. But maybe it was the food from Herr Weber, the extra mouthfuls that he'd provided, that had sustained them.

Today, for reasons that still weren't known, they'd had to make the walk down to the main camp, where they were standing now. And finally, after what felt like forever, names and numbers began to be called out. As Aletta stood, fighting the urge to reach for her mother and Chloe so they weren't separated, women were sectioned off and made to form new groups. She found herself frantically searching the crowd of women for Else and her aunt, but try as she might, she couldn't see them.

The smallest group were Scandinavian women, and Aletta listened carefully as they were told to wait by the fence. Then a much larger group, hundreds by her estimation, were told to wait further away, and before Aletta and the others had even been released, they were marched off.

'What do you think is happening?' she whispered to her mother as fear rose like a snake inside her.

'Nothing good,' she whispered back, and Aletta watched as her mother's eyes followed the women who were being taken away.

Aletta reached for Chloe's hand then, but Chloe pulled away.

'Don't,' she murmured. 'They'll only split us up to spite us if they see how close we are.'

And so, Aletta stood with her hands fisted at her side, almost falling to her knees with relief when they were told to go back to work, and she realised they weren't to be parted.

Women muttered and whispered all around them, but Chloe and her mother stayed silent as they began the walk back to the Siemens factory. That they were still together wasn't something she'd take for granted. She just hoped that the fate of the other women wasn't what she imagined.

But as they began to walk, a piece of paper fluttered from Chloe's coat, darting away on the wind.

'No!' Aletta gasped, knowing what would happen if the guards saw it, if they read it. They'd interrogate them all, or worse.

But a woman a few steps ahead snatched out a hand and caught it mid-air, quickly tucking it into her clothing, as Chloe folded her arms around herself, clearly terrified that another page might fall from her body.

'You need to distribute them among us,' Aletta whispered. 'When we stop, let some of us take them.'

A few other women were glancing at them, and they all nodded. One of them murmured that she would take some, and Aletta realised just how important Chloe was to so many of them. She was holding their memories, and of course they wanted to help her.

The next day, Aletta had that unsettled feeling in her stomach again when the guards came through the factory once more, this time going down the rows and ordering some of the women to go outside for roll call. She saw Chloe freeze ahead of her.

Please not her. Please not her.

But Aletta quickly realised that they were looking for older women, which meant they walked straight past Chloe and her. She'd never been so grateful that her mother had been moved into the office, and hoped that guards didn't go looking in there.

'What do you think they're doing with them?' asked one of the women near her.

Aletta kept her fingers working, threading the steel, not wanting to be caught being idle. She didn't want to think about their fate.

'I don't know,' she said, even though in her heart she imagined they were being taken to their death.

'I heard the ones yesterday were marched straight out of the gates,' another woman said. 'And that the Scandinavian ones were loaded on to buses.'

'Buses?' Aletta repeated, thinking she'd misheard.

'Let's just hope they were taken far away from here,' Chloe said. 'If they've been released, then there's hope for the rest of us.'

Aletta sighed, wishing it were as simple as that but not believing it for a second. If there was any hope of being released from this place, wouldn't they have been let go by now? Were they transferring some of the women to a different camp?

There was a shout then from a guard, telling them that the factory was closing for the day and that they were to return immediately to their barracks.

'Something strange is going on,' Chloe muttered as she turned and waited for Aletta to fall into line behind her. 'There's nothing normal about any of this.'

'Where do you think those women were being taken?' Aletta asked.

Chloe leaned in closer to her, not saying anything. And Aletta knew what she was thinking. In her heart, she knew, too.

'Do you think all of the women yesterday . . .' Her voice trailed off.

'I think that something has happened that has them panicking, and they're trying to reduce the number of prisoners,' Chloe said, and Aletta watched as she touched her breast pocket, the place she knew she kept some of her papers.

Aletta touched Chloe's shoulder as they walked.

'You've done more than most,' she whispered. 'But you need to let the rest of us help you.'

'If something happens to me, if I'm taken, if—'

'Stop it,' Aletta felt as if she couldn't breathe at the thought of Chloe being removed.

'If they take me, you have to promise that you'll share my work with the authorities. When everyone tries to forget what they did to us, they need to know there were real women here, mothers and aunts and sisters. If you survive and I don't . . .'

Aletta quickly wiped away her tears as Chloe turned to her.

'If something happens, I'll find a way to share it. I promise,' Aletta said. 'But can we please not talk about that again?'

'Something awful is happening,' Chloe said. 'It's like they're trying to get rid of as many of us as possible, and quickly.'

Aletta didn't know what to say to that, but she had a feeling that Chloe was right. Being up at the factory usually kept them shielded from the worst that happened down at the main camp.

The crowd shuffled forward then, and she saw her mother, making her forget everything else.

'Mama?' She pushed through the other women until she reached her, noticing how white her mother's skin had turned.

'I overhead them,' she whispered, her face falling as she said the words. 'They were taking them all to the gas. They came for me too, they wanted all the older women, but Herr Weber told them he couldn't do without me.' She gasped. 'He saved me, Aletta. Herr Weber is the only reason I'm still alive.'

Aletta felt as if her heart had stopped beating, and she didn't move even when someone walked into her from behind as she stared at her mother, digesting what she was telling her.

'He saved your life,' she whispered, wondering what they'd done to have a man like Herr Weber look out for them among the blanket of cruelty that otherwise surrounded them.

Her mother was shaking and Aletta moved closer to guide her back to the bunkrooms, keeping her arm around her and refusing to let go even when she was shoved in the back by their *Älteste*.

One comment from a manager had saved her mother this time, but next time?

Aletta swallowed what felt like a rock in her throat.

Next time, they might not be so lucky.

Chapter Twenty-Eight

Chloe

Chloe felt as if she could barely breath. Ever since the additional roll calls had begun, she'd found it impossible to sleep, waiting for one of them to be called away from the other.

And she didn't know how she could live with losing Aletta or Emma now, after all this time together. They'd defied all the odds, they'd propped each other up and fought for every extra scrap of food, for every bit of warm clothing, and they'd had a lot of luck, but it made thinking about being parted now even harder.

'Chloe?' Aletta whispered in the dark, tucking her body even closer.

'It's fine, I just can't sleep,' Chloe whispered back.

Aletta was silent after that, and Chloe curled against her, eyes shut, trying to block out her thoughts. But instead of silencing her brain, the thoughts only multiplied, and suddenly she found herself thinking about her brothers, about her father, about her apartment.

She squeezed her eyes more tightly, but the memories just kept on coming, one after the other. Of what she would leave behind if this was the end for her.

Chloe had thought about her family even more since Herr Weber had posted her letter; imagining them opening it, remembering so much from home that she had tried so hard to forget. She'd said little other than telling them she was alive, and recalling a short poem to write for Adrian so he'd know without doubt that the letter was from her, but the process had brought back so many memories. Memories that she was struggling to ignore.

'Where's Mama?' Adrian asked.

'Mama is in heaven now,' she whispered, stroking the hair from his forehead.

'I miss her.'

'I miss her too, sweetheart, more than anything, but I made a promise that I'd look after you now that she's gone.'

Adrian's blue eyes were wide as he looked up at her.

'I won't ever take Mama's place, but I will spend the rest of my life looking after you and making sure you feel loved. I will do anything for you, Adrian. I promise.'

He snuggled into her and she wrapped her arms around him, wishing she could take his pain, hating to feel his little body shudder with tears.

But she knew that, hand on her heart, she would do anything for him. He was hers now, and she would love and protect him as fiercely as her own mother would have.

Chloe opened her eyes then and stared into the dark. And not for the first time, she wondered if she'd done the right thing when she'd taken the fall for Claude. She'd been prepared to do anything to keep either of her brothers from harm, but after being parted for so long from Adrian, she'd questioned whether she should have stayed, letting her older brother accept the consequences of his actions.

But she also knew there was no way she could have said nothing, that she could not have watched them take her older brother and done nothing to protect him.

She only wished that there was someone to save her. Because she was scared, and she knew that when they eventually came for her, there would be nothing anyone could do to stop them.

But she wasn't alone. She had to keep reminding herself of that. For now, she had Aletta and Emma, her camp family, who would do anything for her, who were hiding papers for her on their bodies, like some of the other women in their barracks, in the hope that they might survive until the end.

If there was an end to this goddamn war.

Chapter Twenty-Nine

Aletta

Aletta had never wished to be back working in the factory more than she did today. She tied her make-shift scarf tighter around her face, trying to block out the stench around her in the main camp, but it was impossible. Usually on Sundays, the factory workers were sent to do physical gardening work around the SS commandant's house or the guards' cabins, but today they'd selected countless women to do the work that no one wanted to be called up for. The guards were keeping to themselves in small groups, and as far as she was aware, no one had been put on gardening duty.

She saw one of the little girls she taught standing in the doorway to her barracks, her sunken cheeks stark as she made a face at the smell. Aletta went straight over to her, ripping a piece from her own shirt so that she could tie it around the girl's nose and mouth.

'Thank you,' the little girl whispered, and Aletta was relieved not to see her dry-chapped lips and red raw nose any longer. Seeing other women looking so alarmingly thin and bedraggled was one thing, but when it was children, it broke her heart.

'You're welcome,' she murmured back, bending to hold the child in a warm hug.

Aletta's back hurt so much she wondered if she'd be able to straighten, but after a long moment she rose, using her thumb to brush away the girl's tears.

'Your mother?' Aletta asked, not wanting to hear the answer, but knowing she wouldn't forgive herself for not asking.

'She has the sick,' the girl replied, standing aside and letting Aletta see past her.

There was a lump on the mattress, on the bottom bunk, that Aletta realised was the girl's mother. She heard a raspy cough and then another, telling her that she wasn't the only woman in there sick. Soon, it would take every last one of them. Usually everyone would be sent outside and the bunkrooms would be turned over and cleaned, but not today.

'She doesn't want to go to the doctor?' Aletta asked.

The little girl shook her head. 'She says no one comes back from there.'

Aletta nodded and gently touched the girl's hair. 'Maybe I'll come and sit here with you later, we can recite some poems together.' She paused. 'Do you know a girl called Else?'

The girl nodded.

'She's still here? She doesn't have the sick?'

The girl shook her head, and Aletta forced herself to walk away before it became too hard, as she thought of how many girls they'd lost, until she could barely stand to teach the new children, for fear of knowing how much it would hurt when they didn't make it. Of how she'd give her own life if it meant getting Else out of the camp and to safety.

'*Beeil dich!*' a guard yelled, waving his hand at her.

Aletta moved as fast as her legs would take her, which she imagined was much slower than it actually felt, back to the group. Sundays were supposed to be their day off, but the work she was doing today was of the very worst kind. Her mother's office job seemed to give her a higher status within the camp, not to mention access to paper that she took whenever she could for Chloe, but Aletta had drawn the short straw, and she just wanted to get it over with.

Other women lined up on either side of her, all of them with their faces covered, and Aletta bent at the knees and reached down to take hold of an ankle of one of the dead. There were piles of them everywhere; some of them shot, some starved to death, and the others killed by the gas.

Aletta refused to look at the woman's face, not wanting the ghoulish skull to haunt her, and it took four of them to drag the body all the way to the furnace, where the fires had been burning for days without stopping. Only a week earlier, hundreds of women had arrived from another camp, somewhere called Auschwitz, all even dirtier than the women around Aletta in their tatty clothing, and even hungrier than the women from Ravensbrück. And it was those women whom she was lifting now; women who'd probably hoped to be coming somewhere better, only to be killed within days. She didn't understand why they had bothered to transport them if they were only going to kill them.

Aletta coughed, sucking back the cloth over her mouth, which only made her cough all the more as she fought for breath. But at least she wasn't inhaling any of the thick ash in the air that was making everything look tinged with grey.

But as she bent over to cough again, a large box marked with a red cross caught her eye from behind a low fence. She glanced over her shoulder, seeing the guards busy talking, and purposely stumbled a few steps so she could see better.

It wasn't just one box. There was a pile of packages beyond that, all marked with a red cross.

Aletta's heart beat a little faster as she wondered what was in there. If the Red Cross had sent them, they had to be packages full of provisions, surely? They had to have been sent for the prisoners?

'What are you looking at?'

Aletta jumped, but it was only one of the other prisoner women. She inclined her head, at the same time holding up one finger to her lips. The other woman's eyes widened but they both stayed silent, instinctively knowing the guards mustn't see them looking. There was a reason all those parcels and boxes were behind a fence.

'What do you suppose is in there?' the other woman asked.

'Food?' Aletta whispered. 'Maybe sanitary items? Medical supplies?' She imagined it might be full of provisions that could be useful, simple things that would seem like luxuries after barely getting by for so long.

Aletta ran her tongue over her teeth, feeling how grimy they were, and noticed that two of her back molars had started to come loose. She couldn't imagine what it would feel like to use a toothbrush or have a comb for her hair, to clean her skin and soak in a bath.

She touched the woman on the shoulder as they went back to move more bodies and, despite the ache in her back, she kept working, moving closer each time to the guards. They were all so exhausted that the only sounds coming from any of the women were grunts and groans, which meant she could hear a lot of what the guards said. Especially now that she was better versed in German and could keep up with much of their conversation.

'They told us to burn it,' one of them said.

'We have enough bodies to burn without adding all of those. Why not just take it for ourselves?'

Aletta gritted her teeth as she walked past them, struggling to carry the weight as she kept listening, straining not to miss anything.

'If we give it to them, they'll only start to get greedy and want more. They might guess what's happening.'

If she'd been braver, she would have stopped and spat on the boots of the guard who'd said that. But she was determined to live, and one glance at their guns told her she'd have a bullet through her brain before she could turn and run.

'We need to just shoot them all while we can, before anyone finds out what we've done in this hellhole.'

She stopped walking and one of the women bumped into her, cursing Aletta as she made her trip. But she ignored her and kept listening, her heart thudding as she realised they didn't expect any of the prisoners to be listening or to understand them. Or perhaps they simply didn't care.

'Did you hear about those other camps?'

Most of the guards were silent then as they listened to whoever was talking, and Aletta hurried to place the body before turning around to retrieve the next one, walking as slowly as she could without drawing attention. She missed part of what was said.

'. . . dismantling the camps and freeing all the prisoners.'

'At least the guards got out of there before they came. We need to make sure nothing is left here before they get to this one.'

Aletta fell to the ground then, her wrists aching as she pushed herself up and received a kick to the stomach for her efforts. The guards laughed, and she took her time getting up, needing to hear more, needing to know what was happening elsewhere. Did this mean the Allies were winning? Was that why the parcels had arrived? Was that what they didn't want the prisoners to know?

'If they catch us, we just say we're only women. We tell them that we were forced to treat them like this.'

'We just have to pick the best of them to send when the buses come,' one of the guards said, looking over and scowling at Aletta as she spoke, clearly not thinking she could understand them. 'They've negotiated for most of the French ones to leave this time.'

Aletta couldn't delay any longer, unless she wanted to be kicked again, so she slowly limped off. For the first time in forever, she felt a lightness rising inside her. Two things were clear to her: there was a chance the Allies would arrive before the last of them perished in this godforsaken place, and she would fight until her dying breath to tell the world how willingly the guards had gone about their jobs. That whatever excuses they claimed were nothing but barefaced lies.

She only wished it was closer to nightfall, so she could tell her mother and Chloe all that she'd learnt. And if it was true that they were going to be releasing French prisoners, there was a chance that Chloe would be leaving soon, so one of them was going to make it out alive.

When Aletta finally found Chloe, her heart sank. She was used to seeing every single woman who'd been in the camp for months or years looking thin and tired, but Chloe had been there longer than most, and it showed. The dark circles beneath her eyes, the hollowness of her cheeks, the slow, almost painful way she moved, as if her joints ached beyond belief – it broke Aletta's heart to see her like that. Herr Weber had kept them alive with his extra rations of food, but now that he'd left the Siemens factory, they were no better off than anyone else. Which meant they didn't have long.

Aletta found the energy to hurry over to them, taking Chloe and her mother by the arms and walking them away from the other women. They were both clutching their tin cups waiting to have them filled, but she didn't want everyone else to hear what she had to say, not until she knew more.

'You look happy,' her mother said. 'Why are you smiling?'

Chloe frowned, glancing back at the soup line. It might be revolting, but none of them ever wanted to miss out.

'I overhead the guards today. The Allies are liberating other camps,' she whispered. 'They must be losing the war.'

Chloe's eyebrows lifted then, her frown gone. 'You're certain you heard that correctly?'

Aletta nodded. 'They have Red Cross packages that have been sent here, and they're stockpiling them behind the crematorium. But there's more,' she said, glancing to check they weren't being watched. 'I heard them say that French prisoners are to be released.'

Her mother's gaze met hers, and her eyes widened. 'That means that Chloe . . .'

'Could be saved,' Aletta said, reaching for Chloe's hand. 'We just have to keep you well enough until they arrive. They don't want anyone knowing how badly they've starved us.'

'I'm not leaving without you,' Chloe said, looking between them. 'I don't care what happens, I couldn't, I—'

'If you can leave, you leave,' Aletta said firmly. 'You can fight for us on the outside, but you do not miss an opportunity to get out of here. Do you hear me?'

In the beginning, it had been Chloe who showed them how to stay alive, who'd fought for them when they needed her, had looked after Aletta when she was sick, but now it was her turn to look out for her friend. It was as if the tiniest ember of fire had sparked inside Aletta, after so many months of feeling nothing.

'We said we were together, that we were all going to—'

'We said we were going to stay alive, Chloe,' Emma interrupted. 'Maybe we don't all leave at once, but it doesn't change that we're all going to make it. But Aletta's right. If you get the chance to leave, you leave. It might be your only chance.'

Aletta took a deep breath, her lungs shuddering, her cough making her almost bend over double. But she rose as soon as she could, wiping her mouth with the back of her wrist. 'We just have to live long enough for this place to be liberated. You can wait for us on the other side.'

There was a shout behind them and they all jumped, shuffling back into the line before they were reprimanded.

'But we have to be careful,' Aletta murmured, leaning in close. 'I think, well, I heard them say that they want to get rid of the evidence. I don't think they'll let anyone see how bad it is here.'

'We need to find somewhere to hide, is that what you're saying?' her mother asked. 'You think they might . . .'

Aletta swallowed, meeting her mother's stare. 'I think that we need to do everything we can to keep our heads down, and we need to stay alert. We need to be careful.' *Just like we've always been, she thought. We need to keep an eye out for each other, listen to the guards, find out what's happening.*

Right now, she was focused on Chloe leaving the camp. She would worry about getting herself and her mother out once they knew Chloe was safe.

Chapter Thirty

Chloe

Chloe froze, along with the other women around her, when shouts echoed through the factory. They'd been waiting for this. Ever since Aletta had told them what she'd heard a few days earlier, they'd started to believe that they might make it out. It had only been a flicker of hope in the darkness, but it had kept them going.

But this couldn't be anything good.

The last time there had been a roll call during the middle of the day, the women taken were never seen again.

'*Beeil dich! Beweg dich!*' came the shouts again.

Hurry up! Move! They were words Chloe hadn't known before coming to Ravensbrück, but they'd been shouted at her so many times over the years she'd been held in the camp that she knew she'd never, ever forget them.

She sought out Aletta, slowly moving closer to her so they could walk out together. Chloe reached for her hand once they were close, and she saw from Aletta's sorrowful stare that she knew what was happening, too.

This was the end. No one ever came back from impromptu roll calls.

There was no more hope, no more belief in the war ending and the Allies coming to save them. It was over.

She held tightly on to Aletta as they shuffled slowly forward, and she only wished that Emma was with them so they could have this last moment together. They hadn't seen her since that morning, when she'd gone to the factory office.

'Your mother,' she whispered.

Aletta had tears slipping furiously down her cheeks, and Chloe held her fingers even tighter.

What was she supposed to say? Maybe this meant that Emma would be saved, that she'd been spared? Or maybe she was already standing out in the cold, awaiting her fate.

Maybe she's already been taken.

Anger speared through Chloe's chest, and she wanted to scream and charge at the guards. She wanted to snatch a gun from them and make her final moment mean something, but even if she'd truly wanted to, she couldn't. She was too weak to run fast; she was too slow to reach them before they shot her; she was too exhausted to do anything other than shuffle along behind the others.

She had lasted longer than most, but in the end, her fate was to be no different from the thousands of other women who'd been killed before her.

When they stepped outside, Chloe lost her grip on Aletta as they were jostled apart, and she was distracted by the sun. The sky was covered in clouds, but they'd parted for a moment, making way for a warm ray of sunshine, and she lifted her face to it, savouring the warmth and closing her eyes.

Chloe smiled as she saw her brothers, watched them as they laughed and talked, and even when she was prodded to move on, she held that memory in her mind. But she was forced to open them when numbers and names were called, and it wasn't until she looked towards Aletta that she saw the white buses.

It felt like her heart had stopped beating.

The white buses were marked with red crosses, and there were people waiting on the other side of the fence who were very clearly not guards. *Who are they?*

Aletta's eyes met hers again over the top of other prisoners' heads, and that little flicker of hope that Chloe had thought lost, ignited inside her once more. What Aletta had overhead that day hadn't been a mistake – maybe there was a chance for them, after all.

She watched, wide-eyed, as all of the French women who'd worked in the factory were called, forming a crude line away from the others; women, she was beginning to realise, who were going to be left behind. It appeared that they were only calling for the French.

And that was when Chloe heard her name and number.

That's me.

She frantically looked around for Emma, trying to see her among the hundreds of women standing in attendance. Chloe couldn't leave without her. She couldn't.

There she is.

Emma's smile was sad. 'Go,' she mouthed, from across the line of women stretching between them.

Chloe looked at the white buses, at the Red Cross workers waiting, leaning against the wire fence as if they couldn't believe what they were seeing. Some of them looked to be crying, others were blank-faced.

But no promise of life after Ravensbrück was worth it if she had to leave Aletta and Emma behind.

Aletta moved towards her, reaching for her hand, urging her on.

'Just go,' she whispered. 'Please.' Aletta's voice cracked. 'Save yourself, Chloe.'

Chloe lifted her chin as her voice and number were read aloud again, shouted this time.

She knew what she had to do.

'I'm here,' she said, calling out loudly and stepping forward.

She kept her fingers looped tightly around Aletta's though, not letting go even when her friend struggled to pull away.

A guard pointed for her to join the others gathered at the side as another name was called. She'd already been forgotten.

'I won't leave without my sister,' she said, bravely facing the guard who was staring at her and telling her where to move. 'Or without my mother.'

It was the first time Chloe had ever stood her ground in the camp. In all the time she'd been there, she'd gone where she was told to go, done what she was told to do. But not today. And with the Red Cross workers looking on, she knew the guards wouldn't strike her or take out their guns and shoot her. There would be no games where savage guards told dogs to chase them as they mocked a prisoner to run; there would be no orders to carry a body that had been shot for the hell of it; there would be no beating her with a baton.

Because now they were being watched, and it reignited a bravery inside Chloe that she'd almost forgotten had existed.

'Names,' the guard said, holding out her list.

Chloe looked to Aletta and then turned to find Emma, holding out her other hand to her, seeing the flicker of hope on both of their faces.

'Aletta Visser and Emma Visser,' she said.

There was a long pause as the guard looked through the list, flipping the pages. 'They are not on the list.'

Chloe held her ground, not moving as the guards looked between them. She saw it then – the way they looked at each other, the uncertainty in their gazes, something she'd never, ever seen before in any of them. Not once.

Except for the new guards who hadn't lasted a day, the ones who'd doubled over and vomited at the sight of so many thin, dying women and paled at the smell of their barracks and the misery before them.

The guard inclined her head and then waved her hand. 'Go,' she said, before moving on to the next name.

Emma's hand slid into hers, and Chloe felt as if her heart might explode, her pulse racing as they walked together and joined the waiting group.

If she hadn't said their names, they would have been left behind.

If she hadn't said their names, she would have lived, and they would have surely died.

'Thank you,' Emma whispered.

Chloe only nodded as tears streaked their faces. But they didn't embrace, they didn't smile, they didn't move beyond where they were told to stand, because there were hundreds of women still waiting for their names to be called, and they turned to watch them. Women and girls who deserved to be saved just as much as they did.

'Are we leaving?' Aletta whispered, her voice barely audible as she leaned into Chloe. 'Are we truly leaving?'

Chloe began to cry then. Big, gulping sobs that she could barely contain, as Emma's hand found its way to her shoulder and Aletta tucked her body close. The three of them, together, not parted even at the end.

'I think so,' she whispered.

Red Cross workers came towards them, some carrying blankets and others stretchers, but the one thing they all had in common were the kind expressions they wore like a uniform.

'Please follow us through the gate to the buses,' a man said. 'We will have food for you soon, and we ask that you share the blankets and share seats where needed.'

Another woman began calling out as she waved at them through the fence. 'We are all from the Red Cross and we will be taking you first to a Danish camp, and then on to Sweden, where you will be safe. But first we need to load you on to these buses, and we need to leave the area as quickly as possible.'

It's almost over. This nightmare is almost over. They can't keep hurting us, they can't touch us again. This is actually happening.

But Chloe knew that she wouldn't truly believe it until they were all loaded on those buses, with Ravensbrück a speck of dust in the distance.

'Please, any of you who are wearing yellow stars or triangles, you must remove them before you leave,' someone else called out. 'I repeat, you must not walk through this gate without removing the yellow star or triangle.'

Chloe watched as perhaps half of the women or more removed their yellow badges, throwing them to the ground. A young woman close to her was so impossibly thin, her arms like twigs, fingers shaking so badly that she couldn't remove hers, and so Chloe stepped forward and did it for her, passing it to her to throw away.

'Why?' Chloe asked, as she moved to help another woman.

'Because no one can know that the guards here agreed to release Jews,' the Red Cross worker said, her voice low. 'Please, it's imperative you do as we ask, for your own safety.'

Chloe ripped her own badge off then, no longer willing to be marked as a prisoner, holding it tight in her palm before throwing it to the ground. They'd taken her dignity when she arrived, but they weren't going to steal it for another moment.

It was time to leave the hell that was this camp behind. She placed her hand to her breast pockets and then her hips, feeling for the paper there, the papers she'd been prepared to die defending.

'I'll never forget what you did for me and my daughter,' Emma murmured beside her as it was finally their turn to amble through the gate towards the closest waiting bus.

'We agreed to survive this place together,' Chloe told her. 'This was me fulfilling that promise.'

Because she would never have left without them. They were her family, just as her brothers were her family, and there was nothing she wouldn't do for those she loved.

Chapter Thirty-One

30 April 2015

Aletta stared out at the barbed wire fencing, swallowing away the lump in her throat. She remembered seeing those white buses waiting, not wanting to believe that the miracle they'd hoped for had finally come true. She closed her eyes briefly and saw Chloe, the way she'd turned and looked at her over her shoulder, smiling, holding out her hand; the hope that had been shining from her eyes.

'We were some of the last survivors,' Aletta murmured. 'Almost everyone else was gone by then. So many of the women we'd met along the way, all gone.'

The tour guide turned to her, his expression kind. She liked this man. He knew a lot about the Holocaust and the camps, but he seemed even more interested in hearing her memories. She supposed that the more she said now, the more he would be able to share once all of the survivors were gone. It was the reason she would keep talking, to make sure that he could pass on her story that so many others from those years shared with her, the next time he was standing here with a group of people interested enough in the past to visit.

'How did it feel, being one of the last survivors?' he asked, softly, as if he wasn't sure whether to ask her or not.

'The truth?' she asked. 'We felt guilty. There was guilt at surviving when others didn't, but there was also just relief, especially on the day we left. The three of us had survived and that felt like a miracle, and at some point along the way you stop thinking about everyone making it, and just think about yourself.'

'But you didn't,' her daughter said, her voice soft, the first time she'd spoken in front of the group. 'You never stopped thinking about your mother and about your friend. It sounds to me as if the three of you never stopped fighting for each other, right up until the very end.'

Aletta let her daughter's words wash over her. 'I suppose, somewhere along the way, I started to think of us as one. There was no me without Chloe, no Chloe without Emma, and they felt the same.'

It had been little more than luck that they'd all made it to that final day, of course. Luck that they had managed to live when others had perished; luck that Herr Weber had been their supervisor, that all three had been able to board those buses together. Luck that Aletta and Emma were even there when Chloe's name was called.

'Ahead of the liberation, more than five and a half thousand women were transferred to other camps,' the guide said. 'The most fortunate, like Aletta here, were handed over to the Swedish and Danish Red Cross, but thousands were killed before then. It's estimated that twenty thousand prisoners were forced on a brutal evacuation by foot ahead of the Soviet Army arriving here at Ravensbrück.'

The guide looked to Aletta, but she simply nodded. She had nothing else to add to the sobering facts he shared.

'I don't know if I'd describe my mother as *fortunate*,' her daughter suddenly said, her voice so quiet and the ensuing silence so loud, that they could have heard a pin drop.

Aletta looked up at her. 'He meant no offence, and he's not wrong. I was one of the fortunate ones, when you look at how things ended for so many others.'

'I'm sorry,' the guide said, his face stained a dark red, but Aletta just smiled and nodded.

'Carry on, please.'

He took a moment to steady himself before continuing. 'When the Soviet Army finally entered the camp, they found more than three thousand sick women and children, left here to die. What they found had a profound impact on those soldiers, and some described it as finding a camp of walking skeletons, tortured and treated more inhumanely than anyone could imagine.'

Aletta looked up at the guide, seeing the tears shining in his eyes, and then at her daughter, who was wiping her cheeks. Her daughter clasped Aletta's hand, the warmth from her skin a welcome reprieve from the otherwise biting cold.

How I ever survived those winters here, in our flimsy clothes. How I kept rising every morning. How I ever believed that we would be saved when so many others were not. They were questions that Aletta had often asked herself, but today, the questions were almost overwhelming. But being with her mother and Chloe had given her the strength to believe. Because she'd been determined to live for them, as much as for herself.

'That concludes our tour,' the guide said, 'although I'd be very happy to answer any questions you might have. I'd also like to thank Aletta for her bravery in sharing her story with us today.'

There were murmurs of thanks from the small circle gathered around her, and she waited until the group fell silent before speaking again.

'But that's not where the story ends,' she said, hearing the shake in her voice and wishing it were stronger, as the small group that had been about to disperse was drawn back together.

Her daughter tucked her blanket more tightly around her legs as Aletta felt her eyes glaze with unshed tears, as she thought back to that day. That day that had felt like a miracle, that *was* a miracle. It was another part of her story that she'd tried desperately to forget, but today, she'd promised to tell the truth and make herself remember.

Her voice quavered. 'There's more.'

Chapter Thirty-Two

Aletta

The last time Aletta had been transported anywhere was by train when they'd been taken to Ravensbrück. Sometimes when she closed her eyes, she could remember what it was like inside the crude wagon made for animals, in the dark and the cold not knowing where she was going. Other days it was as if her mind had blocked the memory and wouldn't let her remember. But today, she could vividly recall the fear; perhaps because she finally, after all this time, felt a semblance of safety. That they were finally leaving the hell of the past few years. That those people who'd been waiting for them weren't going to hurt them, *couldn't hurt them*, anymore.

They were crammed together, reminding her of the last time she'd been transported, only this time they were seated shoulder to shoulder on the bus. And instead of being afraid of the dark, Aletta was able to press her cheek to the cool glass and look at where they were going. Nothing could have prepared her for the bombed-out areas of Germany they passed through, the destruction far more widespread than she could have imagined, the devastation showing her for the first time that the Nazis weren't the conquerors they'd made themselves out to be. They'd been told they were driving to the Danish border, and she knew that the nervous flutter in her stomach wouldn't abate until they reached it.

We're going to make it.

She'd hated the thought of seeing herself in a mirror, but in the window, she could make out her reflection. Her hair was patchy and bedraggled – she'd often felt her scalp over the past months and was horrified by how thin her hair was – but it was her bones that scared her more. She was all sharp angles and stretched skin, although she knew it could have been worse. Some of the women were so sick, their bodies so weak they could barely stand, let alone walk, having only boarded the bus using the same sheer grit and determination that had seen them stay alive amid the horrors of the camp. She knew they would have crawled on their hands and knees if they'd had to for even the slimmest chance of being rescued. If the three hadn't been the recipients of Herr Weber's extra rations for so long in the factory, they would have been just as poorly as the very worst of the other prisoners. If they would have been alive at all.

'We're safe now,' Chloe whispered, seated between them, holding their hands. 'We're going to make it.'

Aletta's fingers were wrapped tightly around Chloe's as she dropped her head to Chloe's shoulder. She shut her eyes, relaxing for the first time in so long that it felt foreign to her. Her lips were cracked and dry, her throat ached for water, and her stomach rumbled, but she was so used to that now that she barely gave them pause for thought.

We're going to make it.

After driving for what felt like hours, the bus slowed and eventually stopped on the edge of a forest. The driver was kindly enough, although quietly spoken, and Aletta imagined he didn't know what to say to the women in his care. But what he lacked for in conversation, he certainly made up for in provisions.

'We'll be stopping here long enough to have something to eat, and for anyone who needs to, to, ah, relieve themselves,' he said. 'Please take your time, we won't leave without you.'

Most of the women were silent, not moving from their seats, even as he opened the door. Aletta didn't want to get out of the bus – it was the first place she'd felt safe in a very long time, and it felt wrong to get out when they could just keep driving as far away from the camp as possible.

'Perhaps you could enjoy the fresh air and stretch your legs?' he suggested, appearing as unsure as Aletta imagined they all looked.

Eventually they did as he suggested, and Aletta held back tears as she looked at the early daffodils in the field, inhaled the smell of the forest and the grass, enough to make her gasp. It was as if her senses had been dulled for so long that experiencing nature again made her want to cry.

'It's beautiful, isn't it?' Chloe said, as she moved past her.

Aletta's mother leaned into her as they gratefully accepted a bread roll and a biscuit, watching as the driver gave the rest of the food to two of the women to hand out so that he could pass around cups full of a sweet-tasting juice.

'It's like we've been living in dirt, everything has been brown and grey, and now someone has turned the colour back on,' Chloe said. 'I've never seen anything like this.'

'Leaves have never looked so green,' Aletta's mother said from beside her. 'And the smell. I can't believe it, truly I can't.'

When Chloe looked up, she had to agree. Leaves *had* never looked so bright and vibrant – it was as if she was seeing them with fresh eyes, and compared to the smells they'd become used to, it smelt like the sweetest of perfumes on the edge of the forest.

'Thank you, Chloe,' Emma said. 'Without you, we wouldn't be here.'

Chloe's smile was warm, her expression showing just how content she was. 'I was never leaving without you, Emma. You should both have known that.'

'Well regardless, we're grateful.'

Aletta gently patted Chloe's back. Her mother wasn't wrong; if Chloe hadn't insisted, they'd still be in that bleak, lifeless camp. They'd done a lot for each other in the years they'd been together, but this final act from Chloe had changed everything. She would never stop thanking her friend for what she'd done.

She chewed the bread slowly as they stood and stared at the forest, savouring every soft mouthful. This was real bread, not the tough, sawdust-filled chunks they'd been served in the camps, and she took tiny sips of her drink in between mouthfuls. When Aletta glanced around at the other women, she saw some place bread in their pockets, presumably for later, and she wondered how long it would take them to accept that food wasn't going to be withheld, that they didn't need to squirrel away rations for another time. Aletta knew it was a habit she would find almost impossible to break.

'Sorry ladies but we'll need to keep moving,' the driver called. 'If you could all get back in the bus. There will be more food at the camp.'

Aletta looked behind her one last time, trying to commit the forest to her memories, to replace the terror of Ravensbrück with it before finding her way back to her seat. She had the window again, and she shuffled over as far as she could so her mother and Chloe could fit beside her.

But just as they were settling in, their bellies full for the first time in years and their hearts even fuller, a loud noise made Chloe snap her head up. The thud that followed made her teeth rattle, and Aletta's jaw clenched tightly as the bus rocked, fingers clutching desperately at Chloe's.

What the . . .

'Take cover!' someone yelled, as panic filled the bus like thick smog, women still hurrying to get in and falling over each other in their desperation to reach safety.

They fell on to their knees, hands pulling apart as they scrambled forward, bracing themselves as the bus lurched. Aletta had known fear, what it was like to think she was going to die, to wonder whether she would live to see the next morning, but she'd never known the gut-wrenching panic of what was happening to her right now, when they'd finally believed they were safe. It was like someone had dangled safety in front of them long enough for them to grasp hold, and now it was being ripped away.

There was yelling from someone at the front of the bus, and then the sound of rapid gunfire, and Aletta winced at the impossibly loud ringing in her ears at another series of what she could only guess were shots from above. Was a plane firing at them? Were they under attack?

She clasped Chloe's hand as they squashed into the footwell, and stayed there with their arms braced above their heads until well after the firing had stopped. And even then, when she rose to take her seat and the driver called out that they should expect a fast and bumpy trip, Aletta barely breathed she was so scared, her heart thundering in her chest and goose pimples covering her skin.

'Who was firing at us?' Chloe muttered. 'Why did he even stop there if we weren't safe?'

Aletta just shook her head and exchanged a worried look with her mother over the top of Chloe's head.

Perhaps we were too quick to think we were safe. Perhaps it's all just an illusion and we're not safe at all.

Hours later, with their nerves still on edge, they finally reached the camp, which was more like a canvas city. There were rows upon rows of tents, with Red Cross ladies handing out packages containing thick woollen socks and scarves, and ladling soup into tin cups. But unlike the soup at Ravensbrück, this soup made Aletta's heart sing. It warmed her belly and eased the gnaw of hunger in her stomach, reminded her of what food was *supposed* to taste like when it was made to nourish a body rather than slowly poison it. They were still shaken up over what had happened earlier, and someone said that one of the other buses had sustained a direct hit, but no one had spoken about it again.

'I can't believe it,' Chloe said, braving a small smile at Aletta over her cup as she took little sips. 'When did food taste so good?'

'I heard them saying that they learnt from the last women who'd come through and decided to make soup instead of rich meals with too much meat,' Chloe said. 'It made them all violently ill after so long with nothing when they fed them fancy food.'

'Well, this is the best soup I've had in my life.'

They passed by a small group of British women whom they recognised from the camp and exchanged smiles with, but mostly Aletta, Chloe and Emma kept to themselves, making their way to their tent. They'd also been given a piece of bread covered in something that looked like butter but wasn't, and Aletta took small nibbles as they walked, her stomach groaning from being filled with food after suffering from starvation for so long. But still, she couldn't stop.

When they eventually lay down in an unoccupied corner, their food finished, the little glimmer of hope that she'd felt earlier returned, that they might finally be safe, after all.

'What are you most looking forward to?' Aletta asked as they lay together, their bodies exhausted from the day of transport.

'Seeing my brothers,' Chloe whispered. 'I have to believe that they survived, that my little Adrian has grown into a young man and hasn't ended up . . .'

She didn't need to continue for Aletta to know what she meant. They knew the reality of the camps, how few had survived, and what a miracle it had been that all three of them had made it. But if Chloe's brothers had been imprisoned . . . Aletta took a breath, her thoughts immediately turning to Harry, and whether he might have met the same fate, if he'd even made it out of her apartment alive.

'I just want to walk through that door and find them how I left them, I suppose.'

'I hope they're there waiting for you,' Aletta finally said. 'I hope they're waiting with open arms for their brave sister to come home.'

Chloe turned, her eyes searching Aletta's face. 'I hope Harry's waiting for you, too.'

'I think it would be a miracle if he was,' she said, even if she had hoped for that to be true. 'Part of me keeps wondering if he survived, and if he did whether we'll ever be able to find each other again. I wouldn't even know where to start looking for him.' Aletta had asked herself so many times whether it had just been something forgettable to him, just a moment in time, or whether she'd meant as much to him as he had to her. She didn't exactly have a lot of experience with young men. So long as he'd survived, she would be able to live with it. But she wanted to know what his fate had been, so she didn't have to spend a lifetime wondering.

'Miracles happen every day,' Emma said. 'Don't either of you lose hope, not yet.'

Tears prickled in Aletta's eyes at her mother's words, because no amount of hope was going to bring the man they'd both loved so much back to life.

'I'm sorry he's not going to be there waiting for us,' Aletta said.

'I had twenty-two years with your father, Aletta. Twenty-two beautiful years. And I won't let that one night be the memory that stays with me, not when I have so much happiness to look back on. I refuse to let them take that from me.'

Aletta smiled, despite her tears. Her mother was right, of course she was, but it sounded easier said than done, especially when that night was still a memory that haunted her dreams and woke her in the dead of night.

'I know it doesn't make up for the people we've loved and lost, or what we've been through, but the war has given me a mother and a sister, and for that, I will always be grateful,' Chloe said. 'I will never forget either of you, for as long as I live.'

'You'll always be my daughter, Chloe. Whether we find our way back to each other again or not once this is over, we will always be family. *Always.*'

'Thank you,' Chloe whispered. 'If my brothers aren't there, if . . .' She let go of a breath. 'It's just reassuring to know that I can find you, that's all.'

Emma's words hung between them, because it was something they'd promised each other for longer than Aletta could remember. They were family, and no matter what, they would always be there for each other, their homes open to one another whenever they needed it.

'Can you give me the papers you're carrying?' Chloe asked. 'I want to collate them, so that I can find someone to give them to.' She glanced up at Aletta. 'I was starting to think that it was a fantasy, that I'd risked so much and we'd never leave that place.'

Aletta took the papers she'd hidden in her clothes, and so did her mother. There were other women who'd held some too, but she'd already seen Chloe ask for theirs. Altogether, it was quite the bundle.

'Maybe, if this war truly ends, you could have them published into a book,' Emma suggested gently, as they all stared down at the dog-eared pages. 'A memory of those who perished, and those who survived. The records of women.'

Chloe just nodded, clearly lost in her own thoughts about the project she had ahead of her.

'That soup has gone straight through me,' Aletta said, sighing as she forced herself to her feet. She was exhausted after the day they'd had, and ready for sleep. 'I'll be back soon.'

Aletta made her way through the tent, standing outside in the cooling early-evening air as she stretched. It was strange to look out and not see walls or barbed wire, guards or dogs, or even watchtowers, and she began walking to a treed area nearby to relieve herself. It wasn't ideal, but she wasn't complaining. To her, this camp felt like the height of luxury.

She continued, her legs a little unsteady, when she heard a low rumble. Turning, she realised that the rumble was becoming louder, and soon there was a plane fast approaching, flying too low through the sky. Terror filled Aletta when she realised what was happening, and she turned on her heel and ran back to the tent, screaming as loud as she could.

'Get out!' she yelled. 'Run!'

Aletta hadn't made it back when a shot and then another rang out in the otherwise still air. Women began to pour out of tents all around them in a panic, and when she finally saw Chloe and her mother she moved as fast as her legs would take her, clutching their hands and hauling them in the opposite direction.

But they weren't fast enough.

Another plane, or perhaps the same one as before, flew towards them, even lower than the first. Shots echoed out, pelting the ground around them, and from the corner of her eye Aletta saw a woman fall. But she couldn't stop. Fear kept her running as she pushed her mother ahead of her and grabbed for Chloe's hand.

They ran as a flurry of more shots fired near them, one sounding far too close for comfort, and Aletta stumbled as Chloe threw herself forward, covering Aletta as they hurtled towards the ground. They landed with a thud and Aletta felt as if all the bones in her body had broken – she had so little fat left on her that she endured every inch of the fall. But miraculously there was silence, and when she looked up, spitting out dirt, she saw the plane flying away, disappearing into the distance.

'Why do they keep shooting at us!' Aletta cried.

Chloe had been holding her hand, but Aletta felt her grip loosen and she tried to turn beneath the weight of her friend.

'Chloe, get off me,' she groaned, trying to wriggle out and wondering why Chloe wasn't moving. 'I can't breathe.'

It wasn't that Chloe was heavy, she was as thin as Aletta was, it was just that Aletta had such little strength left to move herself. Not to mention she felt like being sick, the food from earlier sitting like a lump in her stomach, and her body crying out from having to use energy she didn't have.

'Chloe!'

Aletta finally pulled out from beneath her, at the same time as her mother spoke her name.

'*Aletta.*'

It was one word, her own name, that she'd heard her mother say countless times. But the quiet way she said it this time sent a bone-deep shiver through Aletta; it held a note of caution, of pain, that told her something was very, very wrong.

Aletta sat up and watched as Chloe moved, looking like she was about to push up to her feet before sinking back down to her knees.

'Chloe?' Aletta's voice caught on her friend's name.

And then she realised what Chloe had done when she'd thrown her to the ground and covered Aletta's body with her own. What she'd sacrificed. Why she hadn't moved straight away.

'Oh my God, *Chloe*.'

Everything around them went silent then; the cries of other women, the wails of those who had been injured.

The sight of the dead.

But all Aletta could hear was her mother saying her name, cautioning her.

And all she could see was Chloe.

Chapter Thirty-Three

Chloe

Chloe saw Aletta's eyes widen, and she slowly looked down at her own middle. She'd known it was bad when her body had been hit with such a burning, intense pain, but this . . . she swallowed, surprised when the pain lifted somewhat. It still hurt, but the pain was no longer searing like it had been. When she'd fallen, it had been all consuming, stopping her from being able to take another step, but now it was only a dull thud, even though she still couldn't move.

She placed her hands to her stomach, knowing from her friend's pained, *desperate* reaction, that her not feeling it as acutely as she had wasn't indicative of the wound not being so bad. Because the bullet had ricocheted straight into her torso, and she knew there was no way anyone could survive a shot like that.

I'm dying.

Tears pricked her eyes and she closed them, trying to accept what she knew to be true. Aletta dropped to her knees before her and opened her arms, cradling Chloe to her chest as she cried, her hands pressing against Chloe's, trying to stem the blood flow. Her hands felt slippery from her own blood, and she found she had to focus on every breath now, on the pull and push of every movement of her chest.

'We're so close, Chloe.'

She looked up and saw Emma. The woman who'd become like a mother to her. Her friend. Her *confidante*. Her eyes were glistening with tears.

Emma knew that she didn't have long.

'Just hold on, Chloe. You just need to hold on,' Aletta begged.

But Chloe knew that she couldn't fight it, that no matter how hard she wanted to stop what was happening, she couldn't. Her body was too cold. It was as if she'd been plunged into winter; icy fingers danced across her skin and left her shivering, her breath coming in little pants now. But she couldn't feel the pain, not now. All she could feel was Aletta's panic, listening to her frantic sobs as her chest rose and then fell; all she could see was the sadness in Emma's gaze; all she could hear were the shouts and cries of others, of the other women who were supposed to be safe. She could still hear the gunshots echoing in her mind, even though she knew the planes were gone, and she closed her eyes tightly now, not wanting to imagine how many other women had been shot.

We were supposed to be safe. We were finally supposed to be safe from harm.

'Chloe, you listen to me, you need to hold on until we can get help.'

'I can't,' she whispered, as Aletta's hold on her tightened, as her own fingers slipped from her middle. 'You need—'

'No!' Aletta cried. 'Don't say that! You can, you *have* to hold on. Please, Chloe, *please*.' Her friend's voice broke then as emotion bubbled into her words, as her tears seemed to choke her.

'Aletta, you need to—' She gasped and forced in a breath. 'You need to live for the both of us.'

She heard Aletta's fresh sob, but she felt so cold that she could barely swallow now, let alone reach out to her. It took everything she had to try to form fresh words, to make her tongue move and her voice obey her as Aletta folded her body over hers.

'You can't leave me, Chloe. Please, stay with us. You have to stay with us,' Aletta begged. 'I can carry you to safety, we can get help, we can . . .' Aletta's voice drifted to silence and Chloe wished she could comfort her. That she could wrap her own arms around Aletta and hold her close, that she could say something to make these last moments easier.

Emma was on her knees now, tucked in beside them, her fingers gentle as they stroked Chloe's hair, smoothing it from her forehead. It was a mother's touch, and one she craved. Emma's warm gaze, laced with sorrow, told her that she knew this was the end, that there was nothing anyone could do to save her.

It didn't matter how hard Chloe wanted to fight; she couldn't. Death was already reaching out to her with its ice-cold touch, calling to her.

'Don't ever let them forget,' Chloe rasped, as her hands fell to her sides, while Aletta frantically grabbed for her and pressed both their hands on her wound, as if she could single-handedly force her to stay alive, to keep fighting. 'You find your Harry. Do you hear me?' she coughed, the words almost impossible to expel. 'You don't stop until you find your Harry. And the papers . . .'

She heard Aletta gasp; she heard the pained cries of the two people who'd loved her so much, who'd cared for her and pulled her through her darkest times; her little camp family. She felt their hands on her skin, felt Emma's lips press against her forehead, felt the warmth of Aletta's breath as she collapsed over her again and begged her not to go. She felt every wave of their pain as her own shuddered through her.

And as she drifted away, as her pain eased completely and warmth finally surrounded her, she knew that she could face her maker with an open heart, knowing that she'd done everything she could to save the people she loved. Knowing that she'd lived her life with love and compassion, with as much sense of duty as had been within her power.

She'd saved her brother, had given herself to protect him, and now she'd saved Aletta, too. And she'd do it all over again, in a heartbeat.

Perhaps this was what she'd been placed on this earth to do: save the lives of those she loved.

Chapter Thirty-Four

Aletta

'Aletta, we have to get back to the camp.'

She heard her mother's words, but couldn't bring herself to rise. Her fingers grasped the front of Chloe's shirt as her tears continued to fall.

'Aletta.' Her mother's voice was more forceful now and Aletta felt herself being pulled backwards.

Aletta stared down at Chloe, barely breathing, her eyes burning from the tears she'd shed and the ones that kept appearing. *Chloe can't be gone. She can't be.*

'I can't leave her here,' Aletta whispered. She found it impossible to believe that her friend was gone. Her blood-stained shirt was all the reminder she needed, but she'd slipped away so quickly. After everything they'd been through, after everything that they'd survived, it didn't seem fair or just to die at the final hurdle. Although nothing about the last few years had been just or fair.

'We need to go and ask for help,' her mother said, her hand rubbing circles on Aletta's back. 'We need to—'

'How can you just leave her here?' Aletta cried. 'We can't go!'

'Chloe was like a daughter to me,' her mother said, and when Aletta looked up, she saw her mother's tear-stained face and the pain in her eyes, saw the tremble of her hands as she wiped her cheeks. 'But you're my daughter too, and we need to get out of here before we're shot at again. If they come back, we need to be somewhere safe, or Chloe's bravery will be for nothing.'

Aletta nodded then, knowing she needed to move. 'We'll find someone to move her body?' she asked, swallowing and trying to tell herself that Chloe would have wanted them to be safe, that she would forgive them for leaving her. 'We'll come back for her?'

'We will.' Her mother held out her hand, but as she was reaching for it, Aletta saw her frown. 'Where are her papers?'

Chloe's records. Of course they needed to find them. Aletta had made her a promise that she would make sure the records were shared, and if her mother hadn't mentioned it, she would have forgotten all about them in her grief.

'They might be back at the campsite where we were sitting, but . . .' Aletta felt sick as she reached into the oversized jacket Chloe was wearing, one they'd been given by the Red Cross when they arrived at the site. Bile rose in her throat, hot and acidic.

I've found them.

Aletta took out the crudely bound papers, her heart settling as she realised they could at least do this for Chloe.

'I have them,' she said, hating that she'd smudged the papers with blood. But it was Chloe's blood, and they were Chloe's words, and somehow it seemed almost fitting.

'We'll find the right people to give them to,' her mother said, her voice husky. 'We'll do that for her, Aletta, I promise you. And we'll find the poems she spoke of, the poems she wished could be published. We'll find her family and we'll do everything we can.'

'We'll make sure no one forgets,' Aletta sobbed, reaching for her mother, the papers tucked tight to her chest, her other hand going around her mother's waist as much for comfort as to stop her from falling. Even as guilt rushed through Aletta, she knew that the only way she could thank Chloe was by fulfilling the promise she'd made.

Someone was running towards them. A well-dressed man with kind eyes who looked straight past them to Chloe. Her breath caught as she looked back herself, wishing she hadn't when she saw her friend's crumpled body on the ground. But the man put himself between Aletta and her mother, letting them lean on him as he helped them to walk away, and she noticed that he didn't look like any of the other volunteers.

'Why were they firing at us?' she heard her mother ask, her voice verging on hysterical. 'Who were they? Why are they shooting!'

'They thought we were Germans,' he said, and she heard the anger and frustration in the man's voice. 'They were our own.'

'You'd think RAF pilots would be trained to see the cross on our buses!' her mother said through thick tears. 'Can they not see the red cross? Do they not understand what it means?'

Our own men shot Chloe down. Aletta might have laughed if they'd come away from the gunfire unscathed, but now, all she felt was rage. Pure, white, blinding rage. That after so long of praying for their own to come and save them, they'd ended up being the ones to kill Chloe.

'Our own men?' Aletta repeated. 'Was it them who shot at the buses earlier, too?'

He nodded as they reached the tents again, his expression solemn. 'I knew this rescue mission would be our most dangerous, I was warned, and for that I'm sorry,' he said. 'But Himmler . . .' He shook his head, and Aletta tried to grasp what he'd been about to say. 'They weren't going to leave anyone there alive. The other camps have all been liberated now, but Ravensbrück is one of the last and . . .' He paused. 'Nazis have been painting red crosses on trucks to try to escape to other areas, and I think our pilots are so determined to shoot down every last one of them. I'm so sorry, truly I am.'

Aletta nodded, wiping away fresh tears. She didn't need to hear any more. She knew they had to be grateful, but still, it hurt more than anything to know their own had been the ones to shoot at them.

'If those buses hadn't arrived today, if . . .' She couldn't even continue, her heart aching for Chloe. She fought the urge to look back at her.

'I don't think you would have been alive by the end of the week,' he said, gently. 'You were the last group to be saved. We can't go back again.'

'Thank you,' her mother said, and Aletta watched as she held out her hand.

He did the same, smiled and then gently touched her mother's arm. She wouldn't have blamed him for being repelled by their appearance, but he didn't waver.

'I'm sorry, for what's happened to you both. My only hope is that tomorrow we can transport you to Sweden, where you'll truly be safe.' He smiled again. 'The war is all but over, but I know that's no consolation for those who perished today.'

He glanced at the papers she held to her chest, and Aletta found herself holding them even tighter as the weight of his words hit her. *The war is over.* All these years, all the suffering they'd endured, and it was almost over.

'Are they important documents?' he asked.

'They are memories of the women we've been in the camp with,' her mother said. 'Our friend kept them at great risk to her life.' She paused, and Aletta almost broke at the pain in her mother's voice, at the way she sobbed out the last word. 'Our friend who was killed.'

'Then they're very important documents indeed,' he said, as if understanding their pain. 'There will be authorities waiting to greet you on arrival in Sweden. Tell them that Folke Bernadotte wants the records you hold officially documented.'

Aletta watched, her body beginning to tremble as they stood and watched the man walk away, but she continued to clutch the list so tightly as if her life depended on it.

Chloe was the sister she'd never had.

She was the second daughter her mother had never had.

And now she was gone and there was nothing Aletta could do to bring her back.

We'll make sure they never forget, Chloe. We'll make sure that every recipe, every poem, every note is remembered, and never, ever forgotten. Even if it takes me a lifetime, I promise you that no one will forget.

Chapter Thirty-Five

Aletta

They'd been told they had to leave at eight, so Aletta and her mother had risen at dawn. Chloe's body had been taken, wrapped in a white sheet for burial, but neither of them had felt right about leaving without marking the spot where she'd passed.

'Here,' her mother said, stopping at the place and staring down at the ground.

The lump in Aletta's throat swelled, and she took a shuddering breath, trying to block out the memories of the day before, not wanting to relive that moment ever again.

They stood side by side until her mother took her hand, and Aletta followed like a child beside her. In her other hand, her mother held a small cross that had been made for them by the camp volunteers.

'Why don't we place it here, by this tree,' her mother said. 'I think Chloe would have liked it here.'

Aletta had cried so much during the night, her body so used to having Chloe's beside it, the loss of her warmth a constant reminder that she wasn't with them any longer, that she'd thought she wouldn't have any tears left. But they still fell, slipping down her cheeks, the salty taste on her tongue.

She bent when her mother did and they dug the cross into the ground, kneeling in front of it for a moment before slowly rising.

'Chloe, you were my daughter in every sense of the word,' she murmured. 'We will never forget you.'

Aletta found that she couldn't say anything, so she stepped forward instead, kissing her fingers and pressing them to the cross.

I love you, Chloe, and I don't think I know how to live my life without you.

Chapter Thirty-Six

Aletta

Aletta held tightly to her mother's hand as they stood on the Malmö docks two days later. She was still numb, and she balled her other hand into a fist when she thought about Chloe. *Chloe, who would be holding my other hand if we were all here together.*

They'd all been so close to surviving, and the only thing that had saved Aletta from giving up at Ravensbrück were the papers in her pocket and the promise she'd made to Chloe, even though Aletta knew how much Chloe had struggled as the keeper of those words.

Aletta glanced at the other women around her. There were so many, and she remembered the last time she'd stood on a platform not unlike the docks where they were now, waiting to be processed. She could understand why some women screamed when the nurses here reached for them, why so many were fearful of what was to come, that nothing was more terrifying than being told of the delousing chambers in the next tent. They'd all been told lies before about what happened to fellow inmates, and until they saw the first women emerge out on the other side, unscathed, she doubted anyone would trust what was happening, would truly begin to believe their nightmare was over.

There was a woman beside her carrying a tiny, yawning infant in a box, and Aletta smiled at her, sensing her relief. But it also broke her heart, because if Chloe had been there, they would have smiled down at the little baby together, imagining the life she might have now that she'd been rescued.

'I just want to go home,' Aletta murmured, not even realising that she'd said the words aloud until her mother leaned into her and replied.

'So do I. Just remember that we're closer to going home now than we've ever been.'

She nodded. They were safer in Sweden than they would be anywhere else, she supposed, but still. She wanted to leave all of this behind and take her mother home. To try to rebuild what they had left of their lives. To forget the ordeal they'd suffered.

'Come this way,' a nurse said, and like many of the women they'd come across, this nurse had tears in her eyes as she helped them. Another had fainted when she'd seen the first skeletal women step off the boat, and at least two had run away, not able to cope with what they saw.

They shuffled forward, thanking the volunteers who came up with little cookies and other baked goods, nibbling at them slowly as their stomachs groaned in pain. Aletta wasn't sure what hurt more – being so violently hungry or feeling food regularly landing in her stomach after so long being empty.

'Come this way for delousing,' the woman said. 'Once you pass through here, all your clothes will be burned to get rid of the lice, and new clothes and provisions will be waiting for you in the church and the town hall.'

'It's all right, no one is going to hurt you,' said another. 'We're going to look after you. There is nothing to fear here.'

Their words were kind, but still Aletta tightened her arm around her stomach, not wanting to change out of the only clothes she had, even though they were little more than rags. The Red Cross workers wouldn't understand that talk of burning was enough to make most of the prisoners instinctively run away, that the last time they'd been told to take off their clothes and part with their belongings, they'd been left with almost nothing. It took everything she had not to turn on her heel, and if she hadn't been the caretaker of Chloe's papers, maybe she would have.

'Excuse me,' she said, beckoning to one of the volunteers.

The woman came over. 'I have something important that I need to give to the authorities,' Aletta said. 'Important documents.'

'There'll be time to—'

'I don't want them to get damaged in the delousing chamber.'

The woman looked confused, and Aletta wondered if she would even be able to comprehend the number of women who'd been murdered, or how important the list truly was. No matter how kind they were or how passionately they wanted to help, she doubted that anyone who hadn't seen the camps first-hand could ever understand.

'These records are all we have left from many of the women at our camp,' Aletta's mother said beside her, her voice quiet but steady. 'It is of great importance that these are preserved.'

The woman nodded, her eyes widening as she listened, as if she was trying to understand. 'Then let me find someone who can help you,' she finally said.

'A man named Mr Folke Bernadotte wanted these papers passed to the highest level of authority,' Aletta added, thinking of the kindly gentleman from the tent camp. She had no clue whether his name held weight here or not, but she was certainly going to try.

The woman's eyes widened even more, and Aletta knew she'd made the right decision in mentioning him. 'You met Count Bernadotte?'

Count? He hadn't used a title when he'd introduced himself, but she didn't doubt the sincerity of the woman standing before her.

'He personally aided us just two days ago,' her mother said. 'You speak as if he's well known to you?'

The woman swallowed, looking between them. 'You truly don't know, do you?'

Aletta frowned. 'Know what?'

'The Count is the reason you're standing here. He negotiated for your release and organised the white buses.' The woman's smile was warm when she reached for Aletta's hand. 'Why don't you come with me, and I'll find somewhere safe to place these papers of yours while you're treated.'

Aletta's instinct was to trust this woman, and when she glanced at her mother and received her little nod of approval, she decided to give them to her. Aletta took the papers from her inside pocket, her fingers trembling as she held the documents out. They were smudged with blood and looked so battered she was surprised the pages were still holding together, that the words were even legible.

'I promise I'll keep them safe,' the woman said. 'You follow your way into the tent, and I'll wait for you on the other side. Then we can take it to the authorities together. Someone in processing will be able to help us.'

Aletta nodded, resisting the urge to reach over and snatch the papers back.

'May I look?'

The woman's softly spoken words took her by surprise, but Aletta nodded, watching as she unfolded the papers. Her eyes tracked over the first page, and then the next, and the next, until tears filled her eyes as she read a recipe with the name Anna printed at the bottom.

'Your friend . . .'

Aletta shook her head. 'We lost her. But this is her legacy.'

She watched the woman fold the list again and placed it with the other papers safely in her breast pocket. 'I understand.' She gently touched Aletta's shoulder, her smile kind. 'Once we have these in the right hands, we're going to take you to the hall and find you a bed and some nice new clothes. Someone will take you to a hot bath when you're ready, and there will be food for you whenever you need it. You're safe here, truly you are.'

They stood for a moment, the woman's kind smile never wavering, before Aletta's mother took her hand and tugged her forward. And Aletta had the most overwhelming feeling as they entered the tent and stood behind a screen to remove their clothes.

That it was almost time to go home. That after so long, when home had seemed like somewhere she'd never see again, it was almost time.

Her father was gone. Chloe was gone. But the horrors of war, of the Nazi camp and its endless cruelty, were finally over.

The people she'd loved and lost would never be forgotten. The friends she'd made, the children she'd taught, they would live in her heart forever, and those she'd lost would surely haunt her dreams.

Once Chloe's papers were securely with the Swedish authorities, it would be over.

Aletta stood up straight then, looking at the women ahead of her and behind her, feeling an inner strength that she'd long since forgotten she possessed. And that was when she saw her.

The girl with the big blue eyes. The little girl she'd worried about since the very beginning of the war.

Aletta held up a hand, laughing when the girl, now a teenager, smiled back at her and waved.

Else had survived. She'd made it.

In a world that held very little hope and so much heartache, the fact that the little girl from her past was standing there, safe, felt like the biggest miracle of all.

Chapter Thirty-Seven

Aletta

When Aletta and her mother finally made it home to their apartment, neither of them was certain what they were going to return to. The occupation had only just ended, their city and country finally belonging to the Dutch people once more, and as comfortable as they'd been in Sweden in their temporary accommodation, nothing had been more exciting than finally being told they could return. But there were a myriad of questions running through Aletta's mind now, including just where they would go if they couldn't reclaim their apartment straight away, although the most perplexing issue was that she didn't have a key. She kept slipping her hand into her jacket pocket as if expecting to find one there, as if she were returning from shopping or teaching college, and then she'd have to remind herself why there was no key to feel for. For her jacket was borrowed, and there was no key to be found.

'What do we do if someone else is living in there?' Aletta asked.

Her mother's eyes met hers, and it was clear that she'd been wondering the same thing.

'Honestly? I don't know,' she said with a sigh. 'The old me would have passively stood there and asked them to leave.'

'And now?' Aletta asked.

An unexpected smile spread across her mother's lips, despite everything. 'Now I think I may just stand in my living room and scream at them until they leave. No one is keeping me from my home, not now. I'm taking our apartment back, Aletta, one way or another.'

Anyone hearing them might have laughed. They were two women with sharp bones protruding from beneath their clothes and gaunt faces, their cheeks hollow with dark marks below their eyes still. They had to link arms just to walk the length of the street, and even then they struggled and had to constantly stop and rest, but they'd both survived too much to falter now. And if her mother had to scream and fight someone to reclaim their home, then she'd be there yelling right alongside her.

They hadn't survived Ravensbrück to be turned out on to the streets. Her father had worked hard to buy their apartment, and so long as her family's name was still on the deeds, then it belonged to them, war or not.

The climb up the stairs was brutal, but they held on to each other, pausing more than once before they finally stood at the door. Aletta forced the memories away, refusing to let her mind take her back to the last time she'd been standing there, to what had haunted her relentlessly almost every night since.

Just walk through that door.

She took a deep breath and placed her hand on the handle before finally opening it, relieved that it wasn't locked.

'Hello?' she called out, listening carefully to see if anyone responded.

Her mother inched in beside her, and they both stood and stared. At the blood stain on the carpet, the place where her father had fallen; at the hole in the wall her father had erected, where boots had kicked their way through to Harry; at their furniture haphazardly moved around and what was left of their possessions scattered everywhere. But as far as Aletta could tell, there was no one occupying their home, at least not anymore.

'It looks like the place has been turned over,' her mother said, her voice low.

Aletta nodded. Then she swallowed, forcing down her emotions as she looked around their living room and slowly took step after step into their apartment, refusing to look at the spot where she'd last seen her father.

'Everything of value has been taken,' she whispered. 'They've looted the place.'

There were faded squares on the wall where paintings had once hung; there was an antique sideboard once covered with treasures, collected by her mother over her lifetime, now empty. Her heart ached for what they'd lost, for the mess they'd come home to, but she supposed she should be grateful that they at least had a home.

'They are only things,' her mother said, her hand brushing Aletta's arm as she moved past her. 'We have our home, and we have each other, and that's what matters. After what we've survived? This is nothing.'

Aletta opened her mouth to reply, turning to her mother, but the gasp that came from deep within stopped her. She found herself out of breath, like she'd been punched in the stomach, as she reached for a chair, holding on so tightly that her knuckles turned white.

'Breathe, Aletta,' her mother murmured, her hand warm against Aletta's back as she rubbed in gentle circles. 'Just breathe.'

She gulped down air as she fought against wave after wave of emotion, and eventually she was able to breathe again and straightened, turning and placing her arms around her mother. They stood like that for what felt like forever, Aletta with her eyes tightly shut and her mother's tears damp against her skin, cheek to cheek. But eventually they both slowly let go.

Her mother smiled at her, despite her emotion. 'We start with one thing,' she said. 'Today, we wash the sheets on one bed and tidy one room. Then tomorrow we start on another room. We will tackle it one bit at a time, and we'll do it together.'

Aletta nodded. 'One room at a time,' she repeated.

'This is our home, Aletta, and no amount of looting or damage is going to make us feel otherwise,' she said. 'Your father would have wanted us to stay here, so that's what we're going to do. He worked too hard to buy this apartment for us to do anything else.'

Aletta's throat was thick with emotion again, but she nodded and placed her hand on her mother's arm as their eyes met. Her mother, who'd proven herself to be the strongest person Aletta knew.

This *was* their home, and her mother was right. No one could take that away from them. They'd survived the worst, but it was time to start rebuilding their life again, room by room.

◆ ◆ ◆

Aletta and her mother had barely finished cleaning the bedroom, a task that should have taken a couple of hours and yet had taken them almost all day, when she heard a noise, followed by a call.

'Hello? Aletta? Is anyone here?'

Her heart picked up speed and she hurried down the hall. Or at least she tried to hurry. Her body moved like an old lady's now, and she realised then that they hadn't eaten since early that morning. She supposed it would take them some time to get used to the idea of eating or drinking whenever they wanted.

'Aletta?' the voice called again.

Aletta stopped when she saw the immaculately dressed young woman standing in her living room, a grocery bag slung over one arm. It was like seeing a photo from the past.

'Cecilia?'

'Aletta!'

Her friend's eyes widened as she looked at her, and Aletta knew what Cecilia was seeing. A girl who was barely half the weight she'd been before, almost unrecognisable as the young woman who'd last been in Amsterdam.

'I can't believe you're home,' Cecilia whispered as she drew Aletta into her arms, holding her as carefully as one might an injured small child, her voice laced with tears. 'I thought I was never going to see you again.'

Aletta had thought she was all out of tears, but seeing Cecilia again had her fighting back emotion. All those months and years she'd been away, one of the things she'd hoped for most was to see her friend again, and here she was.

'This place,' Cecilia finally said as she turned and looked around. 'It's a mess. I can't believe people went into homes and stole so much.'

'Even the paintings from the walls,' Aletta said, smiling despite her emotions. Cecilia kept one hand on her while she looked around.

'You look, well . . .' Cecilia frowned. 'You look like you're in need of feeding and pampering.'

'That's putting it nicely,' Aletta replied, as her mother appeared and was the recipient of one of Cecilia's warm hugs.

'My mother told me to leave you be, but when I heard you were home . . .'

'Who told you we were home?' Aletta asked, confused. 'We've only been back since this morning.'

Cecilia grinned. 'I paid the boy in the apartment next door to come and find me if he saw you. It's the best money I've ever spent.'

Aletta laughed. 'It's so good to see you again.'

Even though she knew it must have been hard for Cecilia to see them, given the way they looked, her smile was unwavering as she marched into the kitchen, leaving them to trail behind. Cecilia didn't gawk at them or ask questions, she just made herself busy.

'I'm going to fix you something to eat, because I have some groceries with me, and then I'm going to get a casserole in the oven for you,' Cecilia said. 'I've spoken to my doctor about your . . .' she turned to glance back at them, 'well, people with your enormous weight loss, and you need to eat just a little amount often. We need to be very careful not to overwhelm your bodies, to fatten you up nice and slowly.'

Aletta looked to her mother, who seemed to know what she was thinking and nodded.

'Cecilia, you don't have to—'

'Look after you?' She sighed. 'Don't even start with that. I'm going to clean this apartment until my fingers are raw and cook you everything you need, and I don't want to hear a complaint from either of you.'

Aletta laughed then, and so did her mother. And it was so unexpected that it only made her laugh all the more, until her stomach ached and it made her cough.

'What's so funny?' Cecilia asked.

'You,' Aletta said, her hand to her chest as she smiled, something she'd feared she'd forgotten how to do. 'I don't recall you being so bossy, that's all.'

'Bossy?' Cecilia huffed. 'My best friend in the entire world survived one of those dreadful camps. Do you truly think I wouldn't insist on looking after you? I spent years grieving you and believing I'd never see you again, so please don't take this away from me.'

Aletta nodded and leaned against the wall as she watched Cecilia take out items from the grocery bag. Even the speed at which her friend was moving gave her a headache and made her want to lie down and rest.

'After you eat, I'm going to wash your hair and give you both haircuts, and then I'll set to cleaning. And I'll be back again tomorrow to do the rest, and the day after that if I need to. I don't want either of you lifting so much as a finger.'

'Cecilia, I know you're Aletta's oldest friend, but—'

'I won't hear of it,' Cecilia said, not letting Aletta's mother finish. 'Now, you two sit down and let me look after you.'

Aletta saw the tears in her friend's eyes as she turned away, and so she obediently sat down. If this was what Cecilia needed from her, if this was her doing her best to make them all feel better, for her to be able to cope with what had happened to them, then she wasn't going to argue.

'I truly thought I'd never see you again,' Cecilia said quietly, her back still turned, her shoulders trembling. 'Whole families disappeared and never returned, the things they did . . .'

Aletta beckoned for her mother to sit beside her, hoping that Cecilia never learnt even half of what had truly gone on at Ravensbrück.

'So please, just let me show you that I love you,' Cecilia said. 'I felt helpless for so long, I felt like a coward for hiding away in the countryside, but taking care of you is something I can do. So please, let me.'

Aletta's heart felt full, despite her pain. Because Cecilia had always been a good friend to her, and this was testament to exactly what kind of a friend she truly was.

'Cecilia, did Peter or Thomas make it? Did any of our Jewish friends survive?' Aletta asked. 'The families we went to school with?'

Cecilia's shoulders dropped. 'Peter and Thomas both made it, but not the Jewish families we knew. Not one of them,' she said. 'A while after you were taken, they started making all the Jews wear the yellow star, and then they made them turn over all their property and money. By the time they rounded them up and sent them to the camps, they'd been stripped of everything.'

Aletta blanched at the mention of the camps, and she could tell that Cecilia had seen the change in her.

'I'm sorry, I didn't mean to mention the—'

'It's fine,' Aletta said, before she could say the word again. 'You know, even though I was there, it's still hard to believe what happened to them. Most were murdered before they even knew where they were going.' *But we survived, Aletta thought. Else survived. Not everyone is lost. Most, but not all.*

Cecilia's eyes met hers, but it was as if neither knew what to say.

'I'm sorry, Aletta. For what happened to you.'

Aletta's smile came easily then, because she knew how much Cecilia cared, how long she'd probably been waiting to say those words, even though she had absolutely nothing to be sorry about.

'How about you let me just do a little bit of the cleaning,' Aletta said. 'I don't know how long I can sit here and do nothing.'

'You can stir the casserole and make some coffee for us,' Cecilia said. 'Then you can go straight back to sitting and listening to me prattle on.'

'Or we could play cards?'

Cards reminded her of Harry, and just thinking of their last day together stung, but she wasn't going to let her memories ruin the time she had with Cecilia.

'Cards it is then,' Cecilia said. 'But not a spot of cleaning, do you hear me?'

◆ ◆ ◆

Two hours later, once Cecilia had fed them and watched over every mouthful, and moved around the house righting things and tidying, Aletta answered a question she'd known was coming. The words had been heavy on her tongue, and as Cecilia turned to her, standing in front of the damaged wall, she knew it was time to tell her when she asked.

'I don't want to ask anything you don't want to answer, but this wall,' Cecilia said. 'Was it a hidden space?'

Aletta found herself nodding, but the words still didn't come. There was so much she needed to tell Cecilia, but she just wasn't ready to relive most of it. Not yet.

'Do you remember Harry?' she finally asked.

A fist closed around Aletta's heart as she spoke his name, and Cecilia's eyebrows rose in answer.

'I lied to you back then,' she said, taking a deep breath before continuing. 'The last time we saw each other, when you came to visit, Harry was hidden in there, and I wanted to tell you so badly, but we'd agreed to keep him secret from everyone. Even from you.'

Cecilia's face softened and Aletta watched as her friend turned back and looked at the space before sitting beside her and taking her hand.

'They took him, your Harry? When they came for you?'

Aletta nodded, her throat thick with emotion again. 'I don't think I'm ready yet, to talk about him, or my father,' she whispered. 'Or what happened to us. But I just wanted you to know that that was his room. That's where we tried to hide him from harm.'

Cecilia wrapped her arm around Aletta's shoulders and pressed a kiss to her head. 'One day you'll be ready to tell me, but until then, we can just sit in silence if that's what you want.'

Aletta let herself be held, inhaling the familiar, sweet smell of her friend's perfume as they sat together on the sofa. Her mother was asleep already; darkness was starting to blanket the sky outside, and Aletta had never been more grateful to have Cecilia holding her close.

'There is actually someone I'd like to talk to you about,' she whispered. 'I'm afraid that if I don't talk about her, I won't be able to keep her memory alive.'

Cecilia's arm stayed warm around her shoulder as they sank back into the cushions. 'What was her name?' Cecilia asked.

'Her name,' Aletta said, summoning all her strength, 'was Chloe, and she was the bravest girl I've ever met.'

Chapter Thirty-Eight

Aletta

Aletta walked slowly up the stairs, a bag of groceries in each hand. The first few times she'd barely been able to take more than half a dozen steps without pausing, her body exhausted from the incline and her lungs heaving for air, but today she'd only had to pause twice, which seemed like a small miracle. She still felt as if she were panting, but after four weeks back at home, she was beginning to feel a little more like her old self. The colour had come back to her cheeks, and she was slowly but surely putting weight on her bones, although she still had to summon all her strength to walk through the door to their apartment without seeing those last moments with her father. The physical wounds, she knew, would heal much faster than the evils that haunted her mind.

She caught her mother sometimes in the middle of the night, when she couldn't sleep either, scrubbing the carpet for the hundredth time where Aletta's father had been killed. There was no stain of blood that Aletta could see, not anymore, but still her mother cleaned it, as if doing so might erase the memory of what had happened there. And every single time, Aletta would drop to her knees and join her, until her fingers ached and her mother's silent tears had stopped. They'd both go back to bed then, often curled side by side, and eventually fall into an exhausted sleep. They'd been crammed together at Ravensbrück for so many nights, over so long, that it almost felt impossible to sleep without the comfort of another body pressed to her side, and she knew her mother felt the same. Even though they were no longer cold or terrified of what might happen, it was still hard to be alone, especially when nightmares would wake them, leaving them both drenched in sweat and gasping at the thought of being back there.

When she finally stepped through the door, Aletta was lost in her thoughts, but she glanced up when she heard her mother clear her throat.

'I was able to get a fresh loaf of bread and a piece of beef today, so it—'

'Aletta.' The tone of her mother's voice made her look up, but it was the man sitting at their kitchen table who made her stop moving. The last time her mother had said her name like that . . .

'We have a guest.'

It can't be.

Aletta's breath caught and the shopping bags slipped from her fingers as the man pushed back his chair and rose. She couldn't tear her eyes from his face, and when his gaze met hers, as he stood by her table and blinked at her, tears filling his beautiful blue eyes, a cry lodged in her throat.

'Harry?' She finally said his name as a question, frozen as she stared at him.

'Hello Aletta.'

No. It can't be.

Harry. It can't be my Harry.

But it is.

'Harry!' she cried this time, racing across the room so fast she barely felt the carpet beneath her feet and throwing herself into his arms. 'Oh my gosh, Harry, I can't believe it.'

His arms closed around her, his lips against her hair as she wound her own arms around his waist. He was too thin, just as she was, but his embrace was as warm as it had always been, and the way his lips brushed her forehead before he pulled away was exactly as she'd remembered. She ignored the sharp angles of his bones beneath his clothes, feeling as if she'd almost knocked him off his feet with her excitement, but Harry didn't seem to mind one bit.

'How, I mean . . .' She didn't even know what she was trying to say as he held her at arm's length, his eyes seeming to rove over every inch of her. 'I can't believe it. I can't.'

'I'm here,' he said, his voice raspier than she remembered. 'That's all that matters.'

He was right, of course he was right, and she knew that whatever he'd been through in the time they'd been parted, he likely didn't want to talk about it, just as she didn't want to talk about where they'd been and the horrors they'd endured. She stepped into him again, lifting her hand and placing it on his cheek. She forgot that her mother was watching them, or maybe it was just something she wasn't worried about any longer, not after what they'd been through together. Happiness wasn't something she would hide ever again.

'I can't believe you're alive,' she whispered, wishing his cheek wasn't so gaunt beneath her fingertips. 'I can't believe either of us is alive.'

'You're the only thing that kept me going, Aletta,' he said, folding her into his chest again, his arms warm around her shoulders as his lips whispered against her hair. 'I kept telling myself that we'd see each other again. That one day, I'd find you.'

Aletta blinked away tears, holding on tight to the man she'd never expected to see again, to the man she'd loved for so long. She closed her eyes and felt his body against hers, heard footsteps as her mother walked away and murmured something about privacy, listened to the steady beat of his heart.

Harry didn't speak again until she pulled back enough to look up at him, and he gently touched his lips to hers in a kiss that she felt all the way to her toes, one she'd imagined in her mind every day since they'd been parted.

'I'm not going to let anyone or anything part us again, Aletta,' he whispered against her mouth.

Words failed her, and so she raised herself on tiptoe and kissed him, her arms looping around his neck, their smiles the only thing interrupting what would have otherwise been a perfect kiss.

'Now we just have to convince your mother to let me stay,' he said, making her laugh. 'I kind of went out on a limb here when I made my way back to Amsterdam, and I have nowhere else to go.'

'You're staying,' she said, holding him tight and swallowing away fresh emotion as she savoured the feeling of being in his arms. 'I'm not letting you out of my sight ever again.'

Epilogue

Aletta

Aletta smiled as the sun reflected off the water. She held Harry's hand, his fingers linked with hers as they strolled along the canal. Amsterdam was always beautiful, but in the springtime with the sunshine on her shoulders and a bright blue sky above, it was magnificent. When they slowed, she looked at the buildings surrounding them, stretching out on either side of the canal, and it struck her just how miraculous it was that where they were walking was almost entirely untouched by the war. There were no crumbling buildings opened up like doll's houses, no demolished bridges or even so much as a flattened tree. Physically, the Amsterdam she loved was unharmed, but she knew that for the people who lived there, the wounds ran deep. But at least they could rebuild their lives without also having to rebuild their city – here, it was almost possible to believe that the war had never happened.

It was that realisation that left her tinged with a deep, overwhelming sadness which tugged at her heart, that so many people had to rebuild a life that was absent of so many loved ones. But it was still quite something to be able to look out and not be visually reminded of the war at every turn, when so many other cities throughout Europe had been left in pieces, with destruction everywhere.

Harry squeezed her fingers, and she glanced up at him. His smile warmed her and pulled her from her thoughts, making her forget about the war and think only of him. It was something that he'd been able to do since the day he'd walked back into her life . . .

'Shall we stop here?'

Aletta nodded, tears filling her eyes as he passed her the beautiful flower wreath that he held in his other hand. She took a deep breath, leaning into Harry as he pressed a kiss to her temple, his lips lingering, his fingers still brushing hers until she let them go. She still craved his touch, never taking it for granted.

It had been three years since the war ended. Three years since she'd staggered on to the bus taking her from Ravensbrück. Three years since she'd returned home and been reunited with Harry.

Aletta swallowed as she stepped forward and crouched down, leaning to place the wreath of pink and white flowers in the water. Her fingers clasped the edge, waiting for a long moment before finally releasing it.

It's been three years since I said goodbye to you, Chloe.

Aletta felt Harry beside her, and she knew that he would be remembering the people he'd lost, too. Just as she knew her mother would be thinking of not only her husband and Chloe, but of all the people and children they'd come to know over the years at Ravensbrück.

As if sensing her thoughts, her mother's gaze met hers and at the same time her grasp on Aletta's daughter slipped as the little girl fought to run away, and Aletta opened her arms as her daughter skipped towards her. But she only stopped to give Aletta a quick kiss before running alongside the canal, squealing with delight at the flower wreath as the wind sent it moving through the water, her little legs going as fast as they could. And it was a sight that brought a smile to Aletta's face, watching her own daughter.

'She would be so happy to see you now.' Her mother's hand came to rest over her shoulder as she joined them. 'You were born to be a mum, Aletta. Children saved us in there, and your little girl is saving us now.'

'Our little miracle after so much loss,' Aletta murmured, watching as her daughter turned and began to run back towards her. 'Our little Chloe.'

Her mother smiled as Harry's arm went around Aletta. His lips brushed her hair as she wiped her damp cheeks, catching a fresh tear with her thumb as she watched the disappearing wreath and whispered, 'A more fearless name there never was.'

AUTHOR'S NOTE

All of my WWII novels are inspired by true events, and this story is no different. When I read about a large group of women who were saved ten days before Germany surrendered in the Second World War – of French, Polish, Dutch and Norwegian nationalities – I knew I had to write about it. There was something about this real-life account that made me want to find out as much as I could, and then of course I was compelled to write about it for my readers.

Despite most other camps at this time having already been liberated by advancing Allied troops, Ravensbrück was still under Nazi control, and in the final desperate weeks of war, more than 6,000 women were murdered by gas. Others were shot, starved or forced to go on a death march, as the Nazis tried to destroy the evidence of what had happened at the camp, realising that the world was about to find out what atrocities had been committed. But around 7,000 women were saved by the Swedish Red Cross, taken by buses and driven across Germany, some to the Danish border and then on to Sweden via boat. More women followed in the coming days. Many of the women were skeletal, many had to be carried on stretchers, and some (miraculously) had babies with them, but what became known as the White Bus rescue became the biggest humanitarian mission inside Germany of WWII, and it was all because of a Swedish man by the name of Folke Bernadotte. Bernadotte was shot dead by Jewish extremists after being appointed UN mediator to the Arab-Israeli conflict a few years later. I was saddened to learn that a man with such compassion and dedication to saving others was killed in such a way.

This Swedish Count also saved at least 14,000 prisoners from other concentration camps, including several thousand Jews, and in 1944 he persuaded the Germans to free Allied airmen shot down in Germany to be taken to Sweden. When he first began to negotiate the release of prisoners, Bernadotte famously met with Heinrich Himmler himself, who ran the camps. It is said that the Swedes agreed to send Bernadotte because they thought his royal bloodline and confident demeanour would appeal to Himmler, and this theory proved correct.

The first prisoners to leave Ravensbrück were Scandinavian, and even though it was thought to be impossible for Bernadotte's buses to go back for more women, they returned undeterred and began to save thousands more, including Dutch women. These survivors associated transport with death, and they were terrified of the gas chamber and the crematorium, but when they saw the tears in the eyes of the bus drivers and nurses, and were told they were going to be transported to Sweden, they bravely chose to go with them. The Jewish women who were saved were stripped of their numbers and yellow triangles, so that no one who saw them would know Jews were being released – the SS didn't want word to reach Hitler's people. Among the thousands saved from Ravensbrück were twelve British women, who were almost left behind. It's worth noting too that even when the gas chambers had been dismantled at Ravensbrück on Himmler's orders, to try to prevent the world from knowing what had been done at the camp, gassing was still being conducted on mobile trucks. That was also something I learnt for the first time while writing this book – that mobile gassing trucks even existed.

Although this rescue is only a small part of my novel, I wanted to explain the history behind the final chapters, and also what inspired me to write this novel in the first place. It may seem fictitious that such a rescue took place, or that these prisoners were mistaken for the enemy and shot at in an Allied air attack during their rescue, but it's all based on fact, which only makes it all the more heartbreaking. I would also be remiss not to mention the poems and recipes that were recorded by women in the camps, at great risk to those involved. Recipes were particularly special to many of the female prisoners, as they were a memory of their lives before the camps; of meals they'd once cooked for those they loved. This meant they were often written down and shared in secret, and many biographies about Ravensbrück make mention of the pieces of paper passed between the women in private.

I must also mention the Siemens factory where Aletta, Chloe and Emma worked. While the mentions of the factory are historically accurate, I had to change the timeline slightly to work with my story, which means I have this work commencing in late 1940, rather than in 1942 when the factory was opened near Ravensbrück camp.

This year I visited Dachau Memorial Camp while I was in Munich, and I can honestly say that no amount of research can come close to witnessing the camp first-hand. To stand in the bitterly cold wind and imagine the prisoners there; to place my hand on the wall of the crematorium and experience the silence and sadness there; it was a memory that will stay with me forever.

As a final thought, I feel that I need to share some numbers and statistics with you, which were hugely moving to me when I was researching this novel. In total, 132,000 women and children were imprisoned at Ravensbrück, and it is estimated that up to 92,000 died. In the earliest years of the camp, most babies and children were either drowned, poisoned, buried alive or strangled – this was something I chose not to write about in this novel, because it was just so horrendous. Many young girls who were permitted to live were sterilised, and there were countless horrific medical experiments conducted on prisoners. It is almost impossible to comprehend the cruelty, the death and the heartache that happened during those years, and that was only at one camp.

ACKNOWLEDGEMENTS

This book wouldn't be the story it is today without my incredible editors, Victoria Pepe and Sophie Wilson. I am so fortunate to work with these two amazing women to produce each of my historical WWII novels, and Victoria and Sophie are both so talented at what they do. Thank you both for everything! Huge thanks also to my long-time copy editor, Sadie Mayne and proofreader Swati Gamble.

I would also like to thank the wider team at Amazon Publishing for their ongoing support, including Sana Chebaro, Sammia Hamer, Nicole Wagner and Bekah Graham Pickering. I'm so happy to have you all in my corner! I'm also very grateful for my long-time agent, Laura Bradford.

Huge thanks to my team closer to home as well . . . my husband Hamish, my boys Mack and Hunter, my parents Maureen and Craig, and my assistant Lisa Pendle. I'd also like to make special mention of my writing friends who help to keep me sane during the writing process – Natalie Anderson and Yvonne Lindsay.

But of course, as always, my biggest thanks go to you, my readers! Without you, I wouldn't be able to write the books of my heart, so thank you for choosing my books to read.

Soraya x

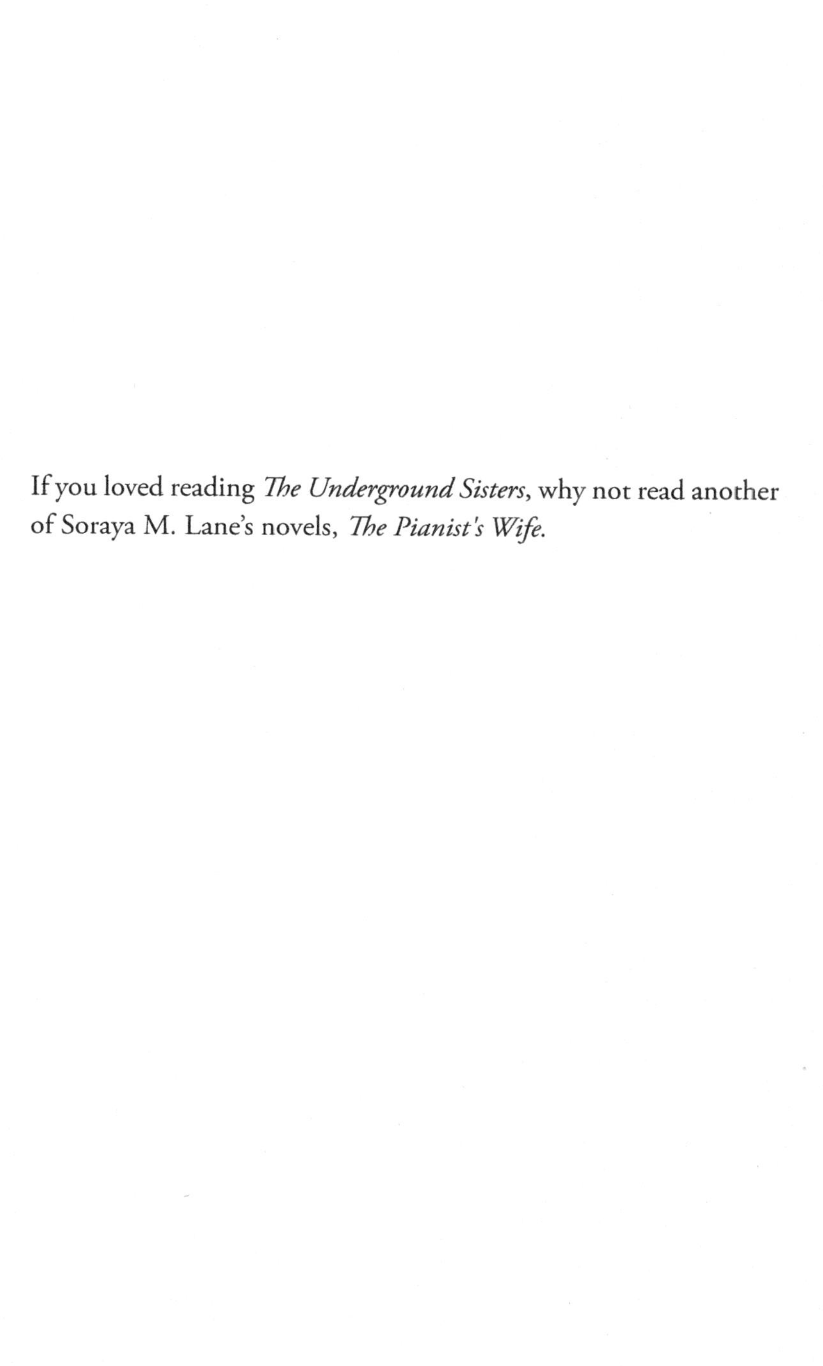

If you loved reading *The Underground Sisters*, why not read another of Soraya M. Lane's novels, *The Pianist's Wife*.

Chapter One

New York, 2006

Amira lifted her gaze and caught a glimpse of herself in the mirror across the room. She barely recognised the white-haired reflection looking back at her; the lines around her eyes, the narrowness of her shoulders, they seemed to belong to another. She still expected to see the thick dark hair and plump skin of her youth, but instead there was an elderly lady blinking back at her.

She turned away when the young woman beside her spoke.

'Amira, are you ready?' Madison asked.

Amira cleared her throat, reaching for the glass of water on the nightstand and taking a small sip. 'I am.'

'Is it okay if I record our interview? So I can listen to it later?'

She looked at the little machine Madison was gesturing at, her finger hovering over the button, imagining her words being played back at a later date. She hoped her voice wouldn't sound as shaky as it felt.

'Yes, I give permission for you to record me.'

Madison nodded and pressed down. 'Well then, let's begin,' she said with a warm smile. 'Amira, tonight you've been honoured for your work raising money for underprivileged and orphaned children in New York. I know you and your husband have both been very private about your joint philanthropic endeavours until now, so I very much appreciate the opportunity to speak with you.'

Amira nodded and instinctively reached out a hand to her husband's. It was warm, his skin almost feathery it was so thin, and she kept hold as she replied to Madison. When she'd agreed to the interview, her only condition was that it had to be conducted at his bedside – she didn't want to do it alone.

'Is there a reason you decided to open up about your work now, after all this time?'

'My greatest concern,' Amira said, 'is that if we don't speak now, if *I* don't speak now, then we may miss the opportunity to encourage others to step forward and follow in our footsteps. I believe that everyone is capable of making a difference in the lives of others, be it with donations or the giving of time, and I hope that in sharing my story with you, I may be able to influence others.'

Madison nodded, her pen poised above a little leather-bound notebook, taking notes even though she was recording their interview. Amira had thought about her answer to that question all day, preparing herself for what she intended on saying, but as she spoke she realised she sounded over-rehearsed.

'From what I understand, you grew up in a village in Germany and lived in Berlin during the war,' Madison said, 'which is where your passion for helping children began.'

Amira sighed. It wasn't that she hadn't expected to be asked, but hearing someone say those words after all these years . . . it made her feel as if she were somehow back there, as if she were still the little girl holding her father's hand, believing that somehow, everything would be alright.

'Can you explain to me what it was like to live in Germany, during those tumultuous years? And how that shaped the woman you are today?'

'That time in my life, it's almost indescribable,' Amira replied. 'Berlin during the war and even before, it was a place full of hate and terror, but now I look back, I suppose it was also a place just like any other. Not everyone experienced such hardship as I did.'

She reached out and took another sip of water, reluctantly letting go of her husband's hand, and when she looked up, she saw that Madison was waiting, leaning forward in anticipation of her continuing.

'In many ways, life in Berlin went on as normal, particularly for those families with what the Nazis considered pure German bloodlines, and most especially those who exemplified what the party stood for, but for others, it was a reign of terror that felt as if it would never end. For the marginalised . . .'

'But what was it like for you personally, Amira?' Madison asked. 'Could you share your own experience with me?'

'Well,' Amira said, her voice cracking slightly as she spoke, 'if I did, it would be a very long story.'

Madison's smile was kind as she leaned back in her seat, appearing to make herself comfortable. 'It just so happens that I have all day, if you're willing to share it with me, of course. I would very much like to hear as much of your story as you're willing to tell. It's why I'm here, after all.'

Amira's gaze found its way to her husband's face, as it so often did when she sat beside him, and she wished he would simply open his eyes, that he could be part of telling their story with her. But she knew that likely wouldn't happen, not now.

I think it's time, my love. After all these years, I think it's finally time that I told our story. Because if not now, then when? I only wish you could open your eyes and tell me that you give me your blessing.

'For me,' Amira finally said, looking up as a wave of nostalgia passed through her body, 'life in Germany changed in 1935, when I realised that the country I loved had a reason not to love me anymore.'

ABOUT THE AUTHOR

Photo © 2022 Jemima Helmore

Soraya M. Lane graduated with a law degree before realising that law wasn't the career for her and that her future was in writing. She is the author of historical and contemporary women's fiction, and her novel *Wives of War* was an Amazon Charts bestseller. Soraya lives on a small farm in her native New Zealand with her husband, their two young sons and a collection of four-legged friends. When she's not writing, she loves to be outside playing make-believe with her children or snuggled up inside reading. For more information about Soraya and her books, visit www.sorayalane.com or www.facebook.com/SorayaLaneAuthor, or follow her on X @Soraya_Lane.

Follow the Author on Amazon

If you enjoyed this book, follow Soraya M. Lane on Amazon to be notified when the author releases a new book!
To do this, please follow these instructions:

Desktop:

1) Search for the author's name on Amazon or in the Amazon App.
2) Click on the author's name to arrive on their Amazon page.
3) Click the 'Follow' button.

Mobile and Tablet:

1) Search for the author's name on Amazon or in the Amazon App.
2) Click on one of the author's books.
3) Click on the author's name to arrive on their Amazon page.
4) Click the 'Follow' button.

Kindle eReader and Kindle App:

If you enjoyed this book on a Kindle eReader or in the Kindle App, you will find the author 'Follow' button after the last page.